16 SOULS

New York Times Bestselling Author
John J. Nance

WILDBLUE
PRESS

WildBluePress.com

16 SOULS published by:
WILDBLUE PRESS
P.O. Box 102440
Denver, Colorado 80250

Interior Formatting/Book Cover Design by Elijah Toten www.totencreative.com

ACKNOWLEDGEMENTS

As always, this work required my reliance on a cadre of people for help from the technical to the lyrical. First and foremost, of course, is Kathleen Bartholomew, without whose love and support and editing, Marty's story would not have seen print. I am very appreciative of the contributions and encouragement of two of the earliest fans and progenitors of this story, Bianca and Dave Vanderwal. I also greatly appreciate the time and effort expended by Arna Robins, Arthur Ferreira, Curt Epperson, and especially Debbie Haagensen, and the excellent assistance of Annie LeFleur, JD, in helping this Texas lawyer navigate Colorado's legal system.

And thanks especially to Steve Jackson, Michael Cordova, and Ashley Butler at WildBlue Press.

This work is dedicated to the memory of a great literary agent and friend, the late George Wieser of New York's Wieser and Wieser Agency, who started it all 35 years ago.

CHAPTER ONE

August 14th

Marty Mitchell awoke and pulled himself up to peek over the ancient slab of granite that had concealed him all afternoon. Strange he'd slept so long. A glance at his watch told him it was half past five. To his relief, the gaggle of climbers who'd been milling around, celebrating their summit, had long since moved on. Now there was no one left on the 14-thousand foot plateau to wonder why *he* hadn't departed.

He'd be gone soon enough anyway.

Marty filled his lungs with the crisp, rarified air as he took in the cobalt blue sky overhead and the gentle breeze. For his last afternoon on the planet, the conditions couldn't be better. In a weird way, this place felt like a launching pad – his own Kennedy Space Center from which to soar safety home.

His eyes instinctively tracked an inbound jetliner descending toward Denver International, fifty-five miles distant, and the mere sight roiled his stomach. It was a 757, the same model he'd been flying last January when his world imploded.

Marty struggled to ignore the Boeing and ditch the negative thoughts as he looked east, focusing on the edge of the boulder-strewn plateau where the path back down the mountain began, the so-called Keyhole Route. He assumed that all the other climbers had heeded the park rangers' warnings about getting off the summit of Long's Peak by one. Even experienced climbers were eager to pick their way down the steep rock face along the "trough" before any freak afternoon thunderstorms had a chance to pop up out of nowhere – lightning-charged storms which too often flailed the rocks with sixty knot winds and stinging rain, raising the stakes by making each footfall exponentially more slippery and treacherous. Beyond that, a mile distant, there was a narrow, challenging trail laterally along the southern rock face which climbers had to traverse to get back to the Keyhole, the jagged and natural passageway leading back to the north side of Long's Peak.

The dangers along that backside path were very real – a major stumble could mean a seventeen-hundred foot plunge down the mountain. And, truth be told, he'd originally considered that an option.

But this is better, he thought. *Much more elegant to go out on top. And,* he thought with a rueful chuckle, *a rather classy way to get the last word without fear of contradiction.*

The morality of his fury had already been decided. If, by some galactic miracle, he could teleport the Denver District Attorney to the rock next to him, Marty would have absolutely no hesitation and even less remorse about tossing Richardson off the edge of the vertical east face of the mountain. The sound of the shyster's body splatting on the granite below would be the equivalent of a symphonic masterpiece.

I'm entitled to a few impossible daydreams, he thought. *I'm alone and doomed, but in complete control!*

But the word "control" triggered an icy flash through his bloodstream and a feeling of loathing. He'd never lost control…control of himself, or control of his aircraft, and for that very reason, Richardson wanted him in an orange jumpsuit and caged like an animal for doing his job.

After several minutes, the anger that had masked his pain began to subside with the setting sun, and his heart ached in sorrow. His entire life had been marked by an intense determination to do the right thing. He'd grown up with a sense of integrity and an unquestioned intent to contribute something good to the world. How could it have come to this?

A brief coughing spell distracted him, and when it had passed, Marty reached down to rummage through his backpack, reviewing the plan, searching for the small vial of pills and the unopened bottle of his favorite bourbon alongside a bottle of wine…

And, there was the varietal cigar he was anticipating – a real Cuban.

First a snack and a little wine, then – as the sun went down – there would be time for the last cigar accompanied by the liquor, and then the deepest of sleeps. He regretted the fact that the rangers would be forced to clean up after him, but that couldn't be helped. Despite his best logistics planning, that detail remained unsolvable.

Marty stood and stretched, keenly aware the thin air at 14-thousand feet was contributing to his lightheadedness. It was easier to look outward, then inward. To the north, he could see almost all the way to Laramie, and at night, the town would be clearly visible from such a high vantage point. Back to the west and northwest were the sister peaks of Rocky Mountain National Park, familiar even from this angle of dominance. Hallet's Peak in particular triggered a fond memory of standing on its summit with a girl he hadn't thought of in years.

What was her name?

He shook off the memory. The Never Summer range was off to the northwest, and, of course, the sprawl of Denver to the southeast.

For a reason he could neither explain nor ignore, the more contemporary thought of Judith Winston popped into his consciousness. It wasn't her image, or the memory of her voice that caused him to tense. It was what Winston represented: The do-good lawyer dutifully trying to save a client she obviously detested. A tough broad when crossed.

He could see the cynicism in her eyes the first time he'd refused to play the game.

More accurately, when I tried not to, he thought.

A caution light went off somewhere in the cockpit of his mind as he realized he'd missed a basic courtesy. Winston hadn't done anything to deserve complete silence, yet among all the other notes he'd carefully placed on his dining room table, he'd forgotten to leave one for her.

Marty knelt by his pack and rummaged until he found the small, leather-bound diary he'd been counseled to fill and hadn't. Oh, a few items were inscribed, like his grocery list, last minute chores, and a feeble attempt at recording his feelings which carried all the passion of an engineering log. But now, for a brief moment in time, that little book would have center stage.

He pulled out a pen and wrote the goodbye note he should have left for her back home. At least there was no doubt she'd get it. Anything he wrote would find its intended recipient.

(Broomfield, Colorado – 5:40 pm, August 14ᵗʰ)

Punching off her smartphone for the fifth time in fifteen minutes, Judith Winston paced back and forth across her veranda almost knocking over the planter on the western wall of her condo.

Where the devil is he? she wondered. Despite the fact that it was Sunday afternoon, Marty Mitchell had agreed to a conference call and she absolutely had to wring out some very specific information from him before they got too close to the trial. Somehow the fact that he was out on personal recognizance – thanks to her impassioned intervention – gave a proprietary feel to her irritation. If not exactly waiting for her command, he at least should be locatable.

Judith was feeling like a fidgety six-year old, sitting, then jumping to her feet to pace some more, stopping to examine the contents of the fridge before continuing her holding pattern and sitting again. The idea of driving to the ungrateful pilot's house was rising past the level of silly to the status of potential intent.

How dare he not answer! If she could disrupt her weekend to work on his case, he could at least have the courtesy to keep the appointment, Judith thought, toying with the idea of attacking a pint of unopened ice cream in the freezer.

The sliding door to her north-facing deck was open and she stepped into the pleasant temperatures for a moment, feeling the light silk blouse she was wearing flutter in the breeze, her eyes drawn to the stark clarity of the front range some thirty miles distant. There were still times she longed for someone to share such moments with, although the solitude these days was good – especially after the last relationship had collapsed with such a deafening roar. Deciding now to be alone was more a capitulation to reality than a choice, but she knew it would still be painfully reviewable from time to time, and usually without warning.

The vista was timeless and awesome. On the west side of Boulder the Flatirons – giant slabs of near-vertical granite – defiantly stabbed the sky, as if guarding the entrance to the high mountains beyond. Further west she could see the sheer, vertical east face of Long's Peak – the so-called "diamond" that rock climbers loved – a vertical granite wall thousands of feet high.

Judith's mind snapped back to the dilemma of locating her truant client, and just for a second, the destabilizing thought that Marty Mitchell might not be answering because he *couldn't* flitted across her logic circuits.

His house was ten miles distant, in Boulder itself and not far from her office. Given her growing unease, it was probably worth the drive to motor over and pound on his door. But what worried her the most was the realization that he hadn't been a second late in any of their past encounters, a fact she attributed to his military training.

No, this was too uncharacteristic. Something had to be wrong.

(Denver – 5:40 pm August 14th)

Scott Bogosian had been thinking about fate lately, but not the fate that had almost become fact.

Now, as he stood alongside his aging Volvo, his legs shaking, the concept of fate was taking on a far more personal and sinister meaning. That stop sign he had raced through was right there, right behind him, clearly marking the intersection, its command to "STOP" big and red and undeniable.

But he'd never seen it until now. Why? Sun in his eyes, not concentrating, sleepy, *what?*

Scott realized he was panting, not exactly like an overheated hound, but not far from the analogy, feeling desperately short of breath.

What was it, two minutes ago? he wondered.

The minivan approaching the same intersection at a ninety-degree angle had barely registered in his peripheral vision, but the automatic assumption that any car approaching from the side was going to stop was automatically unquestioned. After all, no transportation authority would design an intersection in which traffic was allowed to approach from four directions at once without a stop sign or a stop light or something. Yet his path had been clear of signs or signals, or so he thought, as the part of his consciousness assigned to driving presumed an unchallenged right of way, right up to the moment of impact that hadn't occurred.

Fate had written a different script, and the screeching, gut-wrenching four wheel emergency skid into the intersection to avoid the minivan had been a success measured by millimeters.

Mom's taxi had sped on, miraculously untouched, the startled, unforgettable faces of two tiny passengers staring at him from the back seat through the very windows he would have crushed. Those faces were now etched in his memory as permanently as those impacted by the midair collision of Regal Airlines Flight 12 and Mountaineer 2612, an incredible accident he'd spent the better part of the past six months researching.

Scott looked down at his shaking hands. Limping through the empty intersection afterwards and pulling over to the curb, he wondered why everyone else's world – and heart – hadn't stopped as completely as his.

No one had come running to scold, condemn, or support. The McDonald's customers across the street continued waiting for their Big Macs, the do-it-yourself gas station across the way was filled with oblivious customers, and even a police cruiser motored by without a second glance, flush in the uninterrupted flow of this alternate reality.

What almost happened in his universe hadn't, and therefore life moved on, only Scott was now awash in a flood of unbidden adrenaline.

He forced his aging body back behind the wheel and studied the ashen image in the little mirror on the visor. No question he'd been getting rougher around the edges and, to admit it, somewhat seedier since the Rocky Mountain News folded in 2009, almost taking his career with it. A year of struggle had landed him a part time position with the Denver Post – a permanent probationary toehold which kept him breathing, and eating. But essentially the door to being a mainstream, byline newspaper reporter had slammed shut without jarring another open, and Scott, the fading newspaperman at age 58, was experiencing an eerie mix of fatigue and anxiety.

Of course, working now meant making rent with magazine articles, local professional journal writing, and a growing involvement with a digital news service started by other furious Rocky Mountain News alumni, in addition to his new part-time position with the Post. But he'd been spending an inordinate amount of time digging hard with a determination to tell the story of Mountaineer Flight 2612 and Regal Airlines Flight 12. Yes, it was possible he was becoming myopic – fixated on the story, a crowd of one who thought it could support a book. But the story was so incredibly multi-dimensional, and those faces in the windows of the other airplane were indelible, too. Like all airline accidents, there were so many contributing causes it was hard to put in perspective, especially when an out-of-control headline grabber like Grant Richardson seized the opportunity to prosecute an airline captain for murder – the same DA who'd pursued several nurses recently for an entirely innocent but fatal system mistake.

There was a key still missing in the Regal Air crash, something just out of reach that no one had yet discovered or put together. Call it a hunch. Several nights he had awakened with a startling idea of what might have contributed to the crash, but each time it had slipped away as the fog of sleep lifted – if, in fact, there had been anything there to begin with. Maybe it was a reporter's instinct for an incomplete explanation, or perhaps it was nothing more than wishful thinking. What was propelling him forward was the certainty that an accident that convoluted couldn't possibly arise from a single mistake.

He thought of the lengthy, tear-stained interview he'd just completed, and that thought in turn sparked a moment of panic: what if his recorder had failed? His handwriting was so lousy these days even *he* couldn't read the notes he scribbled during interviews, notes taken as he locked eyes with the subject. His traditional steno pads were dwindling in importance. The recordings made him a better writer, but violated one of the orthodoxies of newspaper reportage – that real reporters took notes by hand with the ease of breathing. The tradition would brand him a less professional reporter, and losing an interview tape would mean losing half the information and the very essence of the interview.

Who cares if I use a recorder? he asked himself. There was no longer a city editor to contend with, or even peers to pressure him.

Scott reached in his shirt pocket to check the tiny instrument, triggering a few seconds of sound to reassure himself. The woman's words were clearly audible.

Martha Resnick had been the daughter's name. A pretty 14-year old diving into life. Her mother's post-divorce existence, by contrast, had become more invested in Martha's teen years than her own re-entry into single life. Amanda the mother struggled not to hover over Martha the precocious daughter, and that one snowy afternoon – to her eternal sorrow – she had succeeded.

Letting Martha visit her father in Orlando had seemed a reasonable request when the skies were clear, but that afternoon, leaving Denver by air had become a mounting challenge with snow flying in every direction and the planes doing anything but. Martha, however, refused to concede her carefully planned weekend. Seven days in Florida and then back with Mom for Christmas had been programmed into her iPhone for weeks, and she wouldn't hear of a delay.

Slowly, Amanda Resnick had narrated Scott through the pain of her "if-only" memories of their snowy race to the airport that December afternoon, and of her decision to cave to her daughter's desire to go despite the storm. Dedicating oneself to *not* being the overbearing mom meant a follow through that defied all her cautions and protective instincts. But, after all, it wasn't irresponsible to let Martha go, was it? Even in horrible weather, airline flying was supposed to be safer than just driving to the airport.

There had been one hundred fifty-four passengers and crew on Flight 12, and fourteen terrified faces in the windows of the smaller aircraft, every one of them convinced they were going to die.

How many other lives have been shattered or damaged

by proxy, he wondered. With survivors, the torture never ended.

Every interview had poured more depth and understanding into the human stories, but talking to the passengers was getting more difficult. The captain, in particular, had refused all requests for an interview, and even refused legal help.

Scott opened his notebook and looked at the schedule once more, anything to get those innocent faces of the little occupants he'd almost killed in the minivan out of his mind.

Broomfield, 6:30 pm. Lucy Alvarez.

It was highly unusual, but Alvarez had called *him*. She'd heard he was researching the tragedy, and she'd been seated on the right side of the 757 and finally wanted to talk – after months of therapy.

Pulling into her driveway twenty minutes later, Scott grabbed his notebook and recorder and got out, acutely aware his body was still awash in adrenaline. He would have to make a concerted effort to slow down.

"How much do you know?" Lucy Alvarez asked when they were settled in her living room.

Scott fingered the aromatic cup of tea she'd prepared for him and returned her intense gaze. She was barely over five feet in height, shoulder-length dark hair worn with bangs and a classically angular face carefully maintained. A naturally lovely forty-something struggling to stay younger, successfully so far, he judged. Her deep green eyes, though, were clearly haunted.

Scott cleared his throat. "I don't know enough, definitely, which is why I appreciate so much you calling me."

She nodded. "I heard you were a serious journalist."

"I know a lot of facts...I've interviewed dozens, including the families..."

"It was snowing," she began simply, interrupting him, her eyes shifting away to a distant horizon as her mind transported the both of them back to the previous January. "God, how it was snowing! I decided on the trip to Orlando at the very last minute because my fiancé called from New York with the infuriating news that the weekend we'd planned so carefully in Vail had just gone up in smoke. He was coming back from New York on schedule, that night in fact, but going straight on to southwest Colorado to work for a week with a client hospital. Frankly, I was pissed. I got online and found a great give-away, non-refundable fare, and I remember feeling somewhat smug that I'd outfoxed the system. But the moment I got up and pulled the curtains back on the grey skies and snow flurries that morning, there was a...a kind of foreboding. I felt it, but I dismissed it. Regal Airlines has been such a godawful mess of angry people and poor service for the last ten years, but they practically invented airline safety so I wasn't worried about that. Boiler plate predictability, you know? Flight 12 left at seven-fifteen pm and I was planning to drive to Denver International at around five...it's only a half-hour in good weather. I didn't even check on Greg's flight because I didn't want to see him. Around three, the snow became a near-blizzard. I should have just cancelled, but I threw my bags together and headed for the airport instead, thinking rancid things about Denver city fathers who'd built an airport practically in Kansas without a rail line. I have four-wheel drive, and I needed it. Finally made it at five-thirty. Got to the gate at six-fifteen, and the first thing I noticed was a clearly upset captain...*our* captain...talking on the phone at the podium."

"Captain Mitchell?"

"Yes. I only know that from later coverage, of course. I couldn't see a name tag."

"And he was..."

"Worried. You could see the worry in his eyes. And you could barely even see our airplane through the windows behind him even though it was right there at the gate. The snow was literally blowing sideways, one of those really intense storms. I figured, no way is this going to work because it's coming down too heavily, but the flight information screens were showing only a handful of cancelled flights, so I kind of got as close as I could to hear what the pilot was saying and figured I'd wait it out."

"Was the snow sticking?"

"Not really. More like a powder, and great if you're skiing. I had heard snow like that just blows off the wings, although I also heard they would have to spray some sort of de-icing liquid on the plane before we could go."

"Were *you* worried?"

She shrugged. "Not about safety, just about getting to Orlando somewhere close to schedule. Or, I guess I should say, I wasn't thinking about safety until I heard the captain say something really strange to whomever was on the other end."

"What was that?"

"He said, 'We're pressing the margins here, you know that, don't you?' I never knew who he was speaking to, but that twanged me...worried me. *Pressing the margins?* I didn't want to press the margins if it had to do with being safe. But this guy..."

"The captain?"

"Yes. Captain Mitchell. Just to look at him inspired confidence. Like he came out of some Hollywood casting company, you know? Square shoulders, tall and trim, chiseled facial features. Salt and pepper hair, very neatly cropped. That deep, rumbling, authoritative pilot voice. I figured he was in his mid-fifties and probably former military. He just looked like Air Force or Navy. Maybe it's a female thing, but...if a guy like that is willing to fly, I'll be his passenger any day."

"What do you think he meant by that phrase, 'pressing the margins'?"

"You'd have to ask him. But I couldn't help wonder if he sensed something, too. I mean, something beyond the obvious."

"Please forgive the directness of this question, Lucy, but,

I have to ask."

She nodded, all traces of a smile vanishing. "Go ahead."

"You survived, without injury, correct?"

"Not really. I haven't told you the rest of the story."

"You were injured?"

"Not physically." She placed her cup on the table and got up suddenly, walking to the bay window and staring at nothing.

"Psychologically you mean?" he said, cringing at the 'captain obvious' question.

She stood there in silence for an uncomfortable beat before nodding, slowly, her eyes on a distant, ghostly memory.

"I…will never be able to un-see it…what I went through…or forget the captain on the PA explaining the choice he had to make. It was beyond surreal."

"I can imagine," he replied prompting her to turn.

"No, you can't," she said, an edge in her voice that did not invite challenge.

"But, you'll recover with time, right?"

Her eyes went down to the carpet and she stood motionless for what seemed a very long time before meeting his gaze again, shaking her head slowly.

"No."

CHAPTER TWO

The four lane leading from Broomfield to Boulder was nearly at a standstill, the GPS reporting an accident miles ahead. Judith quietly chafed at the delay as she reviewed the irritating sequence that had delivered Marty Mitchell to her legal care in the first place.

She recalled clearly closing the door to her designer-wrought office that day three months ago and pacing around irately, grateful there were no inside windows to broadcast her agitation to the three other lawyers who shared the downtown Boulder office.

A glance at the elaborate brass wall clock had confirmed she had a half hour before the client she did not want to represent walked in. If he was anywhere near as uncooperative and distant as he'd been on their only phone call, this was going to be a struggle.

Whatever aggravation she felt paled, however, in comparison to the combination of embarrassment and upset over the judicial clash that had made a mistake on her part far worse. Never in her years as a lawyer had she crossed swords so directly – or been insulted so thoroughly – by a sitting judge. The raw memory of dealing with Judge Gonzales came back in high definition clarity, churning her stomach with a toxic cocktail of mortification along with an unmistakable whiff of victimization.

Her supreme effort to maintain lawyerly restraint had failed. She'd expected a quick explanation to the judge would spring her from her obviously misguided acceptance of what had turned out to be a major criminal defense case, an assignment to a corporate lawyer cynically engineered by her firm's senior partner. But Judge Gonzales, it seemed, had for some reason developed an affinity for the idea of a big corporate lawyer playing defense counsel, and had decided not to release her. Originally, Judith had asked the district attorney to join her in a hearing in Gonzales' chambers, explaining that she wanted off the case. But when Grant Richardson had refused, she requested an ex parte hearing anyway, and was surprised when the judge granted the request. Now a rising tide of panic was building as Judith realized the judge was actually enjoying her discomfort, and worse, was absolutely delighted at the prospect that the poised and polished female attorney before him might actually lose control. Within the calculating side of her mind she knew an explosion would play right into his hands, but uncharacteristically the emotional side had seized control.

"Judge Gonzalez," Judith had begun, her words metered through gritted teeth.

He cut her off, his voice dripping with feigned concern.

"You have something more to say, Counselor?" The bushy eyebrows arched up in false surprise. "I was very appreciative that you offered your services as a pro bono lawyer, and I accepted, and I do not see any reasonable grounds for releasing you from this obligation."

"I and my firm made a mistake, sir! I should never have volunteered."

"So, why did you?"

"Because my senior partner thought it was the appropriate thing to do and I really didn't understand the scope of this criminal case."

"Well, now you do. And I need you."

"Judge, I'm not competent to try a criminal case!"

"Colorado does not agree with you. You passed the same bar exam as all the criminal defense attorneys in the state, and you raised your right hand and took the lawyer's oath, right?"

"Yes, of course...but I'm trained primarily in corporate law."

"And in Colorado, a lawyer is a lawyer and every one of us is expected to either have the expertise, or be able to study and acquire the expertise. No, you volunteered and I am not letting you off the hook."

"I can't do this, Your Honor."

"Are we having a failure to communicate? Or didn't they teach you about your pro bono responsibilities for this sort of thing at Yale Law?"

She forced herself to ignore the reverse snobbery. "This... this is a murder case!"

"Yes. I believe we've established that. Is there some point you're trying to get to? I'm a busy man."

Judith took a deep breath and tried to concentrate on the overstuffed contents of the judge's office. The thought of insulting this condescending toad was almost seductive, but she dismissed it. Having her defend a crazy airline captain who'd made a stupid decision that resulted in a loss of life would have been bad enough, but running it up into a criminal charge of second degree murder and expecting *her* to defend him – she was in no way competent to try such a case. Conviction would be a foregone conclusion. And that without even considering the massive disruption in her corporate practice. Her partners would be furious. Her *other* partners, she reminded herself.

"Judge," she began again, only slightly more controlled. "You're charged by state law with trying to *assist* the accused, not condemn him! Your DA is trying to convict this airline captain of second degree murder and send him away for a very long time."

"That's right, but it's only second degree, counselor. You needn't worry about the death penalty."

"Your honor, please..."

"Okay, hold it! This defendant is wobbling close to the precipice of diminished capacity. He's fired or refused every lawyer his pilot union buddies have hired, and while the law says he can do so, the self-destructive nature of this is something I can't ignore. I've already allowed two dismissals of counsel, and agreed that since his airline has him on unpaid suspension, he's indigent, and lo and behold I ask for a pro bono lawyer and I get one of the best. What better solution could there be than to have the best from Walters, Wilson, and Crandall, PC, ask for the job? How could anyone object to having an AV rated lawyer like you?" His tone was unctuous, as if he had no idea why she was objecting. "After all, you *were* a prosecutor in Denver once. Correct?"

"A long, long time ago for less than six months! And I was assigned to white collar crime. I never handled anything big like murder."

He's obscenely enjoying this! she thought, powerless to stop the play. She was sliding inexorably, helplessly into his trap.

"Goddammit, Judge!"

"Watch your tongue, Counselor."

"I say again, regardless of the legal theory that we're all competent to represent anyone for anything, you *know* I'm not even remotely qualified to defend this case. For God's sake, I probably couldn't even defend myself on a traffic ticket! I'm a *corporate* lawyer, and not even a regular litigator in civil practice, and you...you...want to *inflict* me on this man as some sort of ridiculous farce of a public defender?"

Gonzalez was leaning forward now, obviously out of patience.

"It's not your choice any longer, Ms. Winston. And in fact you have only two options. One, refuse to serve, in which case I will immediately file a complaint with our Attorney Regulation Counsel – OARC, for violating rules

Rule 1.16, Rule 1.1, and Rule 1.3, or two, take this case precisely as you volunteered to do and do a competent job of being a lawyer, which...oh, by the way...includes being an officer of the court, which includes being competent to represent a criminal defendant."

"I would think as many times as that attitude has been struck down in this country, it would be judicial misconduct to appoint an unqualified lawyer!"

"Thank you for accusing me of judicial misconduct! But guess what? I'm the judge, and this judge can, and will, throw your posterior in jail on contempt if you sass me like that one more time."

She couldn't keep her jaw from dropping slightly. "My... posterior? Did you say...?"

"You're in my chambers, Winston, you're pissing me off big time, and we're off the record. I can say anything to you I decide to say. But relax. I'm just a common street judge retained by the people. Worse, I'm not a member of your waspy, yuppie club. You, on the other hand, are legal royalty, aren't you? The chosen one? The Ivy League lawyer pulling in a half million a year helping corporate fat cats screw those same unwashed and sometimes undocumented people who keep me on the bench? No wonder you don't want to take three or four months out to try a criminal case and get your hands dirty."

"Good Lord, is *that* what this is about? Some sort of class discrimination?"

"No, Winston, it's about public service. Pro bono publico. Not about attending some annual auction for the untouchables and buying a case of Chardonnay for Christ. You know what? Newsflash, lady. You take the same oath the criminal bar takes, and yet you shoulder few, if any of the criminal defense responsibilities. I, for one, have had enough of it!" He was rising from his oversized chair now, his squat frame and overabundant girth failing to provide the towering image that was playing in his head – the omnipotent state district judge about to put the entirety of the fancy corporate lawyers in their place.

"So, make your choice, Judy. Make your head go up and down and say, 'Yes, your Honor, I will faithfully represent this defendant I've agreed to represent.' Or, prepare to fight a professional misconduct charge."

She'd hated herself all the way back to Boulder for caving in, and for a moment had considered storming into the firm's home office in Denver to call an emergency conference. But setting it up by phone on the drive back worked better, and she was loaded for bear when she finally pushed through the doors of her Boulder office. She aimed herself like a runaway train at the plush teleconference room.

It had been Roger Crandall who'd screwed her. The supposedly revered senior partner who had called her in and, she thought, gently rebuked her for falling short of the fifty hours of annual pro bono work. It had been *his* idea to suggest she take a criminal case that was undoubtedly going to get tossed before trial. That assurance made her nervous, but so did Crandall, and in the end it was just another item on the daily agenda to inform the court that she would take the case as defense attorney.

The first few minutes of the conference call were spent on her impassioned and outraged soliloquy, followed by ten minutes of silence while her two senior partners departed the Denver side of the videoconference, allegedly to answer other calls. A thinly disguised ploy, she figured, to let her cool down while they undoubtedly discussed the liability of having excitable women as lawyers. The thought was anything but amusing.

The two men returned to the other side of the screen, one the perpetrator, the other his cheerful accomplice.

"Okay, now we need you to calm down a bit, Judith, and look at this logically."

"What?" She was coming forward in her chair, already

irritated at what they'd probably said in the hallway.

"I mean, really now, just take a breath. I know you're furious, but we need logic."

The impeccably dressed senior partner on the other end of the video connection glanced at the other greying male and toyed with the pen in his hand before looking back at her – or at least at the image of her playing on their corresponding screen. The furnishings of a typically opulent corporate law office were visible in the background through the glass wall behind the men, and she knew they were looking at a much more tranquil scene framing the front range of the Rockies visible behind her in their satellite office.

Judith let out a long breath.

"Okay, gentlemen, I'm breathing. But I'm also seething, because you tricked me! This was supposed to be a grand gesture that would evaporate with this stupid prosecution. but it isn't evaporating! I'm getting the clear impression that neither of you is ready to throw this firm's might behind getting me out of this stupidity."

Jenks Walters, the firm's cofounder chuckled. "Well, the way I see it, other than risking a humiliating defeat at the appeals court trying to get you out of this with the media watching, our choices are rather limited. Essentially, we could offer the judge a job at the firm, or we could have him killed. The first solution would get us a lawyer who hasn't practiced law in twenty years, and I'll bet a sensitive part of my anatomy he'd be a bastard to work with; and, the second option would put us all in prison." He jerked around toward Roger Crandall and arched his eyebrows. "You see any advantage in either of those, Rog?"

Crandall's sharp features and humorless expression didn't change as he stared through the electronic ether to meet her eyes.

"Here's the deal, Judith," Crandall said, his words typically crisp, fired at the screen like small, verbal bullets. "I pushed you to do this thinking it was, indeed, going to go away. Gonzales was asking for help, and…"

"Whoa! Wait!" she said, coming forward in the chair she'd finally sunk into. "He came to *you?*"

Roger Crandall shook his head. "No, we saw each other at a civic function, I've tried cases before him many times, and he was lamenting his inability to get good counsel for this airline pilot."

"You are aware he thinks we're Gucci-clad fat cats, right? You know he loathes us?"

"That's his official attitude. That's the kind of class nonsense that gets him reelected."

"So, what, he's a drinking buddy of yours and a member of the country club?"

"No, Judith, he's a hardworking judge and he was obviously worried about this defendant, and, quite frankly, talking way out of school, worried about Richardson."

"So, you volunteered me? Seriously? Without discussing it? I mean, hell, Roger, I am a partner even if you're the king."

"Judith, I did not volunteer *you*. I told him I might be able to arrange something, and I took a look at our pro bono commitments thinking I could peel away one of our brightest associates, and guess who I found hadn't been holding up her end for the last two years?"

"Goddammit, you lied to me Roger."

"I did no such thing. And I am not about to support any attempt to use the appellate courts to overrule Gonzales' decision not to release you. The appellate judges will not look kindly on our making a big deal out of a case that is already a national embarrassment for Colorado and a narcissistic overreach by the DA."

"Narcissistic is hardy the word for it, Rog," Jenks Walters snorted. "Trying to convict an airline pilot who had to make a tough choice is a gross abuse of power."

Crandall ignored him.

"My point, Judith," Crandall continued, "…is that it does

not serve Walters, Wilson, and Crandall well to give Judge Gonzales the chance to show to the world that we are, in fact, the type of unresponsive, elitist fat cats he wrongly represents we are at election time. If we go crying to the appeals court, even if they grant the motion, we look bad."

"What are you saying?" Judith asked, her voice close to betraying her rising desire to scream.

"I'm saying," Roger continued, "...as clearly as I *can*, that the best thing for this law firm is for you to suck it up and defend the guy. Period."

"How? Would you tell me that? He's guilty as sin of murder in the second degree. He made a conscious decision. He knew if he did what he did that people would die. It may stink and be unprecedented to be going after an airline pilot making a tough call in flight, but the DA is technically, legally correct."

"Give Roger an opportunity to explain," Jenks interjected, earning a none-too-kind sideways glance from his partner over the lack of need for a champion.

Roger Crandall returned his gaze to Judith Winston. "It does not hurt to show that we are lawyers first, and corporate lawyers second, understand? We all took the same bar exam and it had did have a section on criminal law."

"Dammit, Gonzalez said the same thing, but that does not..."

"You're perfectly capable of handling this, Judith."

Just for a second – an interval so short the other two lawyers could not have noticed – Judith felt the full blown emotions of a drowning person, suddenly overwhelmed, her sense of self-esteem flattened by a visceral terror of failure and that same evil little voice somewhere in the back of her consciousness telling her she was faking it and *they* were going to find out! And just as quickly, as if addressing those very fears, Roger Crandall continued.

"You're sharp as hell, Judith, or I promise you wouldn't be here. We'll get you some help...get you tutored on criminal defense...even get you an experienced second on the case, but in the end, it will help our image to have you rise to this challenge. And, if you lose, well, hell, who could be expected to win something this twisted up? And we might ace it on appeal, you never know. I doubt anyone really wants to put that poor flyboy in prison."

"Other than our buffoonish DA you mean," she snapped.

"Go easy on our poor old district attorney," Jenks chuckled, leaning into the picture again. "Fact is, Grant's a politician, not a real lawyer, and he's all wrapped up in running for God."

Judith's head snapped forward as the car's automated system slammed on the brakes to avoid colliding with the pickup that had suddenly stopped in front of her. She forced her mind back to the present, glancing at her watch, relieved to see the traffic jam was finally breaking up ahead.

Finding Marty Mitchell's address on the northern perimeter of Boulder was almost too easy with the GPS on her phone. Judith parked in front of the house and rang his phone again with the same lack of response. The sun was riding low in the west, but over an hour away from descending below the front range, and the house was bathed in natural light, obscuring whether any lights were on inside. She walked to the front door and rang the bell, hearing the sound echo inside, but nothing stirred. He had talked of owning a very loud dog, but she could hear nothing from within.

Predictably, the doorknob refused to yield to her perfunctory effort to turn it, and she re-closed the screen door and moved to what was probably the living room window, shielding her eyes to peer inside at a well-kept interior, with photos on the coffee table and nothing seemingly out of place.

She pulled out her phone and punched in Marty's number again, keeping her ear to the window to see if she could hear a ring tone from inside, but there was nothing. Worried about neighbors misunderstanding what she was doing, Judith glanced around before deciding to circle the house, grasping the knob on the backdoor just to make sure all was secure and giving it a shake.

But the backdoor latch had apparently not seated, and without a deadbolt in place, the door suddenly swung open.

Judith moved inside cautiously, calling his name, listening in vain for a response. She checked the two bedrooms, finding the beds made with military precision, the bathroom towels ready for guests. She stopped for a second passing a floor to ceiling mirror and looked at herself, aware of the extra ten pounds she was always fighting to keep off, yet mostly pleased with the trim and disciplined woman she saw. Trim and disciplined was what any professional woman had to be, and the last thing she ever wanted anyone to know was how much effort it took, and how often the polished and unshakeable attorney they saw doubted herself.

The kitchen was neat and clean, except for a closed, half-eaten jar of peanut butter – a spoon set neatly beside it. She almost missed the several envelopes in the middle of the kitchen table. Each had a name on the front of it, but no address, or stamp, or return…

A sudden suspicion gripped her like a rising gorge, a sick feeling that she knew where this was going, where it had to go given what she was seeing. Each envelope was sealed, but she ripped open the first one and removed three pages of printed verbiage, trying to slow her reading to comprehend that it was a goodbye. Essentially a suicide note, with no indication of where or how.

Judith pulled one of the kitchen chairs and sat down hard, her mind racing. She opened the other three envelopes one by one, finding different messages but no additional clues. He had, however dated the signatures, and when she focused on the date, it was the 13th, one day ago.

How the hell can I find where he went? she thought. *He*

could be anywhere! Think, dammit!

Suddenly her plan to help him feel better with a more optimistic assessment of his chances with his upcoming trial seemed so pathetically short of the mark. He'd needed that assurance before, and now...

There was something she was missing. The feeling was practically shouting at her, quite audible over the pounding of her heart and her breathing as she tried to figure out what to do. Calling the police would be essentially useless, or maybe not. She didn't even know what car he drove, let alone his license plates...but they would.

She placed her cell phone on the table and stared at it, trying to visualize where his phone was, the one she had bought to give him some peace and privacy. That was an iPhone, just like hers. Maybe the cell company could locate it.

Holy crap! I can't believe I forgot!

She toggled on her phone's screen and moved to the note page, thumbing through the various things she'd typed until she found the one that mattered: The ID and password for the "Find My iPhone" function. She hadn't told him about preprogramming it, and in truth, it was because she didn't trust him. If the court had decided to put an ankle locater on him, she wanted a second way to find him if he fled. Maybe, just maybe, she thought, it would tell her where he was.

Judith worked to control her breathing as she togged on the appropriate app and carefully entered the information. The depiction of a compass rotated back and forth for almost a minute as her heart slowly sank.

It would have been too easy, she concluded, failing to recognize at first when the screen shifted to a map with a little green dot in the middle.

She leaned in, trying to interpret the map and the image. It was apparently a satellite depiction, but she had to zoom in and out several times to finally recognize where his cell phone was claiming to be, and as the recognition dawned, she looked up through the front windows of the house to see the big mountain itself.

Oh my God!

CHAPTER THREE

Summit of Longs Peak, 14,255 feet above sea level, 6:40 pm, August 14th

The temperature had dropped maybe ten degrees, prompting Marty to pull on a thick sweater under his windbreaker. Still, all in all it was pleasant, the lengthening shadows of the Rockies beginning to stretch east toward Loveland on the high plains that James Michener had made so attractive in his seminal work, *"Centennial."* Marty loved that book, and as he'd told more than a few friends, it was the allure of northeastern Colorado ignited by Michener's tale that had prompted him to bid on the next assignment his airline posted for the Denver pilot base. Buying a house in Boulder wasn't exactly living the dream on the prairie, but it was close. He'd been happy there, both as a bachelor, and then a married man, although without the kids he'd always wanted. Nevertheless, it had been a blissful existence that hadn't been quite as blissful for his ex.

He winced at the pain of the breakup, and the agony it had been writing a goodbye note to her.

Marty poured himself some more cabernet, amused at the thought that he might imbibe too much, realizing, as he replaced the bottle, that his pack was buzzing. He pulled out the cell phone, wondering why he hadn't turned off the ringer altogether. The screen showed a long list of missed calls, all of them from Judith Winston.

Dammit!

He'd forgotten about their planned phone call. He thought of sending a simple text: "Sorry to worry you, but goodbye," but she'd get the farewell note he'd just written in the little leather journal soon enough.

The familiar sounds of a smaller jet reached his ears and he looked up to track a corporate Gulfstream as it flew westbound thousands of feet above the peak. The sounds, however, immediately yanked him back to the left seat of the Boeing 757, raising his heart rate and triggering the nightmare all over again: The tail of a Beech 1900 commuter appearing out of nowhere just ahead, the frantic attempt to dump the 757's nose in time, the screech of tearing metal...

It was easier to think about his female lawyer, and especially the way he'd tried to torture her on their first meeting in May. Marty took another sip of wine and looked toward Boulder, recalling that morning as he reluctantly parked his car outside her office.

He remembered being puzzled as to why he was standing outside such a ritzy office building. This was an assigned lawyer, a public defender he had been ordered to see. Such people worked out of old store fronts or their mother's basement, didn't they?

But the address was correct, and with some confusion he'd pushed through the door into a corporate world of wealth and opulence he'd always been amused to visit.

It took thirty minutes and a desultory perusal of three fancy magazines before he was escorted into what resembled a board room. Marty took one of the oversized chairs and waited, somewhere between irritated and bored. He was aware the assigned lawyer was a woman. Probably some bespeckled little inge'nue, with her hair in a bun fresh out of law school and working a hundred hours a week as a drone hoping for partner status and a life someday. If he was dumb enough to let someone like that represent him, he'd probably end up in the gas chamber, or whatever Colorado used.

A door opened and Marty looked up in time to see Judith Winston enter the room accompanied by two male associates. The fact that she was beautiful had survived a concealment attempt – hair back, glasses, a stark business suit instead of girl clothes. Her honey blond hair alone was all but iridescent. Marty had to remind himself he was here to reject her, even insult her, but there was also something about the force of her commanding presence that left him off balance.

She had offered her hand as if forced to greet a leper, and when he'd given it a perfunctory shake, she withdrew and slid into the chair opposite his, already immersed in the paperwork. He half expected her to pull out hand sanitizer.

"You're Martin Mitchell, correct?"

Why else would I be sitting here, Babe? he thought, suppressing the retort in favor of a single word response. "Yes."

"All right. I, for some unknown reason bordering on insanity, have volunteered to represent you and have been so appointed by Judge Gonzales."

"Got it. You're fired."

Her head came up slightly in surprise, but she forced her eyes back to the legal pad, an elegant pair of gold-rimmed half-glasses professionally balanced on her nose .

"Sorry, but I won't permit you to fire me, primarily because I don't work for you, I work for the judge," she said, her voice matter-of-fact and devoid of any emotional ripple.

"Hey, in Colorado I have the right to fire my counsel! I checked on that."

"Yes. You do. But you've claimed that you're indigent and with your wild pushing away of everyone who's tried to help you, if you insist, I'll ask the judge to declare that you are of diminished capacity which would mean that you can't fire anyone. Not that I wouldn't appreciate being fired," she added. "but the judge has made it clear he won't let me withdraw. So, we're stuck with each other."

Her eyes remained on the papers.

Apparently, Marty thought, she was going to keep her distance by never looking at him.

"Look at me."

"I have no desire to engage in a staring contest, Mr. Mitchell."

"Captain."

"Okay. *Captain* Mitchell." She glanced up, quickly scanned his face and looked at her associates, who were doing their best to look obedient.

"Alrighty, then!" She said, eyes back on her papers. "Now that we're past the 'you're fired' nonsense, would you care to tell me why, if you're determined to spend the rest of your life behind bars by mounting no defense, you don't simply plead guilty?"

"Obviously, you wouldn't understand," he shot back. "You and the rest of this stupid legal system already think I am guilty."

She looked at him now, fixing him with an uncomfortable, emotionless gaze. He could actually feel the loathing.

"Captain Mitchell, what I do know is that you are *technically* guilty of the specific charges the DA has filed. You made a conscious decision to do what you did. Your company ordered you not to try it because people would be killed. You did it anyway, knowing the consequences, and they were dead right. People died as a result of your conscious, premeditated decision."

"Hey! Regardless of which choice I made, people were likely to die!" he shot back.

"Understood. Nevertheless, this out-of-control idiot DA wants to ride your conviction to higher office. What happened, unfortunately, can be viewed by criminal law – and a jury – as murder, although the death penalty is not on the table."

He began to get to his feet. "Thank you kindly, ma'am, but we're done."

"Sit down, Captain Mitchell."

"Screw you, lady."

"Wow! Such an irresistible invitation. But I'm no lady,

I'm your lawyer, so if gender is a problem for you, get over it. We've got bigger issues on our hands."

Marty remained on his feet, calculating the path of least resistance. He wanted to leave and slam the door behind him for effect, but something about her attitude was keeping him in place, and that didn't make sense.

He turned back to her. "Counselor, I don't care about your gender. I don't care if you're a lesbian, a shemale, or a hermaphrodite on heroin. I don't need your so-called help and I don't want it, and, as I said, we're done here. If the damned judge wants to throw me in jail for contempt, what the hell. I'm already more dead than any corpse you've ever encountered."

"Why?"

"*What?*"

He could see real anger in her eyes. "Sit your ass down right now, Captain!"

He should have barked back, but instead he shrugged and pulled out an adjacent chair. "If it pleases your majesty."

"Answer the question. Why? Why are you dead? Why do you want to give up? Are you that furious with being prosecuted, or is this some kind of pitiful survivor's remorse?"

"What, now you're a psychologist?," Marty snapped, "Because, lady, I've been rejected by the best."

"Wrong answer. Why?"

"You don't give up, do you? Don't you get it? The mere act of criminally prosecuting an airline pilot in the United States for doing his job the best way he could and for using his blanket emergency authority is so horribly assaultive and third-world banal and wrong…there's just no way to respond other than to say that I will not play your damned game. If America is dead and justice is dead, do what you may. I don't care. I *refuse* to play. Clear enough?"

"Not even close," Judith responded. "Tell me what happened."

"What?"

She cocked her head slightly and almost smiled as she sat back. "You didn't understand the question, Captain?"

"Give me one reason why I should go over everything with you? You're not even on my side. What did you take this case for, anyway? To make headlines? Are you some sort of an associate on the make in this law firm?"

"I'm a full partner."

"Really? Well then, this must either be some sort of exile for you, or you've got an angle. In any event, lady..."

"Judith."

"Excuse me?"

"I have a name, Captain Mitchell," she sighed in practiced contempt. "You may call me 'Judith,' or 'Ms. Winston, or 'Counselor.' You may *not* call me 'lady,' 'ma'am,' or for that matter, 'honey,' 'darling,' 'sweetheart,' or 'babe,' and no matter how upset you might get, you may never use the 'C' word or refer to me as 'bitch.' Clear?"

"Clear enough...*Ms.* Winston."

"Thank you, *Captain* Mitchell. Now, please, tell me what happened."

He snickered. "You don't know?"

"Of course I know, in gross terms, but I haven't heard the full story from my client. So maybe we could rectify that before the next ice age."

"And, what? You're going to get me off?"

"Probably not. But we'll see. I'll do my best."

Marty sat forward, almost leering at her, his index finger stabbing the polished surface of the conference room table.

"And that, Ms. Winston, is my story as well. Plain and simple."

"Excuse me?"

"I did my best. And now some slimeball DA wants me in prison. One hundred fifty-three people inside that 757, fourteen on my wing, and most of them made it home because of my decisions."

"Not all made it home."

"That's true...." he began, his voice choking off the remaining words. He swallowed hard and fought to re-compose himself. She could hear the deep, ragged breath as he forced his eyes back to hers. "I did my best. I tried my best to save everyone....every *one*." His eyes flashed with anger and impatience, his temper rising like an over-stoked fire. "You getting this?" Suddenly he was on his feet again, eyes blazing. "YOU GETTING THIS? I did my goddamned best with the hand they dealt me, and I will NOT be second guessed by someone who wasn't there!""

"You also climbed your jet to the wrong altitude."

The words stopped him cold, and Marty sank back into the chair like a deflating balloon, his fingers drumming an absent tattoo on the table before looking up at her, his voice noticeably subdued.

"Yes, we were at the wrong altitude."

"We? Not 'I'?"

He shrugged.

"Then tell me your story. All of it."

CHAPTER FOUR

Seven Months before — *January 21ˢᵗ*
Regal 12

LUCY ALVAREZ

Captain Marty Mitchell had shifted the phone to his right hand and sighed as he nodded to a female passenger standing nearby and then tried to catch the young gate agent's eyes. The agent seemed oblivious to his presence and he smiled a conspiratorial smile at her, a collegial attempt to share the pressures of upset passengers and disrupted schedules.

The agent looked up at last and smiled at him.

The dispatcher on the other end of the phone was taking his own sweet time coming back on the line after Marty had pushed him for answers. But as captain, he'd meant every word, even if he sounded overly demanding. Until they gave him the time he was supposed to have the airplane started and waiting at the "wash-rack"- the deicing hard stand near the end of the ramp - he simply wasn't going to leave the gate. The snow storm was too intense, and the absolute FAA prohibition about flying with any snow or ice on the wings was a rule he was not about to bend.

God, he was tired of such battles! Why couldn't he have been a pilot back when captains had some respect and authority, rather than being treated as disobedient peons every time they had the audacity to make an autonomous decision?

He watched the young agent dealing with the passengers with a friendly demeanor and a constant smile, obviously enjoying her job. It was a deeply refreshing sight, since too many of Regal's gate agents were smoldering with discontent over years of incompetent management or past mergers that hadn't worked out well. Good people, bad system, he thought, wishing for moment he could have flown for a really professional carrier like Delta, or a great company like Southwest or Alaska. Regal was always on the bottom in customer ratings, and they simply refused to spend the money necessary to change it.

"Captain Mitchell, you still there?" the dispatcher's voice snapped him back from his thoughts. The voice was pained.

"Yeah."

"Okay, I dropped everything else to get this, because you asked, but your time for the de-ice rack is eight-twenty. Normally you get that number right before push-back from operations."

He ignored the dig. "Any change in the forecast?"

"Don't you have the paperwork?"

"Yes."

"Well, it's all in there. But...I'll verbally re-brief it if you insist. It's just...we're really busy down here."

"No. That's okay. We'll be ready. Hope things get quieter for you guys." He replaced the handset behind the podium and looked around for Ryan Borkowsky, his copilot, who was treating the storm as if it were some sort of fun opportunity.

He'd noticed Ryan drifting off to one of the nearby coffee stands a few minutes back, presumably to buy his irritatingly predictable triple-shot, skinny, no-whip, one-Splenda mocha and another oatmeal scone. There was a yawning generational gap between the two of them, and it showed clearly in the younger man's attitude. Borkowsky was one of the small percentage of airline pilots who had signed on because flying was convenient, not because it was a life force. Marty had been startled to hear that he'd never spent time as a kid hanging around airports, pumping gas into light airplanes, or otherwise just being in love with flying. How was that possible? How was it possible to be a pilot and not be in love with flying? The very concept was offensive.

"So, what's the story, fearless leader?" Borkowsky's laconic voice reached him from behind. Marty turned, wincing internally at the unprofessional image before him. Borkowsky's blue uniform coat was unbuttoned, revealing his slowly exploding girth and a badly wrinkled shirt, and he was munching indelicately on a scone like a hungry horse cropping grass.

"I wondered where you were," Marty said, trying to keep his tone friendly, "Then I remembered, they sell scones in the terminal."

"You ever lose track of me, that's where to look. I love these things."

Marty suppressed the word "obviously."

Twice he'd flown with Borkowsky. He could be engaging and funny and he was obviously a competent airman, but what rubbed Marty the wrong way was his disengaged attitude, as if he was just going through the motions. Far too blasé.

The thought of their Orlando layover hotel entered Marty's head and he wondered if he'd be able to drag himself to the 24-hour hotel gym once they got there. After a tense evening like this he'd need a workout.

The ancient 24 pin printer positioned for the pilots behind the gate podium was chattering again, and Marty waited for it to stop before ripping off the latest opus: a hardcopy of the weather report. Buried in the verbiage was the news that many of the airports in a four hundred mile radius of Denver were closing because of the storm. Salt Lake had been overwhelmed much earlier in the day. Colorado Springs had just closed, their last runway hopelessly behind the snow removal abilities of their exhausted crews, and the storm was marching like a ravenous beast on everything to the east. All the private fields, and even Buckley, the Air

National Guard base nearby, were closed, their runways now drifting dangerously with accumulated snow. Denver International itself was down to two operating runways, and if the dispatcher was wrong, they could end up with only one in operation before the evening rush was done. Inbound flights were stacking up in holding patterns in four directions and the disruption to Regal Airlines' intricate schedule was beginning to get serious.

The gate agent stepped toward him. "You ready to board 'em, Captain?" she asked sweetly.

"Yes, I guess we are. About time to get out of your hair."

The copilot was watching her approvingly as the agent turned and left to open the jetway door.

"So, I guess it's time for me to go out in the blizzard and do my Eskimo impression," Ryan said.

"What?" Marty managed, trying to fit the words with realistic meaning.

"You know. Put on a parka and kick some tires," Borkowsky said as he slurped down the last of his mocha and made an unsuccessful attempt to arc the wadded up scone wrapper into the nearest trash can.

Marty turned away, working to generate his own smile at the passengers as he picked up his brain bag and headed for the jetway. This was no evening for apathy, or a lackadaisical first officer. He made a mental note to double-check everything Borkowsky did.

CHAPTER FIVE

Seven Months before — *January 21st*
Mountaineer 2612

At the same moment Captain Mitchell was settling into the left seat of Regal Flight 12, the captain of Mountaineer Airlines Flight 2612 stood crammed into Mountaineer's tiny operations office two concourses distant, wondering why the Durango, Colorado, airport wasn't on the list of snowed-in airfields. Apparently, the huge storm was moving more to the north and east than to the south, but the blizzard was so all encompassing it was hard to imagine anywhere in the western U.S. being spared the rapidly developing snowdrifts.

Michelle Whittier finished studying her paperwork and signed the release form. If they could actually get out of Denver, there was no reason they couldn't get their passengers to Durango – and God knew the struggling little regional airline she flew for needed every dollar that each of those passengers represented.

Not that many of those dollars were going to Mountaineer's pilots. Then again, she appreciated the fact that she was still employed and sitting in the captain's seat. Too many captains – even those with major airlines like Delta and American – had watched their salaries slashed in massive give-backs or otherwise been forced over the years by layoffs to return to the copilot ranks flying for half their previous paychecks. The airline industry seemed determined to destroy itself insidiously by giving away its product in an endless, lemming-like march to lower and lower fares, while killing off any remaining passenger loyalty with nickel-and-dime charges for bags, food, and soon probably even seat belts and emergency oxygen masks.

In fact, Michelle thought, she was plain lucky little Mountaineer was still in business. Too many regionals weren't, and too many regional airline copilots were making less than twenty-five thousand a year – some getting by with food stamps. More than a few regional pilots were moonlighting at other jobs just to make ends meet, and even though the long-predicted pilot shortage was already upon them, the owners of too many regional carriers were still paying their pilots the lowest wages they could get by with while trying to stay profitable flying as surrogates for major airlines that were very accomplished at playing one regional off against another.

In the pilot ranks, it was a shared agony, and there was a stoic tendency to adopt workarounds in support of each other, workarounds borne of sympathy for exhausted moonlighters when they showed up all but brain dead and the other pilot quietly flew solo in order to let the fatigued airman doze most of the way to destination.

Tonight, Michelle had a green copilot still on probation, but the young man was wide awake, sharp and enthusiastic. That was a relief! They were going to need all the coordination and alertness they could manage.

"Michelle, good to see you," one of the ramp guys said, brushing past her to move behind the counter. She waved and was jostled again as another ramp agent came through the door tromping snow from his shoes and complaining with a big smile. The copilot, whose name she had momentarily forgotten, was already outside in the teeth of the storm preflighting the small twin engine turboprop. Michelle checked the paperwork to locate his name, embarrassed she couldn't retain it for five minutes.

Luke! Luke Marshall. Okay.

She had to greet him by name when he reached the

cockpit. That was important. There was nothing worse than forgetting a crewmember's name if you wanted to form a real team.

The desire for coffee suggested itself, but the thought of pushing through the crowded and anxious energy of the concourse again to reach Starbucks squelched the idea. Better to get to the aircraft and get ready. Provided her little airline could afford another round of deicing fluid and get the attention of the contractor who took care of their deicing needs at the gate, she had a chance of getting out on time.

CHAPTER SIX

Seven Months before — January 21st
Air Traffic Control Tower, Denver International Airport

"Regal Twelve, Denver Ground. Runway Two-Six is now closed. You're cleared to Runway Two-Five via Taxiway Golf. Caution, snow removal men and equipment off to the east of Golf."

"Roger," the unseen pilot reported, his tone slightly more cheerful than the situation justified. "Regal Twelve is cleared to Runway Two-Five via Golf."

The shift supervisor in Denver International's control tower had been pulled into the ground control position when two of his controllers couldn't get to the airport. Now it was getting irritating with the airport progressively losing control of the blizzard's assault. The last straw was hearing one of his controllers replace the approach control tie line and announce that one of the regional flights was coming back.

"Who?" Jimmy Toulon asked, a bit too sharply. Too much time in the office and too little in a control position meant his temper was unduly short.

"It's Mountaineer 2612. He can't get his gear to retract. Tracon wanted to bring him back to Two-Six, but..."

"Runway Two-Five is all we got."

"They already know."

"But," Jimmy added, "Tell Tracon to give me at least ten minutes to clear out these other departures."

"Will do."

The controller picked up the tie line again as Jimmy struggled to make out the fuzzy lights through the snow obscuring almost all the visibility from the tower cab. The ground radar was the basic tool they had in situations this bad, and he was appreciative of how easy it now was to see the data block of each moving aircraft.

The voice of the snow removal boss came through his headset at the same moment.

"Tower, be advised, if it keeps up at this rate, we've got, tops, an hour before we're going to have to give up on Two Five between Bravo Four and Golf."

Great! Jimmy thought. *We'll be down to nine thousand feet of slick concrete on one remaining runway.*

Complete closure of the airport before 10 pm was a real possibility.

Several floors below in the Terminal Approach Control Radar room the computer-generated blip representing the Beech 1900 regional airliner known as Mountaineer 2612 had completed the course reversal ordered two minutes before. The controller issued a turn for an inbound British Air Boeing 777 before refocusing her thoughts on Mountaineer. He was doing around a hundred fifty knots with the gear hanging out, but he'd undoubtedly have enough fuel, and the tower wanted an extra ten minutes, so...

I'll bring him northwest past the airport, then I'll turn him east, she decided. "Mountaineer Twenty-six-twelve, Denver Approach, turn left now Three-two-zero, maintain twelve thousand."

"Roger, Mountaineer Twenty-six-twelve, left to Three-two-zero, maintain twelve."

The controller mentally acknowledged Mountaineer's compliance and focused on the approaching 777. "Speedbird Sixty-two, cleared ILS Runway Two-Five now, contact Denver Tower One-three-two-point-three-five."

"Speedbird Six-two, cleared approach, Tower on One-three-two-point-three-five. Cheerio, ma'am."

She started to respond in kind, then stopped herself. Too much competing traffic and a rapidly deteriorating airport for casual exchanges. Keeping the picture was more important than radioed niceties, even though she always loved acknowledging the professionalism of the British crews.

In the tower cab, Jimmy Toulon verified the position of the outbound Regal 757 and issued the directive to contact the tower controller standing next to him. He heard the pilot acknowledge in that same too-happy voice and wondered why it irritated him so.

The controller in the tower position issued the takeoff clearance along with the standard warnings about slick concrete and poor braking action, and Jimmy noticed the electronic blip begin moving down the east-west runway as the big Boeing accelerated to flying speed and lifted off to the west.

In many ways, he envied the pilots climbing out of a storm. In thirty minutes they'd be miles above the weather and looking at stars, and he'd still be in the middle of an arctic blizzard, all his instincts on red alert against anyone making a mistake. A complete airport shutdown would be a relief. Nights like this really worried him.

CHAPTER SEVEN

Seven Months before — January 21st
Regal 12

Marty Mitchell glanced over at the copilot, wondering why he hadn't reacted.

"Ryan? I said flaps up, set Two-Ten."

"Oh! Sorry!" Ryan Borkowsky replied, hurriedly raising the flap handle before reaching for the dial on the forward panel to set the airspeed for the autothrottle system. "Flaps up and setting Two-Hundred-Ten."

There was nothing but snow streaking past the cockpit windows now, the lights of Denver lost in the surreal streams as the tower controller handed them off to the departure controller. Marty was still flying it manually, holding his altitude at fourteen degrees nose up as they climbed.

"Regal One Two, contact departure now, One-Twenty-Three-Five."

"Regal one-two to one-two-three-five," Ryan responded. *"Have a great night,"* he added, changing the radio frequency. *"Denver departure, your friendly Regal Twelve with you, climbing through seven for eight thousand."*

"Regal twelve, radar contact. Turn right, Three-Two-Zero degrees, climb to and maintain nine thousand."

"Roger, cleared to nine," he said turning to Marty. "One to go, *Cap-i-tán.*"

Marty nodded, ignoring the copilot's attempt at humor. It was grating on his concentration.

"Passing eight thousand for nine thousand," Marty

confirmed, reaching out to rotate a small knob on the forward panel to bring the target to 9,000 feet. He clicked on the autopilot and verified that it was set up to capture the new altitude as a melodic chime confirmed they were one thousand feet below level off. He glanced up at the same moment, confirming all the 757's anti-ice systems were working, porting 300 degree centigrade hot air from the engines to the leading edges of the wings and tail, and the forward lips of both engines.

The big jet began automatically shallowing its climb to level at 9,000 feet as the controller returned, his voice a rapid-fire series of instructions intertwined with each reply from the various flights he was handling.

"Frontier Sixty-Two, right turn now to Zero-Eight-Zero degrees, descend to and maintain one-two thousand."

There was a sudden loud squeal and heavy static in their headsets as two radios tried to transmit at the same time. The squeal diminished but didn't disappear.

"Frontier Sixty-two, Zero-Eight-Zero and one-two thousand."

"All flights, we have a stuck mic on the frequency... please check your radios," the controller said. "Alaska Eighteen, right turn now to One-Eight-Zero, descend to nine thousand."

"Ah, Alaska Eighteen, say again approach? Lot of noise in the background."

"Roger, Alaska Eighteen. Turn right now to One-Eight-Zero, and descend to nine thousand."

"Roger, Alaska Eighteen down to nine thousand and right turn to One-Eight-Zero, correct?"

"Affirmative, Alaska."

The squeal and static on the frequency was intensifying, and the controller was seriously considering shifting everyone to a different frequency if it continued. A scratching and voices could be heard in the background, characteristic of a microphone stuck in the transmit position.

The controller tried again: "Everyone on frequency, we have a stuck mic…please check your transmit buttons. Break, Mountaineer Twenty-Six-Twelve, maintain one-one thousand."

"Denver, Twenty-Six twelve is level one-two thousand. You want us at one-one?"

"Say again, Twenty-Six Twelve?"

"Affirmative. You want us to descend?"

Ah, Twenty-Six Twelve, negative. Break, Regal Twelve, continue your climb to one-two thousand, correction, one-one thousand."

Ryan punched the transmit button.

"Regal One-Two climbing to one two…one…one two thousand."

Marty pressed a finger to his earpiece and glanced toward the copilot. "Was that one-two thousand?"

Ryan returned the glance with a confused expression as he reached for the altitude knob.

"Excuse me?"

"Was that one-two, or one-one?"

"That was for one-two," he replied, hesitating before dialing 12000 into the window as Marty watched to verify it. "There's another flight they're descending to one-one, but there's so much damned noise with that stuck mic…"

The 757 responded obediently, continuing the climb as the controller's voice returned, apparently dealing with a precautionary emergency.

"Mountaineer Twenty-Six Twelve, do you need the equipment?"

"Ah, negative, approach. We just can't retract our gear. It's down and locked."

Suddenly the stuck mic disappeared and the frequency returned to the normal quiet between transmissions.

"Mountaineer Twenty-Six Twelve, please say fuel remaining and souls on board."

"We've got four thousand pounds of fuel and sixteen

souls on board, including the crew."

"Okay, Twenty-Six Twelve, descend now and maintain nine thousand."

There was no answer from the other flight, but at the same moment the mechanical voice of the traffic collision avoidance system suddenly rang through the 757's cockpit.

"Traffic. Traffic."

Marty squinted at the glass display before him at the yellow tagged target ahead which just as quickly disappeared. The TCAS had fallen silent, indicating, he figured, some sort of radar ghost and not a real aircraft.

"What was that?" Ryan asked.

"Don't know. I had a target ahead of us for a split second, but I didn't see an altitude and it's gone now. Let's hope it stays gone," Marty replied, his eyes riveted on the screen in front of him where the vanished target had been.

The controller was still calling for the Mountaineer aircraft without success. "Mountaineer Twenty-Six Twelve, do you read Denver Approach? We've lost your transponder. If you hear Denver, turn right now to zero-nine-zero degrees."

On the flight deck of Mountaineer 2612, Captain Michelle Whittier was working by battery-powered lights as she stuffed a small flashlight in her mouth trying to bring at least one of the aircraft's generators back on line.

"What the hell happened?" her copilot was asking.

"We lost both generators. I don't know why. Better get out the checklist."

"I lost the approach controller, too. Aren't the radios on your side supposed to still be useable on battery?"

"Yeah...hold on." Michelle raised the toggle switch to reconnect the left starter-generator, but it snapped off line instantly, just like the right one. Something was badly wrong. "We've got some sort of short. Hey, were you using number two radio?"

"Yes. I'll get his frequency in your radio...yours *is* on

battery, right?"

"Should be. Give me the checklist. Was he trying to give us a clearance when it went off?'

"He said to descend, but it went off before I heard for sure, but I thought he was saying nine."

"Okay, Luke, you've got the aircraft. Fly cross-cockpit on my panel while I try to get him back."

"Twelve thousand?"

"Yes, maintain our last assigned altitude."

"I think he was going to clear us to nine. I heard part of nine."

"Yeah, but he didn't complete it and we didn't acknowledge it. Our last assigned is twelve. Maintain twelve."

"Yes, Ma'am," the copilot said.

"I'm not getting anything on this radio," she said.

"I have a cell phone," the copilot volunteered.

"Yeah, so do I. Good idea. We'll try that if we can't get him."

"They probably still have our skin paint on radar, but the transponder's off if the generators are off," the copilot added.

The captain was already pulling out her cell phone and staring at the buttons, wondering just how to call the FAA's Denver Tracon on a telephone. She punched in "911," wondering if anyone would believe her.

In the dimly lit electronic nerve center known as Denver Tracon, Sandy Sanchez had turned and motioned for his supervisor the moment it was apparent he'd lost contact with Mountaineer 2612 . There was a small knot of apprehension in the pit of his stomach as he turned to vocalize the problem.

"Yeah, Sandy."

"Mountaineer Twenty-Six Twelve...I've lost his transponder and radio contact, but I think I still have a raw radar return. I tried to turn and descend him but that's when I lost him."

"No turn on the skin paint target?"

"Nothing."

"What's the plan with Regal Twelve?" Jerry LaBlanc asked, pointing to Regal's datablock.

"I'm climbing him to eleven."

"Yeah, but he's right behind Mountaineer, who may not stay at twelve."

Someone put a hand on LaBlanc's shoulder.

"Jerry, we've got the Denver police on line twenty-three wanting to know if they should patch through a call supposedly from Mountaineer."

"A call?"

"Cell phone."

"Hell, yes! Which line?"

"Punch up two-three and hang on." The controller turned and motioned to an assistant halfway across the room who spoke urgently into the handset he was holding. Jerry ripped the handset out of the cradle and fingered the right button, listening to a series of clicks before a voice came through."

"Okay, go ahead."

"Is this Denver Approach?"

"Yes! Is this Mountaineer Twenty-Six Twelve?"

"Roger that," Michelle Whittier responded with obvious relief. "Denver, in addition to our gear problem, we've now had a dual generator failure and are on thirty-minute-rated batteries and need to get down. Radios are out and transponder's out."

"Say heading and altitude," Jerry ordered.

"Ah...still at twelve and heading three-two-zero. We need to turn for terrain."

"Standby..." Jerry said, turning back to Sandy. "You want to turn him...*her*...to zero-nine-zero and descend?"

Sandy started to answer, but he was leaning forward, peering at the datablock for Regal Twelve.

"What the...?"

"What?"

"What the hell is Regal doing?" Sandy Sanchez was stabbing at the transmit button. "Regal Twelve, say altitude!"

CHAPTER EIGHT

Seven Months before — *January 21st*
Regal 12

The raw instinct in Marty Mitchell's mind propelled by decades of experience instantly translated the controller's tone as an emergency. If a controller was demanding their altitude, something was wrong – and the most likely cause would be a mistake.

Marty's eyes raked past the altimeter now showing level at 12,000 feet and he glanced at the copilot in an accusatory microsecond. Had they dialed in the wrong number somehow? Time had already dilated for Marty, whose career was on the line for any FAA violation even if his copilot had led him there.

Is 12-thousand right? he questioned himself, vaguely remembering the exchange with the copilot as he raised a finger to keep Ryan from responding and buying further trouble. Marty hit the transmit button himself.

"Regal Twelve is level one-two thousand, as instructed."

He released the button to listen for the answer, inwardly holding his breath, and wondering somewhere in the periphery of his consciousness what the gray shape rapidly coalescing out of the snow might be. He thought he caught a white light, then a red beacon, and in the space of a second it grew into the nightmare shape of an airplane.

"Regal Twelve, descend immediately to eleven thousand! Acknowledge!"

The controller's voice was somewhere distant, trumped

by the rapidly evolving nightmare before him.

Marty's hands grabbed the yoke by instinct, shoving violently and automatically snapping off the autopilot as he threw the big Boeing forward into a negative G maneuver trying to dive clear. But the specter was too close and a bit lower he now realized, and before he could even form the intent to yank back on the throttles and the yoke, whatever it was flashed by on the right accompanied by the bone-crushing impact of metal against metal, head-on into to the nose, an impact that threw them forward and then to the left as a flash of fire accompanied by something scraping over the top of the cockpit as the 757's right wing collided with something big.

There was another momentary flash of flame on the right and then nothing.

The noise and shuddering and cacophony of warnings going off in the big Boeing's cockpit left him nothing to do but react with an aviator's muscle memory, his hands and feet all over the controls urging the 757 back to some form of stable flight, his eyes taking in the fact that somehow both engines were still running, and somehow they were still flying, though the big jet was yawing horribly to the right even with almost full left rudder. Something was pulling down on the right wing as if they'd lost half their lift on that side. The yoke was almost all the way over to the left, the rudder almost full to the left, and it felt like he was millimeters away from losing control.

"WHAT HAPPENED?" the copilot was shouting, clearly panicked. "WHAT HAPPENED?"

Marty checked the altitude and airspeed. They were still flying, but only barely. He goosed the right engine up in power almost to the limit, feeling a bit of relief in the control forces required to stay airborne. The speed had crunched down from the 250 knots to around 200 knots, but the big bird felt like it was wallowing, and he let the speed creep back up to 250, noting somewhere in the back of his mind the more stable feel at the higher speed.

"Midair!" was all Marty could manage.

"THERE'S...THERE'S SOMETHING ON OUR RIGHT WING!"

"Calm down, Ryan! Tell me what you...you're seeing."

The copilot was swiveled around in the right seat, straining against his seat belt to look out the side window.

"THAT'S ALL I CAN SEE!"

Intercom call chimes were ringing but Marty dared not let go of the controls.

"Ryan, pull yourself...together...answer the, uh, intercom. I have to know..."

"OKAY!"

"...know...what's back there. What's going on. How bad are we hit?"

His own words sent another chill down his back. Wasn't that the phrase the doomed crew of a Boeing 727 used seconds after hitting a light plane over San Diego years ago...a disaster no one survived?

"Ah...Ryan...you may have to go back and look yourself."

The copilot was nodding vigorously enough to register in his peripheral vision, and his eyes were huge when Marty glanced at his face. Slowly, Ryan reached over and fumbled with the interphone panel before remembering to pick up the handset.

"Y-yes?" he stammered.

The 757 shuddered sickeningly for a second and then stabilized, as if something was still happening on the right wing. He glanced at the Master Caution light and realized his ears had been popping. The cabin had been breached and they were depressurizing. Must get the oxygen masks on, he thought, before remembering they were only at 12,000 feet. That could wait.

Marty tried to force himself to calm down and think. He had it under control for the moment. Both engines were running. He had her fairly level, even if his left leg was beginning to shake against the force he was using to hold the left rudder in.

Trim! He remembered, holding back the urge to pull his right hand off the yoke and motor the control for the rudder trim full left. Gingerly he transferred all the force to his left hand, realizing the control forces weren't that excessive. Full left rudder trim was helping his leg now, but not much else.

Marty glanced at the center panel to read the warnings that had popped up automatically on the computer display screen. Thank God the hydraulic systems were not part of the list, he thought. All flight controls appeared intact. But whatever airplane had been out there they had hit and he was sure whoever those poor people were, they were spiraling to their deaths at that very moment. How his 757 was still airborne was already the stuff of luck, and that luck might not last.

What the holy hell was he doing at our altitude? Marty's mind was screaming, the thought sending another arctic chill through his spine as he connected the approach controller's attempts to reach the Mountaineer commuter, the phantom TCAS warning that had disappeared, and worst of all, the controller's last urgent call asking their altitude.

Oh, God! Did we screw up?

The controller's voice was still in his ear, demanding they descend immediately, as if he already knew about the collision.

Marty worked his finger back to the transmit button on the top of the control yoke as he fought to maintain control.

"Denver Approach...Regal Twelve...declaring an emergency! We've hit someone up here. Midair collision. We think there's damage to our right wing but we're still flying. We're trying to assess the damage."

A few telling seconds elapsed before the controller's voice returned, quieter, tense, and focused. "Roger, Regal Twelve. You need an emergency return to Denver?"

"Yes. Affirmative. We may...need to do a controllability check, but...yes."

There was a flurry of motion to his right and Marty realized Ryan had dropped the receiver and was half out of his seat, obviously intent on getting out the door to the aft cabin.

"What, Ryan?"

"Ah...ah, they...they're telling me...I got to see this for myself, but..."

"What?"

"A PLANE'S STUCK ON OUR WING!"

"*WHAT?*"

"A plane. Whoever we hit. They're...they're out there on the right wing. She says they can see people in the windows."

"That's not possible!" For a split second they looked at each other, the copilot half out of his seat and clearly panicked, Marty in complete disbelief with time dilating and seconds feeling like minutes as the momentary glimpse of the other aircraft flashing by replayed in his mind.

"Go! Get back there and assess it."

"Right." Ryan resumed the uncoordinated scramble to get the cockpit door to open, all but tumbling out into the alcove by the forward galley. One of the flight attendants shot into the cockpit as soon as he was out, and Marty could feel the panic in her voice before he even glanced at her ashen face.

"Captain! We've...got a plane full of people stuck on our wing!"

"Anyone hurt?"

"I don't know...it looks pretty mangled up."

"In *our* airplane?"

"Oh...no. Oh God! What are we going to do?"

"We're going to make an emergency landing. Get the cabin prepared."

"Can we bring them in our cabin?"

"What?"

"Those people?"

"Get...get the cabin prepared for an emergency landing. NOW!"

She nodded and turned, then realized she hadn't uttered an answer and leaned back in, wild eyed. "Yes, sir."

Ryan was back almost as fast, breathing hard, standing between the seats as if he was afraid to resume his position in the copilot's chair.

"What've we got?"

"I've...I don't believe it. It's a Beech 1900 , on our right wing, over the right engine. We're leaking fuel like a sonofabitch...he's gashed a huge chunk of the top of our wing...and his wing and engine on the left are gone, mostly, but the fuselage is intact and, Captain, the people inside I think are okay, or at least alive."

"The fuselage is stuck?"

"It's...I don't know how to describe it...the remains of his left engine cowling are there, the prop and actual engine are gone, but the landing gear on the right side...best I can tell, it's just jammed into our wing. I think it's the only thing holding him there."

"So, he's not going to fall off?"

"I don't know. He's rocking around in the airflow and it's like our slipstream is trying to lift him off. I...I think we're getting lift from his right wing, the way its cocked up. But if they fall off...they can't fly like that."

"Okay."

"Can *we* fly?"

"We are flying."

"I mean, can we get us both down okay?"

Marty looked around, recognizing the all but feral panic in the young man's eyes.

"We'll do out best, Ryan."

"I mean...I mean...Captain, there are people *alive* out there!'

CHAPTER NINE

Seven Months before — *January 21st*
Denver TRACON (Terminal Radar Control Facility)

Denver Approach Controller Jerry LaBlanc responded to Regal 12's midair report by raising the tie line to his ear – the connection with Mountaineer's cell phone – hoping for audible confirmation that the regional was still airborne and talking and perfectly okay. He could feel himself praying for reassurance with the same desperation of a gambler hoping for a jackpot with his last dollar.

But Regal had overrun Mountaineer's faint radar return, and now there was only the 757 on Sandy's datascreen. And there was the possibility they'd screwed it up somehow as controllers, and that was unacceptable.

"Mountaineer, you still with me?" Jerry asked, his voice clearly strained. The line seemed open but all he could hear in the background was...something. Noise. No voices. Like the phone was being banged around. "Mountaineer, do you copy Denver?"

He was standing partly behind and beside Sandy Sanchez who was hunched over his control position. Sandy's eyes were riveted on Regal 12's datablock, his voice issuing the same instruction as a moment before. "Regal Twelve, turn right now to a heading of zero nine zero degrees. Descend to and maintain nine thousand."

It seemed suddenly cold in the darkened control room.

"He said the word 'midair,' right?" Jerry asked, bending down slightly.

Sandy jerked around, startled. "What?"

"He said he'd hit someone?" Jerry LaBlanc insisted.

"Yes!" Sandy replied, taking in the tie line still held to Jerry's ear. "Do you still have Mountaineer on the line?"

"No...well, I'm not sure."

Two other supervisors had silently gathered behind them, listening intently.

"I've lost his skin paint, and..." Sandy added, his words hanging in agonizing limbo between them, as if finishing the sentence might doom the little turboprop by making the midair real.

Regal 12 broke the icy silence. "Ah...Denver, I'm... having a struggle up here just flying straight, but I'll start a slow turn to the right to zero-nine-zero. I...ah...did you clear us to nine thousand?"

"Affirmative, Regal Twelve. And please say fuel and souls on board."

Somewhere inside Sandy knew he was snapping off the routine questions and instructions in order to force the situation itself back to a controllable routine. By the numbers. Get them back by the numbers.

Regal 12 was transmitting again, the voice hesitant and distracted, and almost irritated. "I...the fuel is...I don't have time right now. When I can, I'll...read that to you. Our dispatcher knows."

"What's your status, Regal?" Sandy insisted. "Are you controllable?"

Each question was followed by a deep silence like the agonizing wait for more clues after a scream in the dark. But each time as Jerry Lablanc was sure he'd have to intercede – grab a headset and say *something* – Regal 12's transmitter clicked on again.

"Having a struggle because the right wing's lost...ah... you know, lift, and... we've got all that extra weight out there."

Sandy Sanchez glanced around at Jerry, searching for

help in translating the pilot's words, but there wasn't any. Extra weight? He snapped his gaze back to the datablock as if his concentration alone could help the apparently stricken Boeing.

"You've lost *what*, Regal? Your right wing, or...I mean, lift? What's wrong with your right wing?"

More silence. One of the supervisors was urgently reporting the situation into another tie line alerting a wider circle. Jerry was still pressing the receiver to his ear, almost sure now he heard what sounded like voices among the background noise, and maybe even voices yelling somewhere distant.

"Roger, Approach," the Regal pilot resumed, "...we've got the weight of the other airplane out there, and...I'm having a struggle holding us level."

"What does he mean, 'weight of the other plane'?" one of the supervisors asked as they all looked at each other. But Sandy Sanchez' voice was already asking.

"Regal Twelve, you mean the damage done to your right wing by a collision is giving you control problems? You say you're controllable and want to return to Denver International immediately, correct?"

One of the supervisors behind Jerry LaBlanc held his hand over a receiver and leaned into the group. "There are no reports of a crash in the vicinity of Broomfield. Mountaineer was over Broomfield when you lost him, right?"

"You mean he might still be airborne?" another asked, as Jerry motioned for quiet.

"Regal Twelve, Denver Approach. I need to know what you want, sir, and I need to understand what's going on with your right wing so we can assist."

This time the transmitter came alive with a cockpit conversation – a shrill voice in the background answered by the pilot working the radio.

"........pretty mangled up."

"In our airplane?"

"Oh God! What are we going to do?"

"We're going to make an emergency landing. Get the cabin prepared."

Their transmitter clicked off and Sandy stabbed at his transmit button

"Regal Twelve, Denver Approach, we...heard part of that exchange and copy you need to make an emergency landing. But...I'm still unclear on the nature of the problem on your right wing?"

The pilot's voice came back solo this time, more forceful than before, as if he'd finally gained control over the situation.

"Okay, Denver, I haven't seen it myself...my crew tells me we have the fuselage of a smaller airplane imbedded on top of our right wing from the collision, and that the occupants of that aircraft are apparently alive."

For a few heartbeats the collection of controllers in Denver Tracon stood in frozen silence, their minds trying to pull from the varied richness of their aviation experience an image of what had just been described.

But there was no image, and no precedent.

Sandy turned to the others briefly, reading the disbelief on each face as confirmation he'd have to figure it out himself.

"Regal, is the other airplane intact?"

"If you mean, can it fly if it falls off? No. Their left wing is gone, or mangled, or something."

"Roger...what are...I mean...how can we help you?"

The silence rose to a crescendo before Regal's transmitter cut in again.

"Just...ah...vectors, Denver, to the longest runway you've got at DIA."

Sandy glanced at a note that had been slid in front of him. Denver International had lost the battle trying to keep a second runway open. Runway Two-Six was now closed and they were down to one useable strip of concrete, but the bad news went on: *DIA says they may have to close part of the remaining runway in two hours if the snowfall continues at this rate.*

There was no point in reading the second part to Regal, Sandy figured. They were going to get him on the ground before then anyway.

"Regal, ah...Regal Twelve, Denver Approach. That'll be Runway Two-Five. All other runways closed by snow."

"All twelve thousand feet available on Runway Two-Five?"

"Roger, Regal Twelve. The entire runway is available."

For now, he thought.

CHAPTER TEN

Seven Months before — *January 21st*
Regal 12

For some reason, the right wing was feeling lighter, and for a few moments Marty hadn't any idea why. He was still having to hold a huge amount of force to keep the yoke rolled to the left, but it definitely was becoming easier, and that meant something was changing, which was not necessarily good.

His eyes caught the fuel gauges on the center panel at the same moment the memory of the copilot's voice replayed in his head: "We're leaking fuel like a sonofabitch..."

Jesus! Of course! Marty thought, wondering if he had mere seconds or minutes to change the fuel distribution panel before the right engine started sucking air instead of kerosene. If the right engine flamed out, the prospects for restart would be nil, and the chances for staying airborne and under control with one engine and the wreck of another airplane on the right wing were zilch.

Somewhere deep inside a small prayer of thanks was playing like a mantra that the collision hadn't physically destroyed the right engine. He wouldn't be having this conversation with himself if it had.

I can't believe this is happening!

Marty held the bird steady with his left hand while reaching to the overhead panel to make the adjustments – changing from the tank-to-engine takeoff configuration to have both of the hungry Pratt and Whitneys feeding off the unaffected center tank. That would preserve all

66 | JOHN J. NANCE

the counterbalancing weight of the full number one tank in the left wing. He'd have to get Ryan to help with the calculations in a few minutes – how many pounds were left in the center tank and the left versus whatever their fuel flow was at low altitude in order to figure out how long they could stay airborne. Whatever the answer, it would be measured in hours, and surely they'd be on the ground long before that.

We're supposed to be at nine thousand and we're still at twelve, he reminded himself, his stomach contracting again at the near-certainty they'd created the whole disaster by blundering up to the wrong altitude. Maybe it was an old tendency to fatalism, but somehow – even without reviewing all the details in his memory – he knew. He just damn well knew! He'd promised himself to double check everything this copilot did, and he hadn't.

Slowly Marty let the jet descend, pulling the power back slightly to keep the airspeed within ten knots of where it had been. If he changed anything about the angle of attack – slowed or sped up too much – there was no way to predict what would happen to the changed aerodynamics of the Boeing. But if 250 knots gave them some degree of stable flight, he wasn't about to change the airspeed.

Marty glanced at the overhead pressurization panel. The cabin was essentially depressurized, but there was a very slight pressure differential a result of the air conditioning packs still shoving air into the cabin. Somewhere along the upper right side the fuselage had been punctured, not that it mattered much now.

The copilot had been shuttling back and forth to the cockpit as if manic action could help the situation. Suddenly he was back again, trying to close and lock the cockpit door behind him. The gesture struck Marty as ludicrous.

"Ryan! Stop fussing with the damn door and just prop it open!"

"Really? What about the security rules?"

"What? We're worried about hijackers? Prop it open."

"Yes, sir."

"And then strap in and help me here."

"I'm...sorry...I was trying to figure out..." his voice trailed off with the track of his thoughts as he scrambled to comply.

Marty let his mind ricochet around the cockpit again. He didn't have a plan and he desperately needed one. There were no checklists for what had happened, but there were plenty of smaller checklists to help keep them disciplined. In range. Before landing. And there was probably something more in the emergency procedures to help, even though nothing covered hauling around a parasitic pile of aluminum on the right wing with people still inside.

First, last, and always, he reminded himself, there was order in the way you were supposed to fly even a crippled airliner, and he had to restore his thinking to that regimentation, even if his hands were shaking on the yoke.

"Where are we, Captain?" Ryan asked, the formality registering as a combination of fear and abdication. The subtext was agonizingly clear: *I have no idea what to do now, so please tell me!* Marty felt a flash of sympathy, wishing there was someone *he* could turn to with the same questions.

"Near Boulder, turning east."

Yeah, what the hell DO we do now? Marty asked himself. He turned to the copilot – aware the senior flight attendant had once again entered the cockpit and was standing between them, unwilling to break in until acknowledged.

"Ryan, figure out the fuel and how long we can stay airborne at this fuel flow rate, and get on the controls with me. You need to feel this."

The copilot nodded as his hand went to the yoke, his eyes scanning the fuel readouts. Marty slowly released his grip on the pilot's yoke, letting the copilot feel the artificial feedback and realize how much pressure he was going to have to use to maintain control.

"Jeez! That much?"

"Almost everything. The rudder, too. Almost full left. Got your foot on it?"

"Not...yet. Hold on. Yeah."

"You got it?"

"I think so."

"Okay, you've got it. Remember, you're flying hydraulic valves and artificial feel springs."

They went through the same sequence with the rudders, Marty letting go and feeling the stricken 757 yaw sharply as the copilot first put too little pressure on his left pedal, then muscled it back under control.

"Good God, this is awful!" Ryan gasped.

"Can you hold it long enough to let me run back and look.?"

"I...yeah!"

"Hold your heading and slowly bring us down to nine thousand. Got it?"

"Yeah. Hurry!"

Tell me about it, Marty thought as he snapped open his seat belt and lunged out of his seat, aware the flight attendant was scrambling to get out of his way. The look in her eyes when he glanced at her was pure panic, and he stopped long enough to put a hand on her shoulder.

"I'm sorry, I've forgotten your name."

"Nancy."

"Nancy, what were you going to tell me? You've been waiting."

She pointed toward the cabin. "Just that...you need to see it, Captain!"

He let her lead the way into the forward entry alcove and past the galley, into a first class cabin full of the pasty faces of deeply shaken people. As the captain passed they could see the four stripe epaulets on his shoulder and read the determined look on his face – a contrast to the wide-eyed copilot who had already darted back and forth through their cabin twice. They were all on a ragged edge, he thought.

A PA announcement from him would be needed as soon as possible.

Nancy was all but running aft as he tried to keep up. She stopped adjacent to the emergency overwing exits where she motioned to a gaggle of standing passengers to move back and find other seats. It was against his normal manners to ignore passengers, but the need to see what was sitting on the right wing was all consuming, and he slipped into a row of seats and plopped his knee on the floor to put his face squarely in the window, marginally aware that Nancy was inches behind.

The flash of the red rotating beacon on top of the 757's fuselage was the only light source, illuminating the bizarre image just 25 feet away in garish explosions of light. The shape of the smaller aircraft's fuselage was too distinctive to miss: A Beech 1900, an overgrown King Air, with jagged and torn metal surrounding the stub where the left wing had connected with the left engine. The engine itself *was* still there, although the propeller was gone along with the left wing. And with the next flash he thought he could see the Beech's right landing gear strut protruding down from the engine nacelle into the ugly gash on his right wing. How they had been lucky enough to avoid a major fire with the breached fuel tank?

Marty whirled around, almost smashing his face into the flight attendant's.

"Nancy. Get back up to the cockpit and tell the copilot to turn on the overwing lights.

She started to move and he stopped her. "No! Wait! Instead, tell him to tell *you* where the switch is, and you do it. He can talk your hand onto it. I don't want him to let go of the yoke. Understood?"

She nodded, terrified and silent, and disappeared up the aisle as he turned back to the window, pressing his nose against the plexiglass, aware that the 1900's fuselage was vibrating visibly – not exactly rocking, but shaking and shuddering in the high-speed airflow.

And there was something else, and it chilled him as if the abstract had suddenly become reality. There were lights in the cabin of the ruined commuter – and in the cockpit a flashlight beam suddenly stabbed toward him. Marty could see whoever it was turn the beam on his own face, as if the underscore the fact that he wasn't just dealing with a thing on his right wing.

He could see a cascade of long hair illuminated by the flashlight. The captain was apparently a woman, and somehow that made everything worse.

The white overwing lights on the side of the 757's fuselage suddenly snapped on, flooding the nightmarish scene on the right wing like a single spotlight on an empty stage. He could see the remaining stream of kerosene leaking away into the night from the hopelessly gouged right main fuel tank, and with sinking heart he saw just how precarious the catastrophic mating of the two aircraft really was. The fuselage was just barely stuck on the Boeing's wing. It wouldn't take much abrupt maneuvering to get rid of it.

How the Beech had missed the 757's right engine was a mystery in itself, but right on top of it – anchored tenuously by the wheel less right main landing gear at the end of a channel of ripped aluminum wing surface – was what? Ten thousand pounds of ruined airplane? Maybe more.

"Jesus Christ!" Marty said under his breath, aware every passenger within view was waiting to read his face when he stood and turned around. He had to look calm and in control, which would be a visceral lie.

Nancy was back, waiting quietly behind him, this time not as close.

How long has it been? Marty wondered. It felt like ten minutes since the collision.

"What do you think, Captain?" Nancy's soft voice was holding up well, he thought. She had to be at least as terrified as he was, but neither of them could afford to show it.

He glanced at her, the words he had not wanted to verbalize escaping straight from his thoughts.

"I've got to find a way to get this bird down without changing the angle of attack."

"I'm...sorry, I don't understand that term."

"The angle of the wing into the wind," he said, turning back to the window again, no longer holding a tiny, irrational hope that the specter might have disappeared. *How the hell can I do this,* he thought, his synapses firing on a solution. *Maybe if we milk the flaps down as we slow...*

The way the ruined commuter was jumping and jerking around, if the airflow canted upwards anymore – hit it from a lower angle – the chances of it pulling loose were obvious. He could see the little Beech's right wing occasionally flutter into view on the far side of the embedded 1900's fuselage. That wing was producing lift, which was probably why they hadn't just rolled over to the right and lost control immediately after impact.

But if it produced too much, it could fly them right off the wing. "Can we bring them in?"

The voice came from someone behind them standing in the aisle. Marty turned to find four ashen faces hovering above Nancy's shoulder, one of them belonging to another of his flight attendants.

"What?"

"Captain, if we could open the emergency exit door two rows ahead, couldn't we get those people across the wing and safely in here?"

"No," he said, backing out of the seat row and preparing to dash forward.

"I think we *can* do it!" a male voice answered, two more chiming in for clueless support. The mere idea frightened him, and Marty turned to them. "I've got to get back to the cockpit, but don't even think about opening that door. There's no way."

"Well, wait a minute!" One of the men said, glancing around as if confirming he had allies. "Suppose we could find a rope? Don't you have a rope?"

The sight of the captain raising his hand for quiet had the desired effect.

"Hey! The wind over that wing? It's *two hundred and fifty knots*...almost three hundred miles per hour. That's worse than any hurricane! There's no way to get a rope tied between them and us, and even if we could, there's no way for anyone to hang on. They might as well be on the moon out there."

"Well, then, slow us down, Captain," one of the women said, as if only a moron wouldn't be able to figure that one out.

"If I do," Marty added, choosing his words carefully, "I'll have to pull the nose up, meaning the wing will be at a greater up-angle to the oncoming wind in order to produce more lift, and if that nose-up attitude – what we call angle-of-attack – gets too great, the wind will raise their fuselage from our wing and fling it off. Their left wing is gone. They'll die if they fall away from us."

How could the import of his own words chill him so, Marty wondered, but there it was, in a nutshell. He turned and began moving back toward the cockpit as fast as he could without running, trying with only moderate success to suppress the thought of setting a 757 onto a short, slick, snow covered runway at just under three hundred miles per hour.

CHAPTER ELEVEN

Scott Bogosian had stopped what he was doing, his attention drawn to an array of state-of-the-art flat TV screens hanging across from the City Desk, searching for special report banners or anything that would explain why he had been suddenly attracted. In the middle of a growing blizzard anything could happen in the way of breaking news, although his mental recitation of that grossly overused term made him cringe. Before the end of the Rocky Mountain News Scott had proudly posted a sign over his cubicle that prompted rolled eyes, but he loved it: "When news breaks, we fix it!"

There was nothing on the monitors to explain his sudden shift of attention. Of course, he'd been on alert all afternoon. Too many years of subconscious monitoring, he figured, his ear fine-tuned to police and fire radio channels, and now all of that supplemented by the visual addition of all the local and cable channels with their speakers off.

Something, though, had yanked the chain of his otherwise engaged conscious mind.

He looked around the newsroom, but no one was demonstrating the behavior of a newsroom on the scent of a new story – no one had popped up like a disturbed prairie dog.

There it was again, a short transmission, but coming from a desk to his right, and he realized one of the other long-time reporters – an inveterate pilot – had left his handheld aviation scanner on. That was it! Suddenly it had burst into activity.

Scott moved to the adjacent vacant desk and examined the little radio, reading a combination of aviation-only radio channels. It was jumping from frequency to frequency like any scanner, and once again it snagged an urgent voice.

"Roger...what are...I mean...how can we help you?"

Seconds went by before the reply as Scott wondered what he'd missed, and what phrase had caught his attention. The volume had been so low...how could he have understood anything from the distance of his desk?

"Just...ah...vectors, Denver, to the longest runway you've got at DIA."

That was enough. He turned up the volume and moved back to his desk to trigger his computerized Rolodex and find the restricted numbers he kept for Denver International and the FAA's Denver Tracon facility. The list populated into detail across his side-by-side computer screens and he examined the listings, wondering which ones would generate overly cautious spokesmen with an arsenal of defensive answers. The airline and aviation world were awash in paranoids afraid to even admit there *were* reporters in the world, let alone talk to one.

An unlisted line he knew penetrated deep into the control positions of Denver Tracon caught his eye. He'd surreptitiously copied it down during a tour the previous year. To use it now would be risky, but his internally generated need to know was pegged out, and he sat back down and punched in the number in the one line that never transmitted caller ID, composing what to say.

The line was answered instantly with a no nonsense male voice and a terse repetition of his controller position number, then the phone transmitter clicking off as the man released the little transmit button on his handset.

"This is Bogosian," Scott said, matching the brusk, authoritative air. "What are you working that requires the whole runway? I understand we need to keep it completely plowed?"

"Yeah...he'll need it all. It's a Regal seven-fifty-seven, Flight 12...just took off and may have midaired someone on departure near Broomfield. And...I'm not sure of all of it but he's apparently controllable but asking for the longest runway, so, yeah...we'll need all of it. Can you keep it open?"

"Who did he hit?" Scott asked, instinct overriding caution, instantly aware he'd gone too far. Whoever the controller thought he was talking to, that question didn't make sense, and there was a tiny, telling hesitation on the other end.

"Wait, who is this? Airport ops?"

"Gotta go. Thanks." He clicked the line off and replaced the receiver.

Damn! A Midair! And whoever he hit is probably already on the ground.

Scott wondered whether to alert the paper's television news counterpart and give substance to the loose partnership with the TV station across town. It was probably inevitable, he decided. But handing broadcast people breaking news they weren't aware of always felt like surrendering a once-in-a-lifetime scoop to the infidels. Sometimes they'd throw a crumb and give the Post on-air credit. Usually not. Of course, he couldn't remember a time someone over there had called *him* with a breaking story.

Instead, Scott pulled up the phone number of the Broomfield Police Department and punched it in. If something had fallen out of the sky, 911 should be exploding by now.

CHAPTER TWELVE

<u>*Seven Months before*</u> *— January 21st*
Minneapolis

Headquarters of Regal Airlines – System Operations Control Center

Normally, the Director of Regal Operations Control Center would not be hanging around the airline's huge, mission-control style command center so late in the evening, but the thought of showing up at a wedding rehearsal dinner for a woman he detested was enough to keep him at work for a week. The witch was his wife's friend, not his. It was bad enough he had to put up with her hanging around their house like a dark cloud all the time, bitching and moaning and complaining about life in general. But he couldn't imagine spending an entire evening with the type of people she must attract – including the presumed loser she had convinced to marry her.

Lying about being unable to leave the command center was a ploy his wife would not forgive if she ever found out. But it was a risk worth taking.

Paul Butterfield had been perseverating over his social deception when word came in from Denver that a local TV station was reporting a Regal flight in trouble. It had taken two control room personnel to decide the call needed to hit the boss's ear, and after a minute of questioning the frightened person on the other end of the phone, he realized she was one of their operations agents.

"Wait, wait..hold on...I know you're excited, but I need you to slow down. The TV channel broke in and said what?"

"That our flight twelve has had a midair collision and is coming in for an emergency landing! It just came over the air!"

"We've heard nothing from FAA. Where are you physically?"

"Our operations office in Denver."

"Have you talked to the flight?"

"No, sir. I haven't heard from them, but someone from the airport command post called and says they really are coming back."

"And, the flight said there was a midair collision? With whom or what?"

"I...they didn't say."

Paul turned to one of the supervisors who was wearing a decidedly pasty expression, his eyes wide.

"Can you get Denver ATC on the phone and check this out?'

"In progress," he replied, pointing to three men huddled over a bank of phones. .

"And someone get an ACARS message to the crew to tell us what's going on," he said, referring to the onboard digital datalink letting them send printed messages to the cockpit.

He pressed the phone back to his ear. "Okay, we'll take it from here. Alert your maintenance people to stand by and try to call the flight on company frequency. And go to your emergency checklist, okay?"

"Yes, sir," she replied, her voice trembling. *"I just boarded them all less than an hour ago! All those people!"*

A flash of sympathy nearly pulled him off target, but there were bigger problems to attend to, and he ended the call as gently as possible. Two tiers of consoles down, two of his people had been huddling over another phone. They turned around suddenly, both trying to talk at once, until one gave way.

"What?" the director asked, aware of the irritation in his tone.

"Paul, our flight apparently rammed a Mountaineer regional flight from behind. A Beech 1900. Our pilots are telling ATC the wreckage of the smaller airplane is stuck on their right wing."

"What? Is that even possible?"

They both shrugged. "That's what they told Denver Tracon, and no one can reach the Mountaineer flight, and there's no reported wreckage on the ground."

The thought of one of their airliners being involved in a midair collision and still airborne but without formal contact with the company was unacceptable. Hell, the whole idea was unacceptable. Must be a hoax, or a gross misunderstanding.

Take a breath, Paul thought. The number one checklist item he himself had written for the command post was to take a beat, take a breath, and slow your own heart rate. He let himself stare at the desk for thirty agonizing seconds before looking up and positioning his mouth in front of a small, gooseneck microphone connected to the PA speakers at each position. He pressed the transmit switch and adopted the calmest voice he could manage.

"Okay, folks, this is Butterfield. We're going to a Stage One Alert. Our Flight Twelve out of Denver is reportedly preparing for an emergency return to Denver and has reportedly suffered a midair with a regional airliner. There are blizzard conditions there, as most of you know. I need the roundtable manned in five minutes with open lines to all duty officers, especially maintenance. I need Boeing in the mix for aerodynamics, and run the normal contact checklist for a Stage One. We need to try to get our crew on the satellite phone, send them an ACARS message that we're trying, get maintenance control on alert, and get a line to Denver Tracon. This has already hit local television in Denver, so we need to scramble our communications team, and corporate."

The quiet but intense scramble of control room personnel moving in their appointed trajectories began instantly, yet Paul Butterfield's attention was on the phone number he had to dial next – the one that would presumably grab the full attention of Regal's CEO. That Doug Nielsen was the very last human whose attention he wanted tonight was an understatement of epic proportions, and he girded himself for the experience while ticking off the one positive in all of this: The 'Can't Leave' explanation to his wife was no longer a fib.

CHAPTER THIRTEEN

Michelle Whittier had come back to consciousness slowly, the scene around her as incomprehensible as the muddled dreams of a drunk. She was in the cockpit – *a* cockpit – but it was very cold, and there was a wild appearance to it with papers and debris strewn everywhere, including the glareshield. Worse, there was the noise of a slipstream, but no panel lights. And the cacophonous roar of their twin turboprop engines, where was that?

She tried to raise her head and lean forward, but her right shoulder protested with a cascade of severe pain, and she gasped as she tried to relax back to her original position. Her head hurt, too. She turned her head to the right, trying to make out the face of the copilot who was leaning forward and draped over the controls.

What the hell happened? She wondered, trying to make sense of being apparently airborne with no lights and no engines after...what?

Am I dead? But there was pain, and maybe that meant no. Nothing made sense.

No panel lights! Just a glow...emergency lights overhead.

Yet, there was a glow outside somewhere to the left in her peripheral vision, and braving the new flash of searing pain in her shoulder Michelle forced her head part way to the left, her mind unable to comprehend why a row of lighted airliner windows seemed to be stationary there, where the left wing should be. Were they flying formation with someone? Why?

The pain stabbed at her again and she felt herself drifting back to unconsciousness, relaxing to let it overwhelm her. Take her. Whatever nightmare this was, it wasn't anywhere she wanted to be. Oblivion was clearly better.

But it was so cold, and what sounded like voices from the cabin behind brought her back enough consciousness to spark her to try. She was captain after all, wasn't she? Shouldn't she deal with whatever this was?

Once more she forced her body forward and upright, accepting the screaming pain and finding it not as unbearable as she'd first thought. Her right shoulder, she figured. Something had happened to hurt her right shoulder.

Again she looked left, this time turning her body part way around to get her eyes squarely on what was out there.

The windows of an airliner were now unmistakable. A big airliner of some sort, with faces in the lighted cabin, some staring back at her. She let her eyes move forward and down, seeing the left engine nacelle of the Beech she'd been flying. But there was no buzzing noise of a turboprop, no indication of a propeller, and...no left wing.

She could feel the 1900 moving, bouncing and twisting in whatever wind this was, as if they were sitting on a larger airliner's wing – as if that were possible.

Must still be a dream.

There were more voices from behind her, and Michelle forced herself to accept the massive protest from her shoulder as she swiveled to the right to peer through the cockpit door to where the cabin should be.

In the glow of the emergency lights she could see the cabin was a godawful mess as well, with belongings strewn everywhere, the floor covered in spilled briefcases and coats. There were passengers there, too – several of them awake and looking back at her in wide-eyed, stunned silence.

How many... she wondered, not remembering the number

they'd had aboard.

Painfully she turned back forward, her eyes resting on the copilot's limp form again. This time she tried to get her right arm to move, to touch him, to shake him – anything. But it refused to work.

She tried to call his name but couldn't remember it. Was this the same flight that had started in...where? Denver?

What the hell is his name? she thought, struggling to reorder her mind. The fuselage suddenly lurched as if rolling left. Just a little, but a sharp, startling movement nonetheless. She looked past the copilot's slumped form and through his side window, straining to see the 1900's right wing. It was there, okay, but it was riding up and down on the river of air streaming by. How could that happen, she wondered?

No engine power, no propeller, but our right wing is flying.

Motion in the right seat caught her eye. Just a small movement, but something to indicate he was still alive. She heard him moan.

Luke!

"Luke?" she called out loud, startled at the raspy, guttural voice that had come from her. "Luke? Can you hear me?"

An arm moved, then moved again, accompanied by a low noise of some sort she couldn't quite make out. And without warning the copilot sat bolt upright, his head snapping around to her, eyes wild with fright.

"Luke!"

He was staring at her uncomprehending, blinking in the shadowy light, his head jerking left and right as he tried like she had to force sense out of an insane situation.

"Where are we?" he gasped.

"I...I don't know for sure. It...I think we've been hit by a bigger aircraft, and....and we're on his wing."

"We were hit? Oh, God! What are....what...."

He was struggling to look over her through the left pilot's side at the airliner windows beyond.

"Our left wing's gone, Luke. The props, too."

"Our engines?" Shock, she figured, was fully engulfing him. She watched the younger man glance forward then, his hands moved ever so slightly toward the control yoke as a scream erupted from her. "NO!"

He looked over, totally confused. "Maybe we can pull up!"

"NO!" she said again, shooting her left hand out at him, the gesture falling short but getting his attention. In the space of a split second she had understood exactly what he wanted to do. The control cables would still be connected from the control yoke to the elevators in the rear, if the tail was still there. One hard pull on the yoke and the broken airplane would leap free of the bigger bird to certain death.

'Why?" Luke managed.

"Our left wing is gone. We have to stay here."

"Here?"

"We're...Luke, listen to me. My right shoulder is bad hurt. We can't fly. If we get shaken loose, we're dead. Don't touch that yoke."

"Okay."

"Are you hurt?"

He was shaking his head side to side.

"Okay...unstrap and carefully go back and check on our people. If the fuselage starts to tip, get back up here."

It sounded stupid, she knew, but what else made sense? What was holding them on here anyway? Maybe their tail was hanging out over the back of whatever wing this was. She couldn't tell.

"What are we going to do?" he asked again, his voice a pleading shriek.

"Check on the passengers. Now! That's what you're going to do."

He nodded for an inordinate number of seconds before responding, fear tightening around his throat, inwardly grateful for direction as he released his seat belt and scrambled through the cockpit door to the small cabin behind them.

She was alone again, and the desire to verbally bind with someone outside was growing like an explosion, driving her to search the cockpit for options. The radios were obviously gone since the engines were no longer producing electrical power, but there had to be some battery power. And her phone...where was her phone? Hadn't she been using her phone?

A vague memory undulated in the back of her frightened mind, something about their landing gear being stuck down, and their radios gone. How long back?

Yes!

There had been a cell phone and she'd called...who? Maybe the controller, but the memory ended abruptly.

She tried to look in the shadows by her feet, but if a phone was down there she couldn't see it....or reach it. Maybe Luke had one. Maybe one of the passengers did. Maybe people were trying to reach them right now to tell them to keep calm! Somewhere out in the darkness there had to be a rational answer, if only they could hear the instructions: "Stay put and we'll get you!" They would expect the captain to lead, to make sure no one opened an emergency door or did anything stupid to make it worse. Whoever the pilots of this bigger plane were, maybe they were ready to open emergency doors and come get them. Or...or maybe they'd keep the 1900 attached and just land together. Could they do that, she wondered?

The last thought morphed into an icy feeling in the pit of her stomach as she felt the fuselage rock again. They had to stay attached! But how could she ensure it? The urge to reach someone...tell them she knew what was necessary... was becoming manic. Radio, phone, something.

Michelle looked back at those windows. The glow of the interior looked so warm, and it was so cold in here! There were eyes over there staring at her, too, and one had a face attached she could almost make out. A man with what looked like epaulets on his shoulders!

She scrambled with her left hand to find her flashlight in the left sidewall pocket, yanked it up and snapped it on, playing the beam toward the face in the window and raking it back and forth frantically as if to scream "We're in here! We're here!" The face in the window was still there, but there was no wave, no indication that he understood.

Michelle pulled the flashlight around and shone the beam in her face, relieved at last to see the man nod, then move away from the window.

Somewhere in the back of her mind she understood the impotence of that pilot's dilemma – whether he was the captain or the copilot or just another airman. There were emergency exits on both airplanes, but a no man's land in between – a wind tunnel – and Michelle suppressed the reality of what that meant.

Yet, there had to be a way. They were just a few feet apart!

The airspeed indicator on the forward panel of the captive Beechcraft was in darkness, and she tried to ignore it. But it was no use. She had to know the airspeed, and with the flashlight beam flipped forward, the gauge was visible and reading 250 knots.

CHAPTER FOURTEEN

Regal 12

With the cabin full of anxious, frightened faces Marty had just seen – all pleading for deliverance – the act of selecting the PA position and preparing to speak to them brought its own level of terror. They would be listening to *his* words, and hearing reassurance, but was it enough? And how much of it would be true?

Marty clicked the mic button, hearing the corresponding sound of the PA transmitter through the open cockpit door.

Folks, this is the captain. I...there's no way to sugarcoat anything. You know we've had a midair collision with another airplane, and you're all aware by now the fuselage of that airplane has somehow become attached to our right wing, and as far as we know, everyone over there is alive. We are, of course, flyable, or I wouldn't be talking to you right now. We can land back at Denver, and we're making preparations right now to do that. Denver has closed all but the runway we used for takeoff because of the snowstorm, so...we'll get on the ground as quickly as we can. We have a little under two hours of fuel on board, so it won't take long. My plan right now is to try our best to land carefully and smoothly without letting those folks fall off our wing, but I've got to...we have to get some more technical help from our company on airspeeds and such.

Marty felt his finger weaken on the transmit button and let it pop out. Was he lying to them? No, at least not yet, but how the hell could they keep the same angle of attack and slow down? Chances were not good for landing and getting stopped before running out of snow covered concrete .

So far, no lies, he thought. He hated telling lies to passengers.

Once more he pressed the transmit button.

Okay, there are two things you need to know. First, as tempting as it seems, that we could just open a few emergency hatches and bring those people over here, that's not possible. The wind is going over that wing at just under three hundred miles per hour, and there's just no way. And I can't slow us down enough. Worse, anybody exposed to even half that wind in below freezing temperatures would be hideously frostbitten within seconds, even if they weren't swept off the wing. Now, we WILL need to slow down to land, but if we do it wrong and change the angle of attack...the angle of the airflow over the wing...we may lose them. I'll try to keep you informed, but in the meantime, stay seated, stay calm, and a few prayers wouldn't hurt...mainly for those folks on our wing.

He replaced the microphone and glanced at the copilot, who was grimly hanging onto the controls and doing a surprisingly good job of holding their heading and altitude at 9-thousand.

"You okay for a few more minutes, Ryan? I need to talk to the company."

He was nodding. "Yeah. I'm getting used to her now. We're gonna slow for landing, right?"

"We'll do the best we can, Ryan."

"Okay. Captain, I don't know if our trailing edge flaps will still work, but we can't even try the leading edge devices," Ryan said, his eyes riveted on the instruments.

"They've got to be mangled on the right side, that leading edge."

Marty considered the incongruity of the F/O's flaky, lackadaisical attitude as they left Denver and this sudden burst of cogent analysis. It was as if someone else had slipped into the right seat. Even the panic was gone, or markedly subdued.

"Good point," Marty replied.

"When you're ready to configure, we'll need to deactivate the leading edge devices through the circuit breakers, and they're right behind me, I think."

"Got it."

"And...one more thing, Captain. If the flaps are screwed up, the flap asymmetry protection may not work, so we'll need to milk them down a few increments at a time and make sure they're coming out exactly the same."

"Absolutely. Hang onto her...I'll be on the sat phone. Then we'll brief what we're going to do."

Ryan nodded, his eyes glued on the instruments.

Two flight attendants had moved into the back of the cockpit and Marty turned to face them.

"Can you wait?"

"We've...yes, I guess so," one of them said. "but everyone back there is using a cell phone."

"Let them. Can't harm a thing, regardless of the propaganda they teach!" Marty said as a cockpit chime announced an inbound satellite call from Chicago operations.

In the coach passenger cabin of Regal 12 cellular phones had broken out like a rash in almost every row, some passengers powering them on with success and locking up a signal, and others looking with frustration only at red "no service" warnings. Text messages were streaming from the aircraft like contrails as wives and husbands and lovers and passengers of all ages rushed to reassure parents and loved ones below that they were going to be okay.

Twenty feet away in the unheated, freezing interior of Mountaineer 2612, the same attempt was already underway by three of the passengers as the copilot returned to the cockpit.

"We may have lost one...a man toward the back...I couldn't get a response and his head is at a strange angle. Three others are still unconscious but look okay, and people are...are..."

"Asking questions?"

He was nodding. "I told them to get on any coats they had and just wait, that we're trying to figure it out."

"Good."

"Dear God, Captain, what are we going to do?"

Michelle shook her head, the hollow in the pit of her stomach a black hole. They were all freezing to death with no way to get inside the bigger aircraft, and barely attached somehow to the bigger wing, completely unable to communicate.

"Luke, did you see my cell phone? I remember now I was talking to the controller on it."

He shook his head, his shoulders hunched against the cold soaking the thin white shirt he was wearing. She'd kept her black flight jacket on but he was struggling to pull his on now as he glanced at her feet, and remembered his pocket flashlight. It was already a painful maneuver to lean forward in the mess of the cockpit and try to look at the floor, but the cold made it far worse, and she could see his torso shaking slightly, the leather jacket laid on his seat.

"Luke, get your jacket on first."

"It's okay...I'm already down here." He pushed his body forward, along her left leg, trying to get his head under the dash panel.

"See it?"

"No. I'm sorry."

"Damn."

"I have a cell phone. Want that one?"

"Yes. But get your jacket on."

He complied finally, zipping it up against the deepening chill. It was already well below freezing in the fuselage, the battering, frozen wind sucking out all remaining heat with every passing second.

Luke fished out his cell phone and handed it to Michelle, who punched it on and once again dialed 911.

CHAPTER FIFTEEN

Seven Months before — *January 21st*
Denver TRACON (Terminal Radar Control Facility)

A highly focused group of controllers and supervisors had closed ranks around Sandy Sanchez, one of them quietly asking whether he wanted to be relieved. After all, the supervisor thought to himself as the controller looked around at him with an uncomprehending stare, Sanchez had been the controller working both flights when the accident occurred. Most of his mind, he figured, was probably preoccupied with whether or not he'd screwed something up and caused the collision.

That's sure as hell how I'd feel! the supervisor thought.

"No!" Sandy replied, turning back to the screen as if interrupted by an idiot. "I'm fine."

"I just thought you might be worried about..."

"I said I'm fine! Okay? I didn't make any mistakes here today," Sandy fired back, noting the odd look on the supervisor's face. He was a man who normally triggered deference if not respect wherever he went in Denver Air Traffic Control, but the discipline required to withhold the question "Are you sure?" was almost more than he could manage. The book said replace him, but he decided backing off was the best move.

Two of the assisting controllers were on various phones at the same time: a tie-line to the tower, one to airport operations, and another to Denver Center. Sandy Sanchez was still talking to Regal 12 by radio and vectoring him carefully around to the northeast, setting up a slow turn to the south and then to the west for landing on Runway 25 as fast as possible. Departures had been suspended during the emergency.

Jerry LaBlanc had been standing to one side, holding open the line to Denver International's operational control center as the group there directed the losing battle against the worsening blizzard. He lowered the receiver now, holding the mouthpiece against his leg as he looked for an opportunity to get the others' attention.

"Guys..." he began, realizing it would take more. One by one he reached for the shoulders of those around the seated primary controller, Sandy Sanchez, and they all paused their conversations, one of them tapping Sandy on the shoulder as well.

"What, Jerry?"

"The winds have shifted, 20 knots now from the east and we're going to have to change to Runway Zero-Seven. But... they're not going to plow anymore between Bravo Four and Golf intersection. They've got nine thousand feet of plowed surface left."

Sandy whirled back to his scope. "Shit!" he said, studying the scope for the best way to reverse course and maneuver Regal 12 back to the west toward the mountains, giving him a wide enough berth to make a shallow turn in for landing on a truncated Runway 7.

Another ten or fifteen minutes in the air!

He relayed the news to Regal 12, not expecting the response.

"No problem, Approach. I was going to need more time anyway. I...have to figure out how to land this thing. I can't slow her down."

"Ah...roger, Twelve. Do you want vectors for the new runway or...do you need to hold? State your intentions."

"To get everyone home alive, Approach. Just stand by, please." There was an edge to the pilot's voice, as if he was reaching his pressure saturation point. "I'm working with our company on another phone."

"Roger, Twelve. Maintain zero...no, turn right when able to one five zero degrees and descend to eight thousand."

"Right turn to one five zero and eight thousand, roger."

The blip that represented the combined radar hits and transponder from Regal 12 began to shift its trajectory to the south as directed while the speed block remained constant, and Sandy watched with growing internal alarm. He was only a private pilot but he understood that in the thin air of a mile above sea level, which was Denver, airplanes flew faster over the ground for any given indicated airspeed than at lower altitudes. Damage or no damage, they couldn't keep shoving that 757 along at just under three hundred miles per hour and expect to land anywhere. Let alone a 9,000 foot slippery runway.

"What's he doing?" Jerry LaBlanc asked quietly, his face next to Sandy's as another controller picked up the telephone handset and punched on an incoming call.

"I don't know, man, but he says he can't slow down yet." Sandy looked up, momentarily hopeful. "What's the ground roll distance on a 757 landing at two hundred fifty on a contaminated runway?"

Jerry was shaking his head. "Not possible. You'd need the dry lake bed at Edwards in California, and even then, your tires would probably explode."

The third controller broke in, his eyes wide.

"Guys! I've got Mountaineer on the phone again!"

CHAPTER SIXTEEN

Present Day – *August 14th, 7:05pm*
Summit of Longs Peak

Like a moviegoer struggling to reconnect to reality moments after a gripping film has ended, Marty Mitchell looked up and around, blinking, momentarily confused at the lengthening shadows on the mountaintop around him, and the incredible contrast to a 757 cockpit.

He was aware of being slightly cold, but that reality was fighting the high definition memory of his first hour with Judith Winston months before, that moment when he'd told the story of Regal 12 in such stomach-churning detail. With the National Transportation Safety Board investigators, it had been clinical and technical. With her, it had been emotional, and to a far greater extent than he'd planned.

Marty's physical presence on the mountaintop and what he'd come here to do were mere footnotes to the intensity of that memory. It had been incredibly important to make her understand – to make her see – and he felt the burning intensity of that desperate need again as his sight returned inward.

She had tried to keep her composure, Marty recalled, but clearly the flint-hard lawyer had been shaken by his words. He could tell by the way she had shifted uncomfortably in her plush boardroom chair, her hand tugging absently at a tendril of hair as she asked with feigned detachment, "So, what were your options?"

"I wasn't sure at first. I was in denial, y'know? The jet

was still flying…and both engines were running…but I had this…this *thing* on my right wing and there was no precedent, no training for what to do about that. My jet, the 757, was sluggish and yawing to the right…I could essentially feel the presence of that fuselage in my controls."

"Did the airline help? You called them for help, right?"

"They were trying, but they're only set up for routine emergencies, and this was anything but routine. And to make matters worse, the captain of the aircraft we rammed pulls out a cell phone to talk to the controllers, and then… then, goddammit, she calls *me*!"

"What's wrong with that?" Judith Winston had asked.

He'd paused, grasping for the words.

"How can I make you understand? One moment it's a *thing* out there, a problem I can deal with almost in the abstract, even if my mistake created that problem. I can deal with numbers and abstracts and emergencies. But then her damned voice was in my ear."

"Pardon?"

"The other pilot. The controller asked for my cell phone. He should have asked me if it was okay to pass it on, but he didn't, and suddenly it rings with a frightened woman on the other end, a fellow pilot stranded on my right wing with fifteen others. Suddenly her life is a personal albatross around my neck. She's totally dependent on what I do, what I decide, and worse, I got her into this by ramming *her!* I didn't need that level of pressure! It was hard to even think, the magnitude and gravity of all of it was so profound already. But the moment that happened…the moment a live person invaded my command space…it made it personal and unbearable."

"But…why? I'm struggling to grasp why it made a difference?"

"Because, dammit, that could have been me out there, terrified and barely hanging on and totally out of control! I couldn't keep from being an empath! I felt her terror, and I caused it."

"So, you're saying that affected your ability to make the right decision?"

Marty had met the lawyer's eyes, uncaring that his were probably glistening with tears as he shook with anger.

"There was no right decision. That's the goddamned point! But even if there had been, who am I to decide, y'know? Who am I to decide who lives and dies? Those people on my wing, they have names and families and...and suddenly it wasn't just a number. It wasn't just souls on board anymore. And I couldn't un-ring that bell."

He had let himself submerge back into the narrative of that horror.

"Okay, where was I?"

"You were talking to your company and trying to figure out how to land," she offered.

CHAPTER SEVENTEEN

"Standby, Ops," Marty barked into the satellite handset. "Just...please standby a second."

Somehow he was going to have to slow the pace down. Everything was cascading, and he didn't need raw instinct to know that was how pilots made fatal decisions – including the one that had probably started this whole nightmare.

Once more he felt his stomach contracting to the size of a singularity at the thought that they'd climbed to wrong altitude and were the ones at fault, but he had to shove that aside.

Marty turned to the copilot, who was deep in concentration holding onto the controls in the right seat.

"Ryan, can you hang on a bit longer?"

"I've got her, Skipper. But the controller wants your cell phone number."

For some reason, the request hit him like a stomach punch, the same effect as a control tower asking a pilot to call them after a potential violation.

Marty nodded and toggled the transmit button, passing his phone number to the controller, then punching up the PA.

Folks, this is the captain again. Your two pilots are working hard, but if there are any other airline pilots aboard, or anyone with big jet experience, we could use some extra eyes up here. Just ring your call button.

There was no time to explain it to the flight attendants, but they were savvy enough to figure it out anyway. Marty punched off the PA, surprised that he didn't hear a single call chime from the cabin. Most airline flights were awash in off duty pilots, but then again, who'd be voluntarily non-revving on a night like this?

Okay, think! We have to work out the sequence for flap extension, and I need to know if the speed brakes are useable.

The satellite phone was still in his lap and Marty pulled it back to his face.

"Sorry! There a lot of moving parts up here. Where were we?"

"You tell us, Captain," someone in the ops center replied. "We've got about ten of us on the line here to help you as well as our maintenance and performance people and a Boeing engineer."

Marty was rubbing his eyes and nodding, before recalling that they couldn't see the gesture.

"All right, my main problem is keeping that Beech fuselage on the wing. If we dislodge them, if they fall away, they die. There's no question about that. Worse, I have no way of knowing how secure they are on our right wing. I mean it looks like the strut of the right main landing gear is literally embedded in our right wing. Maybe it's so well stuck that I couldn't blow them off if I tried, but I'm very worried that any increase in our angle of attack, even if accompanied by a significant decrease in airspeed, could lift them off. And it could happen too fast to stop, which means I really can't experiment beyond a certain point. Everyone there understanding all this?"

"We're hearing you, Captain," someone answered.

"Okay...I'm astounded that we haven't lost a hydraulic system, but so far so good. My biggest worry is whether we can milk down the flaps, extend them very, very cautiously, while slowing, and keep the same angle into the wind. The more flaps I can get down, the lower my pitch angle has to be for any given speed. That's why I need to know what the performance figures say about maintaining the same angle of attack at slower airspeeds with the flaps out at different settings. My pitch angle right now is almost zero."

There was a very loud silence on the other end for what seemed like minutes before one of the engineers responded."

"Captain, there are really no easily accessible figures for that in our manuals. Boeing? Do you guys have anything to help?"

"Yeah, well…aside from telling you this sort of situation can't happen and that you can't do what you're doing and stay airborne with wreckage on your wing, all I can tell you is that we're in no man's land. We can dig up test figures and parameters and all that but…zero pitch, did you say, Captain?"

"Yes."

"See, I couldn't even predict that with the graphs and charts I have."

A quick discussion ensued on the other end culminating in the completely useless information that no one really knew what to do.

Obviously, Marty thought, they were struggling to help, but appreciation was overshadowed by a long-ago disaster over Iowa when a United Airlines DC-10 had lost all hydraulics to an engine explosion. The crew of United 232 desperately needed help from their operations experts, but there was simply no data for a total hydraulic failure and now he knew exactly how Captain Al Haynes had felt.

"*Really*, gentlemen?" Marty said, trying unsuccessfully to keep the frustration out of his voice. "Come on. I need analysis. I mean, if we got the flaps down to five degrees, and I keep the same airspeed, the flaps would give me additional lift and I could lower the nose a bit to compensate. But if, as we bring the flaps out, I slow the airplane to keep the same angle of attack, producing equal lift with a slower airspeed and more flaps, how far can I slow?"

"Captain, we'll work on it. We just don't know."

"So I have to play test pilot up here?"

A new voice broke in.

"Captain Mitchell, Paul Butterfield here in Central Operations. I'm the head guy tonight. We're doing and will do everything humanly possible to answer your questions, but we've got no basis for that particular answer. As you can imagine, that's not something we normally need to calculate."

"Okay, I get that," Marty said, "but please do your best as fast as you can. In less than an hour I'm going have to just experiment."

"No...we don't want you playing test pilot up there, any more than you have to."

"Then, gentlemen, get me the figures so I know what I'm doing. Of course, this might all be a moot discussion. I may not be able to physically extend the flaps at all."

Marty could hear a brief exchange from the right seat between the copilot and ATC regarding another heading change. His right hand trembled as it held the satellite phone handset, and a sort of roaring started in his mind, as if everything he was facing was accelerating toward some critical mass.

He forced himself to take a breath and answer a bunch of well-meaning suits who obviously had no clue what he was saying.

"Mr. Butterfield...all of you...I know you're trying to help, but if we can't answer my question about slowly bringing the flaps out, then answer this, please. Let me ask you some stuff based on a no flap emergency landing, cause I know we've got test data on that."

"Yes, we do."

"Captain," another voice interjected, "we've run the numbers for a no flap landing given the one remaining runway they're telling us is still open at Denver, Runway

Seven. Your approach speed – what I guess you pilots call your bug speed – will be one hundred eighty-two knots. With full braking and full reverse and touchdown on or before the numbers, you can just barely stop before the overrun. And, as I'm sure you know, the overrun on that runway ends in a hundred foot downslope."

Marty bit his lip as he watched Ryan struggling with the airplane and ran the statement from Operations through his head.

"Okay, but at that airspeed, one hundred eighty-two knots ... what will my angle of attack be?"

"You have to slow her down for landing, Captain. I don't think there's a choice about that. You can't stop in the available runway otherwise."

"What pitch – what angle of attack or what nose-up pitch angle – would I be using with the gear down and flaps fully retracted in level flight, at one hundred eighty-two knots, versus the angle of attack I'm using right now at two hundred forty?"

More silence from Operations before a new voice answered.

"Captain, you're...you say you're maintaining two hundred and forty knots right now?"

"That's right. I've slowed her down from two fifty. And I don't dare slow any more without risking all the lives in that wrecked Beech on my wing. I have no damned way of knowing what speed would cant my wing up high enough to cause the slipstream to lift them off the wing and kill them."

"Captain, Bill Baxter here at Boeing again. I've got a team working on it right now."

"Thank you, Mr. Baxter. You understand what I'm asking?"

"Yes...but we're going to have to grab for original engineering test flight data. We don't measure things by angle of attack, or nose-up deck angle, as you know."

"Okay. Please keep this line open and let me know the

moment you've got something I can use."

"Captain, Paul Butterfield here. We'll keep the line open of course, but about your speed. I need to emphasize that you're going to have to slow her down."

"Mr. Butterfield, do you want me to describe the faces of the passengers in that ruined airplane on my wing?"

"Captain, your passengers' lives depend on..."

"*Hey!* I'm well aware of my responsibilities, okay? I just picked up some new passengers I hadn't planned on."

"I'm just reminding you, sir, that you can't safely land at that airspeed."

"Don't you think I fucking know that?"

There was dead silence in response for several seconds before Marty forced himself to speak. "I'm sorry. I apologize for the profanity but...I'm the one who has to make the final decisions up here."

He pulled the handset away before Butterfield could respond and turned to motion Nancy, the lead flight attendant, back in the cockpit, to monitor the sat phone as a distant warbling reached their ears.

For several seconds it was confusing: another cockpit warning apparently corking off and he should know what it meant. But he couldn't recall – until the realization dawned that the noise was the ringtone for his cell phone.

The last goddamned thing I have time for! Marty thought, planning to ignore it even as the insistent sound continued. But there was something in the back of his mind screaming at him that this was somehow important, and even in the jaws of the tidal wave of worries trying to engulf him, Marty ripped the phone from its belt holster and punched it on.

"Yes?"

The voice was distant, and female, and very hesitant, like someone coming out of a deep sleep realizing they'd dialed a wrong number.

"Ah...is this...the captain of...I don't know what your flight number is, but..."

"Who the hell is this?" he demanded.

"Ah...I'm...the pilot of the airplane on your right wing."

The roaring in Marty Mitchell's mind reached a crescendo as her words finally registered.

"I'm sorry...I wasn't expecting..."

"I'm...Michelle Whittier."

"You're the captain?"

"Yes, if there's anything left to be captain of."

"I'm Marty Mitchell. Captain as well."

"You guys hit us. I think one of my people may be dead. Everyone else is okay...although we're freezing over here."

"I'm so sorry! I have no idea what happened. I'll get us down as quick as I can, Michelle."

"You think that'll work?"

"Has to."

"I mean, we're really moving around out here...my left wing is gone and my right wing may be structurally broken, and we're being buffeted big time by the wind. I'm not even sure this is all real."

"I get that. Look, I think your right main gear strut is what's keeping you on our wing."

"We've got to be creating huge drag for you."

"Some, yes."

"And when you slow and configure for landing..."

"I'm not going to slow. I can't risk a higher deck angle."

"Ah...Marty, is it?"

"Yes."

"Marty, how...I mean, how can you land if you don't slow? How fast are you going...are *we* going...right now?"

"Two forty. I'm going to try to milk the flaps down to decrease the deck angle as I slow, and hopefully the diminished force of the slipstream will also help keep you there."

"I'm sorry to point out the obvious, Marty," she added, "but we can't fly if we fall off. You know that of course."

There was a rising tide of emotion suddenly choking off

his ability to speak, but he forced himself past the paralysis.

"Yeah. I wish we could bring you across the wing and inside."

"So do I, but we don't have any ropes, and unless..."

"We'll get you down, Michelle."

"I...of course I hope so. Hope so."

"I'll need your help."

"Right. Anything. Sure," Michelle replied, each word an attempt to reinforce the previous.

"We're on vectors right now waiting for our company to get back to me with some of the figures for landing, and we're down to Runway Seven at Denver, and I need to start experimenting to see if we can milk the flaps out. That's when I'll need feedback from you on any movement which might indicate we could lose you."

"What do you mean?" she asked

"Any sudden grinding, or lifting, or shaking, or any indication she might be coming loose."

A long pause and an audible exhale filled his ear until her weary voice returned.

"Marty, I'm not sure we would get any warning. We... the fuselage... could just fall off without any, ah...precursors, y'know? It's constantly shaking right now."

"Got it. We'll proceed extremely slowly."

"I'll let you get busy but...I guess, call back when you need to."

"Okay. My phone captured your number."

"Marty?"

"Yes."

"Ah...look, please do your best. I'll admit I'm terrified. I mean, I know you will but, we're in your hands, y'know?"

"Yes, I know."

Who am I kidding, Marty thought.

There was no one to help. It was as if she was hanging onto his hand and dangling off the edge of a cliff, and yet he was holding on for dear life himself, screaming for help that would never come, grip loosening, voice hoarse – her Gwen Stacy to his Peter Parker.

He had to clear his throat to answer, and the words felt more like a fraud than a promise.

"We'll get you down safely, Michelle. I'm not letting you go."

CHAPTER EIGHTEEN

Seven Months before — *January 21st*
Newsroom, The Denver Post

With the post-deadline newsroom all but deserted in a major blizzard, there was essentially no one for a part-timer like Scott Bogosian to check with on his way out the door. Scott had fulfilled his duty to call the paper's aviation beat reporter and hand off the breaking news, but she was engaged in mortal combat with a nasty version of the flu and her obviously worried husband was stiff-arming any interference.

"I wouldn't wake her up for an interview with Jesus," he snapped. "Whatever the story is, it's yours."

Scott grabbed his parka and lifted the beat reporter's handheld scanner from her desk before heading for the parking structure, unclear where he was racing to. The Broomfield police – in fact the entire matrix of police and fire departments in the Denver-Boulder area – had picked up no trace of a fallen airliner, and the bits and pieces of radio communication he'd heard on the scanner were offering the alternate conclusion that there was no regional twin on the ground because it was somehow being carried on the wing of a larger jet. Not really possible, but...

The snow was blowing horizontally, at least in the downtown canyons, as he literally skidded his aging Volvo onto Colfax, already chiding himself for not replacing a set of slick tires that were far too low on tread. With money an increasingly rare commodity in his solitary life, tires that had the grace to just remain inflated automatically won his loyalty. Other things like food and rent and the occasional bottle of Jack Daniels came first.

Scott guided the Volvo gingerly up the slick ramp onto the Interstate, engaging his mental autopilot as he struggled to visualize what was happening overhead. With no other location logically competing for his presence, the course to Denver International Airport was a given. But precisely what should he do on arrival? That would take more thought, and there was the not-so-insignificant question of whether he could even make it there. The snow was piling up fast and there was only one plowed lane left to navigate on I-25 – and probably the same on I-70 leading to Pena Boulevard, the 10 mile highway from the Interstate to the terminal that was always spring-loaded for closure in a storm like this.

The handheld scanner, programmed for aviation frequencies, was spewing staccato bursts of radio traffic as Denver's approach controllers worked to clear the skies for Regal 12.

Thanks to the warmth of the car's interior, the storm beyond the windshield seemed completely surreal, and the other-worldly aspect of the snow streaking by horizontally just added to the disconnect from reality.

So far, there were no named individuals in peril in the frozen night, just flight numbers and evolving facts. And while his mind gave ritual voice to the prayer that all affected would get down safely, there was still a guilty rush associated with something like this. He hated to admit it, but it was true. The thrill of grabbing his hat – if he'd had one – and racing out to cover something big ahead of everyone else was, in truth, every reporter's primordial wet dream.

Scott's childhood image of newspapermen dated from the previous century. No matter that he didn't own a trench coat or carry a hatband that said "PRESS" or have to find a pay phone to read his story to a copy desk, it all fit nicely into the old-school fantasy images he'd had as a kid of someday being a real newspaper reporter. Even classmates had rolled their eyes at him. They'd get into trouble doing something their parents had forbidden, and Marty would be there with a note pad to chronicle the whole thing. It was when he started actually publishing his reports in a makeshift mimeographed newspaper that life at Kennedy Elementary got really lonely, and no amount of claiming to be a reporter versus a snitch would repair things. Virtually no one was surprised when he landed his first real newspaper job.

True, the stereotyped image had faded – tattered, in fact – and the reality over the last forty years had been startlingly less magnificent than his starry-eyed dreams. But there had been the occasional victory, the occasional scoop as an investigative reporter who never quit – a reputation he valued. And the breaking news rush was still there when he launched on a mission that was his to complete. Tonight was such a moment.

Scott swerved suddenly to avoid a jackknifing semi, barely getting the old Volvo under control and back into the groves of previous tires after the trucker pulled off to the side.

The face of a firefighting acquaintance at Denver's airport crossed his mind. Whatever happened at DIA in the next few hours, the firefighters would know about it and be there. If Josh Simmons by some stroke of luck was on duty tonight, it would be a great help.

The radio calls had quieted markedly as the airborne traffic diminished, but the Approach Control frequency suddenly came alive again.

"Regal Twelve, say your intentions."

"To get everyone home alive, Approach," was the immediate reply, somewhere between a curative attempt at humor and evidence of a distracted airman.

Several seconds elapsed before the pilot continued. "Denver, Regal Twelve should be ready for the approach in about twenty minutes. We've got to do some controllability checks up here."

"Roger, Regal. Please be advised Denver International is doing their best to keep the runway open for you and they are currently plowing, so they need a five minute warning when you're ready for the approach to get the equipment out of the way."

"Roger that, Denver."

Another transmission filled the void, this one used for ground control at the airport.

"Airport Twenty, Denver Ground."

"Airport Twenty."

"What's the runway status?"

"Ground, we've got six plows deployed and we're two thirds down Runway Seven at this time, but it's coming down too fast. Frankly, we're losing the battle. We need to get that bird on the ground asap."

CHAPTER NINETEEN

Seven Months before – *January 21st*
Passenger Cabin - Regal 12

Normally, when Lucy Alvarez scored a window seat *and* the extra leg room of the emergency exit row, it felt like a small lotto win. One hour into the aborted flight of Regal 12, however, 22F had truly become the seat from hell.

It had taken Lucy less than a minute after the collision to regain focus and gaze out the window, directly into the windows of Mountaineer 6212. At first, everything was essentially black. But as Lucy's eyes adjusted to the garish scene, every flash of the Regal 757's red beacon illuminated anxious faces staring back at her, eyes pleading, lips mouthing words she could only imagine.

The captain's explanation of why there was no way to reach them and bring them across that gap to the safety of the Boeing's cabin made sense, but the logic was drowned out by the scream in her mind that those poor people had to be saved. No way could she just sit there and watch them die.

Both pilots, one after another, had come back and leaned in front of her to get a better view of the unfolding nightmare. Most of her fellow passengers had remained reasonably calm, but a tall, broad-shouldered man in his mid-fifties wearing a baseball cap and a checkered flannel shirt – the occupant of seat 21F just in front of her – had been doing a slow burn, muttering and becoming increasingly agitated. Suddenly he jumped to his feet and began pacing the aisle, arms flailing, gesturing wildly to the emergency exits; searching for allies who felt the same despair that was eating Lucy alive. But the man was frightening her, and she couldn't trust him to be her voice. When he looked straight at her, she quickly diverted her eyes, partly out of embarrassment.

"Hey! Y'all! Are we gonna sit here like sheep and let those folks out there die? Come on, people, they're less than twenty-five feet away from the window! There's got to be some rope or cable or something we can use."

"And do what?" a younger, owlish looking male had looked up at him and asked. "You heard the captain. It's like a hurricane out there and even if we could weather the cold, there's no way to attach a line or a cable even if we had one."

"Hell, son, I've worked in Deadhorse in the winter," the man replied. "Don't be a pussy. There's nothing on that wing you couldn't handle in a parka," he added, gesturing to the overhead. "They've got life rafts and all sorts of other equipment in this airplane and all we need is thirty feet of stout line and the determination to do something other than sit here. If we can get a line to them, we can bring them all across. Then it don't matter if the damned thing falls off."

One of the male flight attendants had approached quietly and now put a hand on the pacing man's shoulder. Lucy could see the apprehension in the flight attendant's eyes – the passenger was a half foot taller – and he turned on the crewmember now with a snarl.

"What do *you* want?"

The flight attendant's voice was level and calm, his words precise.

"Sir, I have to ask you to sit back down and fasten your seatbelt. We all want to go get those people, but it is not possible."

"Y'know, I just don't believe that!" the man said, his face a study in contempt as he sized up the challenger.

"Well, sir, you can believe this with absolute certainty. We are legally under the complete command of the captain, and he has ordered all of us to sit down. Failure to comply…"

The passenger rolled his eyes. "Yeah, yeah, yadda yadda! I know the spiel. You'll have me arrested if I don't sit down."

"Yes, sir. Something like that."

"Well, buddy boy, I think instead of threatening me for trying to solve the problem, you and the crew should be tearing this plane apart to find enough rope or cable to use."

"Sir, we're not going out there. Stringing a rope or cable would be impossible."

"Oh, you're buying that pilot crap? Fine, you stay in. Find that rope for me and I'll bundle up in my parka and do it myself."

Two other flight attendants had quietly gathered behind him.

"I'll inform the captain that you're volunteering in case he changes his mind. In the meantime, back in your seat. Please."

He hesitated, trying to stare down the flight attendant who wasn't giving a millimeter. Finally, the passenger nodded and slunk slowly down in his aisle seat.

"I can't believe the cowardice of you people," he snarled, jerking his head around to glare at the passengers around him before muttering angrily to himself.

Such a boor, Lucy thought, comparing her fiancé's impeccable manners to what she'd just witnessed. A deep feeling of guilt suddenly rose around her like dark smoke.

Manners? What about her manners? What if she didn't survive this? She hadn't even had the courtesy to say goodbye to Greg, she'd been so ticked off at him. He wouldn't have a clue where she was!

Lucy pulled her smart phone from her small purse and checked the signal indication, aware she'd forgotten to turn it to flight mode. It was showing two bars, probably enough, and she punched in his number and waited. There was no ringing, but the circuit went instantly to his voicemail, indicating his phone was either not on or not within range of a cell tower.

Lucy listened to the familiar, warm tones of his greeting, then realized she had to say something into the digital recording.

"Greg, Honey, I'm...I'm sorry...I was really mad at you and I caught a flight to Orlando and now there's been a midair collision and..."

She tried with moderate success to suppress a sob.

"...and I'm all right as long as we get down safely. Please try to call when you get this. I'm on Regal Flight 12."

He was probably still in flight, she figured, and undoubtedly diverted somewhere else because of the storm, but she pulled up her calendar anyway to check on his original arrival time back in Denver, which showed as just after 5 pm. There was an app she'd recently downloaded which could track commercial flights and she triggered it now, keying in his flight number and finding it had arrived on schedule.

And he didn't call! He probably had plenty of time before his outbound flight and he didn't call?

The emotional racquetball continued, bouncing between anger, guilt, and fear. She'd been furious and essentially stormed out of town, but she hadn't said a word to him and in the call from New York, she'd been as sweet as ever. He had no way of knowing of her insidiously long slow-burn.

Maybe his outbound flight was cancelled. Where was he going?

She'd been so impacted by the news of the lost weekend ahead that she hadn't paid any attention to whatever he said about location. Wasn't it Durango?

That's right. Durango. And he's probably in Denver right now and not answering. Something's going on! He should already be at my place...

Guilt won the game, then the tears came.

CHAPTER TWENTY

Seven Months before — *January 21st*
Regal 12

"Okay, Captain, I think I have it figured out," the copilot said, a piece of paper on his lap covered with numbers. Marty had been flying for the past few minutes while Ryan worked on how long they could stay in the air with their remaining fuel.

"And?"

"We have less than forty-five minutes. I mean, we wouldn't flameout at forty-five, but there would be no margins left for a go around, for instance."

"Understood. Okay, take her, I'm going to make one more attempt at getting some useful information from Minneapolis and then we're going to get her back on the phone and try to slow."

"Her?"

"The captain out there…Michelle." Merely stating her name inflated a lump in his throat.

Regal Operations was still on the line, but the news was less than useful. Boeing had done their best but there were, as the engineer said, too many variables. Suddenly Marty wanted nothing more than to be rid of the call, and the men and women on other end could sense his mental disconnection.

"Okay, thanks to all of you. We'll work it out from here."

"Captain? Butterfield here again. May I ask what you're next step is?"

"Yes, sir. I'm going to experiment carefully with slowing

and configuring. We have to get down within a half hour."

"Understood, Captain. I...need to relay to you from the head of the airline and myself that despite your heartfelt concern for the aircraft on your wing and those inside, we cannot take the chance of injuring our passengers with a landing speed that guarantees an accident."

"Got it."

"So, you'll be guided by that?"

"I'll be guided by my best judgment, sir. This is a major emergency, however it got started, and I am the sole decider, so to speak. Now I need to end this discussion."

"Captain..."

But Marty had already pushed the disconnect button, the bottomless hole in his stomach communicating clearly that regardless of their success or failure, his career was probably over. He turned to the chief flight attendant who had been holding and monitoring the sat phone and his cell phone.

"Nancy?"

She held out the iPhone and he scooped it to his ear, aware of the pounding in his chest. He absolutely did not want to know what his blood pressure was reading just now.

"Michelle? Are you there"

He turned back to Nancy, his expression needing no words.

"I hadn't heard anything from her for the last few minutes, Captain."

He nodded, working at the screen to toggle the last number received and holding his breath that the call would go through. Cell systems were polarized to suppress calls from the air, but they had been very lucky and flying just low enough to get the signals to connect around the edges.

He heard her answer, her cell phone scraping on something before she cleared her throat and answered slowly, painfully, her voice extremely strained.

"Michelle here."

"How are you holding out?" Marty asked.

She cleared her throat, and he could almost feel her searching for the most useful words.

"We're very, very cold over here, but…we're working on it."

"Okay, Michelle, please listen. I have to try slowing and bringing the flaps out. You and your copilot are the only ones who can tell me when to stop, which will be before you sense that she might lift off the wing."

"I understand. And I have an idea."

"Please tell me."

"Our controls are still connected at least to our elevator on the T-tail. I can feel the airstream in the controls. I can also sense that our center of gravity is behind me and that we're attached to your wing behind the center, still about where the landing gear strut is dug into your wing…which means that if we push the controls forward, we'll tend to rotate the nose down and hold us in position without lifting the strut out of your wing surface…or whatever we're attached to down there. At least I hope that's right."

"I'll go with your analysis, Michelle. But I'll narrate everything I'm doing and I expect you to yell 'Stop' if it feels like we're approaching the limit."

"I understand. We'll start pushing nose down pressure as you increase the angle of attack. How much longer?"

"Two minutes before starting this experiment. We have to land in the next forty minutes."

"Okay. Thank you."

"For what?"

"Just…trying, I guess. Good luck to us all, but I agree you've got to slow."

Marty handed the phone back to Nancy.

"I need you to turn on the speakerphone as we start this and keep it close enough to my ear that I can hear her and vice versa."

"Got it," Nancy replied.

"And, can you get the whole team up here for a second?"

She nodded and turned to one of her crew, who summoned the others. With six flight attendants squeezed into the door and Ryan still flying, Marty pointed to the right wing and explained what they were going to try.

"When we land, it may or may not be smooth, and we may end up going off the end of the concrete. Be ready for an emergency evacuation. Be ready for anything."

He wasn't prepared for the number of reassuring hands on his shoulder, and his emotional response caught him off guard, but he choked back his feelings as he toggled on the PA.

Folks, this is your captain. We will begin our final approach within the next 30 minutes back to Denver International. For the next ten minutes, though, we will be attempting to slow the airplane and change the pitch angle as little as possible to hold the other aircraft on the wing. Even if we could slow to normal approach speed we could not...and I would not authorize any attempt to...open the emergency exit hatch to try a rescue. Everyone's best bet is to set us down on the runway together. Follow your flight attendant's orders to the letter – they speak for me. And when they say tighten your seat belt, really tighten it. As I said before, a few prayers would very definitely be in order. Thank you.

CHAPTER TWENTY-ONE

Seven Months before — *January 21st*
Cabin of Regal 12

Roger was his name.

For some reason, Lucy Alvarez made a mental note of it as the agitated passenger worked himself back up to what was probably going to be another outburst.

She felt sorry for the young woman in the middle seat next to him. Roger had insisted on introducing himself, as if reverting to some form of civilized restraint would erase the first impression of his meltdown.

Once again he gestured across the middle and window seats ahead to point to the fuselage, and once again – despite trying not too – Lucy followed his gaze, pressing her face against the plastic inner layer of the window and straining in spite of herself to make out the faces looking back. There were no cabin lights in the smaller airplane, but some passengers were using their cell phones, and someone in the window directly across from her turned his phone to his face. Lucy's heart froze.

Of course, it couldn't be *her* Greg, but the face looked just like him. She fought down the immediate sense of total panic and tried to think, not taking her eyes off the man, who was nodding for some reason and gesturing something she couldn't make out.

Lucy pulled out her phone with trembling hands and frantically checked the messages. Nothing from Greg. She checked the little indicator next to her text messages, but none indicated delivered. Once again she tried calling, fumbling with the virtual keyboard to enter his speed-dial number and once again heard the system go straight to voicemail.

Twenty-five feet away, the man across the wing was still looking at her, but had lowered his phone. Only the outline of his features was visible. That absolutely could *not* be her fiancé, she reassured herself, but the reassurance was hollow and she fumbled with one of the airport apps to find which flights had left for Durango. Surely the only one he could have caught would have been cancelled.

There it was. His flight had to have been Mountaineer 2612, Denver to Durango.

She entered the flight number in the flight tracking app and read, and then re-read, the result. Mountaineer 2612 had departed on time. She shifted to a different display as Greg had taught her to do to monitor a flight's progress with its altitude and flight track over the ground, and with the bottom dropping out of her world, she realized Mountaineer 2612's flight track had ended just west of Denver less than ten minutes after departure.

There was no arrival in Durango, or anywhere else.

With her hands shaking violently and her heart pounding, Lucy toggled on the flashlight function of the iPhone and shone it on her own face as she faced the window, wondering if he was looking. Greg would have no way of expecting her to be on this flight…at best she would be nothing more than a distraught female face in the window. Her world was now riding on that wing, and the need to get to him, and not just helplessly sit still, welled like a rising tsunami, floating hope and desperation all at once.

The man named Roger had stood quietly and retrieved a bag from the overhead bin. Lucy had only half noticed, but now she realized he had donned a parka and gloves, and as a host of startled passengers watched, he held up what appeared to be a coil of some sort of wire, smiled, and then physically pulled the adjacent two passengers from their seats. Next to the overwing exit now, and with two alarmed flight attendants running forward to reach him, the man pulled the red cover off the latching mechanism and yanked the lever down.

Both flight attendants were yelling, but they were too many rows away.

"STOP HIM! TACKLE THAT MAN!"

Roger had a look of triumph on his face but in a microsecond it changed to puzzlement as he pulled on the plug-type hatch and was unable to dislodge it. Three male passengers were on their feet now and lunging for him, one sailing over a seatback to grab the big man by his waist at the very moment the sound of air pressure being released in a frightening "thunk" was met with him losing his balance and falling back, the hatch in hand, and the deafening roar of the slipstream from the now open hatch drowned out the startled cries all around.

The male flight attendant who had confronted Roger earlier soared over the same seat back and grabbed the hatch, struggling over the now-empty middle seat to shove it back in the hole, and with another solid "thunk" borne of slight internal air pressure, the hatch went back in place. He raised the locking level before turning to see the man named Roger restrained by two passengers and a flight attendant as another rushed back from the front of the plane with plastic handcuffs.

The entire episode had taken little more than a minute, but Lucy realized that for a split second, she had been ready to launch herself out of that hole to get to Greg.

An off-duty sheriff's deputy was recruited to watch Roger, who had now been strapped to an empty aisle seat. The other crewmembers were cautiously returning to their respective ends of the aircraft as the PA clicked on, the captain's voice louder and more urgent than before.

Folks, real quick, this is your captain. I am the legal

*authority right now over everyone, and I'm telling you I
need complete cooperation and understanding. We cannot,
repeat, cannot open a hatch and go get those people.
Anyone else who even talks about trying will be arrested and
prosecuted. Clear? For those who helped tackle that idiot
now in 20D, thank you! The only reason he was able to pull
that hatch open by the way is because we're not pressurized.
Don't touch the doors or the hatches! And 20D? You, sir, are
under arrest and will be federally charged when we get back
on the ground.*

Once again Lucy pressed her face to the glass, watching
the outline of her love framed by the darkened window of
the Beech some twenty-five feet away; feeling the most
profound level of despair she'd ever experienced.

CHAPTER TWENTY-TWO

Seven Months before — *January 21st*
Regal 12

"Approach, Regal Twelve. I assume runway zero seven is still the only one open?"

"Affirmative, Twelve, and the airport is advising that landing sooner than later would be a good idea. They're trying to keep ahead of the snowfall with the plows, but this storm is unprecedented."

"Understood, Approach. Right now, we need vectors for a north-south track with twenty-mile legs for the next ten or fifteen minutes. We're going to try configuring and slowing."

The controller relayed a heading, and with the cell phone connection to the captain of the wrecked 1900 on speakerphone, Marty took control from the copilot.

"Ryan, check the leading edge on your side for ice. I checked the left a minute ago and we're clear, but I am assuming the anti-ice is inop on the right leading edge."

The copilot swiveled his head around, face against the side window as he strained to see the right wing.

"This stuff is too dry to stick, Captain, and I have no idea whether the anti-ice ducting is blown or what."

"At least the engine anti-ice is on."

There was silence for a few seconds before Marty turned to the right seat, suppressing his roiled and conflicted feelings which were mixing a dark anger for the copilot's contribution to this disaster, with contrition for his own failure, leavened by appreciation for the younger man's aeronautical competence under pressure. If they survived, they would sort it all out on the ground. Hell, the NTSB and the airline and everyone up to God would sort it out with dire consequences to be liberally distributed to the offending flight crew, but for right now, the first officer was the best ally in sight. And the younger man was clearly feeling as frightened and hunted and alone as Marty.

"Ryan?"

"Yes, sir?"

"Kill the 'captain' and 'skipper' and 'sir' crap, okay? My name is Marty. Use it. We're working this together."

Ryan met his gaze with the look of a startled owl.

"Okay?" Marty nudged.

"Yes," Ryan answered, nodding. "Thank you…Marty."

"Welcome. And for the record, I'm scared shitless as well. Now, you're one hundred and fifty percent sure you're got the right circuit breakers for the leading edge devices?"

"Absolutely certain."

"Anything else we should be considering or thinking about? Anything we haven't addressed?"

"I don't think so."

"Okay, here we go. I'm going to bring the throttles back incrementally and I want you to start milking the trailing edge flaps out and watch that gauge like a hawk for any asymmetry. Michelle? Can you hear us? Are you ready?"

"We are," was the response.

The sound of the two huge turbofan engines changing pitch ever so slightly met their ears as the copilot lifted the flap lever out of the detent and brought it backwards a few millimeters at a time. He could hear the hydraulic motors begin to turn the torque tubes driving jackscrews that allowed the flaps to descend into a highspeed slipstream. Both of them were well aware that at two hundred forty knots they were going to overspeed the flaps, even though the entire flap system was sufficiently overbuilt to take such a beating.

"We're at flaps one, moving to flaps two," Ryan reported.

"Slowing through two hundred thirty-five knots…" Marty said, "…holding the same pitch angle. Keep the flaps coming…same slow rate."

"Roger"

"It feels pretty much the same out here," Michelle reported.

"Okay, slowing through two hundred thirty knots… down to two twenty-five. Flaps, Ryan?"

"About four degrees…I'm having to interpolate on this readout."

Marty felt a tiny tinge of relief that the leading edge devices in fact had not popped out. Any one of them deploying could have been catastrophic. Obviously Ryan had pulled the right breakers.

"We're at two hundred twenty-five knots and I'm holding the same pitch angle but we're starting to drift down in altitude. Keep the flaps coming, Ryan. I'm holding the airspeed and the power right here, and hoping the flaps will give us more lift at a slower airspeed."

"Coming through flaps five," the copilot reported. "You feel that buffeting?"

"Yes," Marty replied, the disturbed air roiling over the Beech fuselage had changed angle slightly and was shaking the tail of the 757. "It's controllable. Michelle? You agree?"

"We feel the shaking, and we're starting to put some forward pressure on our yoke. Are you changing your pitch angle?"

"Trying not to, but I'm going to have to pull up a bit more."

"We're feeling it shimmy and…and we hear a little metallic screeching, but nothing too alarming."

"Okay, I'm holding two twenty-five knots and the same pitch angle, flaps are at what, Ryan?"

"About seven percent."

"Okay, and we're sinking about three hundred feet per

minute. Michelle, I'm going to increase pitch angle by two degrees."

Gingerly he put back pressure on the 757's yoke, feeling the nose come up slightly, watching the attitude deviation indicator on the screen in front of him to limit the change.

"Ah, we're hearing a lot of metal sounds over here and she's bucking a bit. We're putting pitch down pressure on our yoke. I think we can take some more."

"Okay...keep the flaps coming, Ryan. That pitch angle has zeroed our descent...we're holding altitude. I'm going to try slowing to two-twenty."

"Flaps coming through ten percent now, ah, Marty," Ryan reported.

"Pitch attitude is two degrees and..." Marty began, his voice trailing off as the 757 began rolling to the right.

"STOP THE FLAPS!" Marty ordered.

"Yeah..." Ryan replied, "we've got an asymmetry. Right side has stopped."

"Yes. I'm bringing the flap handle back up...please tell me when we're neutral...when, I mean, the roll moment has stopped."

"Right there! Stop!"

"Okay."

"How much flap do we have out?"

"Ah..ah..eleven percent. But I'm just past the flaps ten detent. If I let the handle go, it could move."

Marty turned to the lead flight attendant holding the iPhone by his ear. "Nancy? Is there any tape of any sort in the galley?"

"I think so."

"Wait, guys," Ryan said. I carry duct tape in my flight bag. Here...I'll tape the lever in place and..."

Suddenly a loud metallic screech and rumble shook the cockpit and the 757 yawed to the right as the voice of the other captain cut through their consciousness from the speaker of the iPhone.

"SHIT!"

A rhythmic bouncing was shaking them as well as another lurch accompanied by a scream from the cockpit of the Beech 1900.

In the Cabin of Regal 12

Lucy felt as if she were descending through the outer circles of hell. She had been watching the Beech fuselage as if her laser-like vigilance could somehow keep Greg safe. It was she who first noticed a dark panel of metal near the front of the ruined fuselage suddenly rise up, shaking violently. The vibrations were followed by a rhythmic bouncing and her heart all but stopped as she saw the structure begin to move, like an injured creature trying to rise where it had fallen. She saw the front end begin to bounce upward, and even being halfway back in the 757 at row 22 she could hear voices yelling in the cockpit as the tail of the parasitic aircraft suddenly rose and the 757 pulsed nose down.

She was losing him. The aircraft would fly up and back and disappear and she didn't need a pilot's license to know they would die if that happened with only one wing. *He* would die! The guy she'd waited a lifetime for who she'd finally found in her early forties was retreating to another dimension in time, like the wrenching scene in her favorite film *Somewhere in Time*. She hadn't even realized her right hand was on the window, fingers spread, in a gesture beyond mere words.

The Cockpit of Regal 12

"LOWER YOUR NOSE...MARTY...PLEASE! It's trying to pull loose..."

Marty had pulsed the yoke forward slightly, relaxing the back pressure to let the 757's nose drop quickly by several degrees, changing the angle of the airflow over the wings and lessening the pressure on the underside of the Beech fuselage.

"What's happening over there?" he asked.

"Oh God...pushing! No, Luke, push more! Help me! "

Her voice was vibrating from the shaking violently bouncing the ruined Beech fuselage before the sound of the phone being dropped and banging around the floor of the cockpit.

"Michelle?" Marty tried.

Suddenly the shaking in the 757 stopped, and Ryan looked at the captain with a feral look of disbelief.

"MICHELLE?" Marty yelled, meeting Ryan's gaze. "Look out there...are they..."

The copilot had already plastered his face to the window.

"Yes! They're still there! I can't see much but they're still with us."

The sound of the phone being retrieved in the Beech cockpit was followed by Michelle Whittier's voice, clearly shaken.

"Oh God! Luke, hold it there. We almost blew off!" Michelle shouted, her voice shaking. "We...I could feel the right gear strut lifting out of your wing and our nose was pulling us up...we pushed hard on the yoke and she settled back in but...it won't take much more...angle of attack I mean. It was so sudden..."

"Our flaps are out as far as we can get them, Michelle, and I'm at two twenty and now speeding up by ten knots to get back to the same deck angle."

"Okay...I..."

"Are you all right?"

"NO! God, no, we're not all right! How the fuck did all this happen, anyway? What did I do to deserve this hell?"

A breaking wave of shame, guilt, and remorse broke

over Marty and for a second deprived him of the ability to speak, but Michelle's voice provided the grace of a reprieve, for the moment.

"Nevermind...that's not...I'm just deeply rattled over here. We were just lucky a minute ago. That came out of nowhere...no warning. We jammed the yoke forward and thank God it worked...for now."

"Agreed," Marty said, his throat even more bone dry now than seconds before. "We're at two hundred thirty knots. Keep forward pressure on your yoke."

"Please don't slow anymore!"

"We won't."

"It's still bouncing out here, far more than before...like the nose is trying to lift again...and making those screeching noises, so it's not as well seated...the gear strut...as before."

"Michelle, is your right aileron controllable? If your right wing is producing lift out there, maybe rolling your yoke to the right could settle it back on our wing more. Your call."

"Already doing it. How long to landing?"

"Ah, ten, maybe twenty minutes," Marty replied.

Her voice came back markedly different, low and metered and somber.

"Okay, we have to face the facts. This may not work, Marty. Even if we can stay on your wing to landing, you'll never get a 757 stopped on a slick runway inside of ten thousand feet."

"That's a chance we'll have to take, and the length is twelve thousand, just...the far end is unplowed."

"They were closing runways behind us. What's left down there? Which runway?"

"We'll come in on Runway Seven."

There was a long pause and what sounded like a sigh before she replied.

"Ah...you do realize there's a dropoff at the east end of seven, right? At least a hundred feet. And to each side...

well, there are the taxiways to the north."

"I know."

"Any other runway would be better."

"All the other are covered in snow, Michelle."

"I think that's my point."

"I'm not following you."

He heard the phone scrape on something again and a cry of pain.

"Michelle?"

"Sorry, sorry! My shoulder is …hurt. I forgot not to move it."

"How are you and your crew and passengers holding out?"

"We won't die of hypothermia before you run out of fuel, but I may move to the Sahara after this. No, we'll…we're holding on…literally and figuratively."

"Just a little longer."

"Look…Marty…I want to live…I want my passengers to live…but I want everyone in your plane to live, too…"

"Michelle! That's enough. I'll get us down. I'm not sacrificing you guys to make a smooth landing."

"What can I do over here."

"Just what you're doing. Now it's up to us."

There was a garbled reply

"What?" Marty asked.

"I just said… 'I *hope* God is with us,'" she replied quietly. "Not my characteristic benediction but, you know what they say: There are no atheists in foxholes."

Mountaineer 2612

"Luke, I have to ask you something," Michelle Whittier said, wincing in pain again as she glanced at her copilot.

"Sure. What?"

"Since we know we've got over twelve hundred pounds

of baggage in the back of this fuselage, and we're trying to keep from tipping backwards, and the weight being so far back is a significant force trying to pull us off this wing..."

"I know where you're going."

"Do you? Because we'd have to use the crash axe to chop through the wall to the cargo bay, and then open the door from inside, which means it will blow off instantly, and if it doesn't, if it just opens into the airstream, it could pull us off by itself.

"But if we could get rid of that weight..."

"Michelle, I know of one 1900 cargo door that came completely open in flight and didn't blow off."

"Yeah, but we'd be guessing as to whether it could affect us."

"Wait, I have an idea," Luke said. "I know I can get into the cargo bay...that wall is flimsy. Instead of changing the cargo door, why don't we relay bags to the emergency exit row, pull the exit open, and dump stuff out there. Even if some of the bags won't fit, we can dump the contents."

"Really good idea," she answered, "...and maybe we can find more warm stuff for our freezing passengers to wear. We also need to move people forward to the extent we can."

"Only three empty seats forward," Luke replied, "...but I'll take care of it. Can you keep forward pressure on the yoke, though?"

"Yes. One way or another."

"Okay."

"How are you holding out, Luke?"

He had been in the process of removing his seat belt and he looked her in the eye now and paused.

"Ah...I'm very cold, like you, and I thought we were done back there, so...every minute's a gift, y'know?"

She nodded. "I do."

"Having something to do, to fight with, is good."

"It is. Go. Quick. Move the people forward first."

CHAPTER TWENTY-THREE

Present Day — *August 14*[th], *7:55 pm*
Summit of Long's Peak

With a deep sigh, Marty pried his mind away from the virtual reality of his memory – his all-consuming mental hologram. Somewhere in his head a small shiver registered that his body was now cold, but he couldn't feel it, even though the temperature on the peak was probably below forty and the wind at least a steady fifteen knots. As the wrenching realism of that January night receded like an evaporating nightmare, it left in its stead a stark loneliness.

I wish Judith was here right now, he thought, *I wish she had understood. Maybe I could have explained better...*

But there would be no need. After all, he would be dead and gone and who gave a tinker's damn in the broader scheme of human existence if some schmuck named Marty screwed up and people died as a result. People died all the time. No, as he'd told her, he would not be a pawn in their game of chess.

But deep inside, Marty Mitchell knew that was a damnable lie. He longed for vindication. Or, perhaps, something resembling forgiveness.

Marty took another deep breath, gazing at the boulder strewn summit, which was now bathed in semi-darkness.

It was time. Yes, he was burning to get all his points across, yet aching for relief from the all-too-vivid replaying of the accident every single solitary fucking night. And that's what he'd climbed this ancient pile of granite to find: relief.

Marty stood and snapped on his flashlight, playing it on his pack as he started to lay out his own last supper. Whiskey and pills. Food of the gods, he chuckled. The only thing missing was peanut butter.

And that thought alone brought a smile…for at least a few seconds.

Marty had never contemplated suicide before, other than to condemn those who had…those who had indulged in it as an ultimate escape clause. Oh, he could understand someone accelerating the process of dying from cancer or Alzheimer's or something else clearly fatal. But to eat a shotgun without warning one morning like Hemingway? Pure selfishness. Pure cowardice, or so he'd thought – until the unbelievable pain of his failures was redoubled by the harsh condemnation of society. Suddenly, suicide made sense.

For some reason he remembered Michelle Whittier's words before the landing. What had she called it? Oh, yeah. Her "benediction." She hoped God would be with them. Of *course* she had to know that there were, in fact, at least some atheists in foxholes. That old phrase insulted atheists and thumped agnostics, and he had imagined himself one or the other. In fact, he'd always worn an agnostic attitude as a slightly snobbish badge of honor. But if his cynical point of view was right and there was nothing else beyond this life, the Marty Mitchell he knew and had once been very proud of was about to evaporate. The irony was, he'd never know it. He'd never know anything. All that life and experience gone. All that training as a pilot. All that memory. Poof. Something was deeply illogical about that, he mused. Maybe in these last minutes he should at least consider that there might be something after this mortal excursion.

Marty looked down at the prepared items and reached for the bottle.

"Time to find out," he said to the wind as he uncorked the whiskey. "Checkmate!"

A frantic Judith Winston glanced at her brass wall clock, stalking around her office, cell phone glued to her ear. It had been less than an hour since she'd rushed back to try to convince someone to organize a rescue to Rocky Mountain National Park. Fortunately, her secretary was working late on a weekend, and she pressed him into immediate service.

A voice returned to the other end of the line, causing a head shake.

"No," she replied. "I need General Stone. I need to speak to the adjutant general of the Colorado National Guard, as I told you. And yes, he *does* know me, and this *is* an emergency, and I can tell you with certainty that someone is going to die if I can't get through to him!"

She rolled her eyes at the response.

"No...no, sergeant, listen carefully. That was not a threat! I'm trying to prevent a suicide on a mountain top that apparently only your helicopters can reach, okay? Now please, drop your defensiveness and call the general!"

Her secretary had been waiting, leaning in the door, and Judith motioned him to come, punching the mute button in the process.

"Anything?"

"This may be his home number. I'm not sure."

"Call it and see if you can get him on the line.

Judith stopped to look at her hastily taken notes. She'd talked to the National Park Service, two hospital emergency rooms, and a longtime friend who owned a jet charter company out of Broomfield, as well as two medical evacuation helicopter operators, both of whom claimed their choppers couldn't go to fourteen thousand feet. She supposed that was truthful, but it was hard to accept, knowing that someone had recently landed a helicopter on Mt. Everest at 29-thousand feet. She'd even seen the YouTube video.

Her secretary was back and holding a portable office phone.

"It's General Stone," he whispered.

"Great. Tell whoever comes on here that we found him. It's on mute." She handed over her cell phone and took the offered portable.

"General, Judith Winston here. We met last fall at the benefit in Cherry Creek for...oh. You do? Good. Well, I'm sorry to bother you at home, but I've got a crisis on my hands and I'm told that only your team can help, but I can't get hold of anyone in your outfit who'll dare to make a decision."

Denver

Across town in the Centennial Airport command post for RescueFlight, the shift chief was drumming his fingers on the desk and thinking about the rescue he'd had to reject. Despite being the primary source of medical helicopters for central Colorado, Long's Peak summit was not a place their choppers could safely reach. What had snagged his attention, however, was the name of the person needing rescue.

He thought for a few more seconds, turning over the question of whether tipping off a reporter he knew could get him in trouble.

Hell, we're not really involved. Not my monkeys, not my circus.

Scott Bogosian answered on the first ring.

"Hey, Scott, Jeremy here at RescueFlight, although this call never happened, okay?"

"Sure."

"I remember you told me you were considering doing a book on the Regal accident, and I've got a bit of breaking news involving that airline captain who's on trial."

Boulder

The callback to Judith from the head of the Colorado National Guard affirming that a powerful Blackhawk helicopter would be airborne inside a half hour propelled her into motion northbound to the Estes Park area. Technically the LZ – as the landing zone they were preparing had been described – was the Long's Peak trailhead parking lot south of Estes. The rescue attempt would be launched from there, and if Marty Mitchell could be found – and if it wasn't too late – there would be an ambulance waiting at the LZ.

Fortunately, the night seemed mild, the sky clear, and no ominous clouds were approaching the front range. *Probably as ideal as it could be for a helicopter rescue*, she thought.

She had checked the GPS location of Marty's phone again before darting to the parking lot, and once again the target had moved slightly, still on the summit of the peak, but at least a few feet away. That had to mean he was still alive, she concluded. At least she *hoped* that's what it meant.

North Denver

Three rings had come and gone on the best number Scott Bogosian had for the Superintendent of Rocky Mountain National Park, but so many people now forwarded one phone to another, he decided to stick with it. On the fifth ring, a no nonsense voice he knew well, a voice laden with a heavy southern accent, barked a hello.

"Joe? Scott Bogosian."

"Hello, Scott! What's up? I'm a bit busy right now."

"Does that have anything to do with someone on Long's Peak?"

There was a distinct chuckle on the other end. "You wouldn't ask me that if you didn't already know. Yes. And this is off the record, okay?"

"Absolutely."

"We're arranging a landing zone for a National Guard Blackhawk...near the Long's parking area. You know the location?"

"I'm a veteran of that lot."

"Thought so. I've got to get moving...I'll be there myself in thirty minutes. You didn't hear this from me, okay? And I do NOT want to hear about it on KOA or KNUS."

"You won't...at least if you do, it won't be from me. I'm a print reporter, not broadcast, remember? And I owe you, Joe."

"You *always* owe me Bogosian! When you gonna pay up?"

"Well, when you tell me in what form payment should be rendered for past intelligence provided? Cash, check, liquor...women?"

"*Women?* Shit, Scott, your sense of humor is gonna get us in deep trouble one of these days when the call gets monitored by NSA or something and someone posts it on Facebook."

"You started it, old friend. Okay, I'm in motion."

Long's Peak Trailhead Parking Lot,
Rocky Mountain National Park

The crew of the inbound Army Blackhawk spotted the LZ almost thirty miles away. Cordoned off by ranger vehicles and sheriff's SUV's, all with red and blue beacons flashing urgently, it was impossible to miss. Using their GPS anchored displays of the terrain, the pilot guided them though the wide valleys leading up to the mountain and settled the twin engine turboshaft machine onto the concrete for a quick pre-mission brief.

The crew had shut the helicopter down and had used the hood of a car to layout and examine a terrain map. Now, a half dozen park rangers pushed in around the pilot and his crew as he looked up from the terrain map they'd been examining.

"Okay, folks, weight is a factor, even for a Blackhawk, but we'll have one flight nurse and the most terrain-savvy ranger with us. So, five of us – two pilots, two crew chiefs, and our one flight nurse – plus Ranger Wilson here, who knows the summit very well. No one else. We're not going to use night vision goggles because we will need to use our night sun to illuminate the area when we arrive, and we've got pretty good moonlight with moonrise in a few minutes. We've been briefed that there is no flat, open terrain up there on which to set the machine down, so I'll either hover just above with the crew chief using the winch as necessary, or I'll balance one of my main wheels on the flattest rock available to get people in and out, and essentially remain barely airborne in the meantime. Weather at the top this evening is very moderate, winds should be no more than twenty knots from the southwest. Any questions?"

Judith could see the position lights and the beacon of the Blackhawk lifting off from the LZ as she turned off the main highway. She had briefed the Guard command post by phone since she knew that riding along was not possible. As she pulled around the circle of ranger SUV's and parked, she could still see the machine climbing toward the north. Judith watched for a few seconds, startled when a uniformed man materialized at her window.

"Ma'am, we have a rescue operation going on…"

"I know that. I called it."

"Sorry?"

"I'm the one that asked for this." She still wasn't making sense and she held out her hand instead. "Judith Winston. The guy we're trying to save on the peak is my client."

CHAPTER TWENTY-FOUR

Present Day – *August 14ᵗʰ, 9:05 pm*
Summit of Long's Peak

Trying to get comfortable enough to die was more of a challenge than he'd expected – dammit! Even the spot he'd used during the afternoon felt like precisely what it was: a bed of rocks!

He stood unsteadily, aware of being at least intoxicated, but wondering why the barbiturates he'd finally received from an offshore pharmacy two weeks ago hadn't kicked in yet. The thought that they might not be as potent as they were supposed to be had crossed his mind, but hey, he had all night.

What had really propelled him to his feet was a growing anger that had harpooned his idea of a peaceful departure – a deep sleep to oblivion. He had been a good captain, dammit! But wasn't he a freaking human being? Weren't humans *supposed* to be imperfect? Yes, he misunderstood a radio call and failed to question his bumbling copilot, but it seemed it was just diabolical chance that put that Beech 1900 in front of them! Chance or a higher power that hated him.

"GODDAMMIT!" He screamed into the wind, the effort making him dizzy. He braced himself on the edge of a huge boulder that had been his companion for hours and stood and railed again. "FUCKING GODDAMMIT TO HELL! WHY? WHY ME? YOU HEAR ME? WHY? THERE ARE WORSE BASTARDS OUT THERE TO TORTURE!"

Maybe it was the lack of oxygen, but screaming felt better than lying on rocks and wondering when it was all going to be over. He let go of the boulder and took an unsteady step forward, shaking his fist at the now starry sky. "YOU BASTARDS SET ME UP! YOU'RE THE ONES WHO SHOULD BE ON TRAIL...TRIAL...WHATEVER. I WAS A GOOD MAN! I WASN'T TED FUCKING BUNDY OR CHARLES MANSON OR SOME SCUMBAG WIFE BEATER!"

Somewhere in the corner of his mind was the question of precisely who he was railing at. Who *were* the stated bastards? But there was a therapeutic impetus to the screaming, and it was like a huge boulder that had started rolling downhill with too much momentum to stop.

More yelling now, shaking both fists, and turning toward where Denver ought to be before realizing he was too dizzy to know which direction to look.

I'd better sit down, he decided, but another idea slowly crawled into his frontal cortex and he summoned the energy and the anger to stand once more, middle finger offered to the skies as he screamed: YOU...YOU COWARDLY MOTHERFUCKERS! I CHALLENGE YOU! YOU HEAR ME? SHOW YOURSELVES AND FIGHT ME! COME ON, BASTARDS! I KNOW YOU"RE UP THERE...OR OUT THERE SOMEWHERE! COME ON! I *DARE* YOU!"

A slightly familiar, rhythmic sound reached his fuzzed up hearing and he steadied himself and turned in that direction, watching something descending toward him as a blinding light hit him like a million suns. He covered his eyes and screamed ineffectually against the oncoming Valkyrie or angry devils or whatever it was that was accepting his challenge. He felt like a mouse flipping off an eagle a microsecond before the talons closed, but that tiny rebellion felt good!

"YEAH! THAT'S RIGHT! YEAH, BABY! BRING IT ON, YOU BASTARDS!"

The light was blinding, the sound apparently the beating of huge wings. What the hell had he summoned, a pterodactyl?

So this is what dying is like! he thought

The breeze had risen to a hurricane and the merciless blazing light was even brighter as he kept his left arm and hand above him, middle finger defiantly thrust toward the invited intruder. He unshielded his eyes and screamed one last heartfelt epithet at the top of his lungs: "**FUCK...YOU!**" as he slowly lost his tenuous hold on consciousness, his eyes rolling back in his head, the bulk of his body slowly oozing down among the boulders like an escaping octopus.

CHAPTER TWENTY-FIVE

Present Day — *August 14th, 9:35 pm*

Thanks to the "he's with me" stewardship of Joe Johnson, the barrel chested chief park ranger now standing next to him in the trail head parking lot, Scott Bogosian had been spared the task of pushing through the normal official defenses thrown up against invading reporters.

Word had been radioed from the flight crew that they had the target on board and were electing to land back at the LZ and transfer the man to a waiting ambulance, a decision Scott interpreted as hopeful.

"Any idea where they'll take him, Joe?" Scott asked.

"Don't know. Usually our mountain rescues are all about broken bones and hypothermia, so helicoptering directly to a Denver trauma center is the best idea, but I don't know what they're dealing with. Could mean he can walk to the ambulance. Could mean they recovered a body." Joe turned and regarded Scott for a few seconds. "So, what's this all about, Scotty? Why are you out here in the cold tonight? I know it's not a social visit because you didn't bring any scotch."

"A book I'm thinking of writing. Maybe."

"Really? Well, that figures. In the old days you would have never shown up without a photographer rattling at least one bag full of Nikons. You aren't acting like you're under deadline pressure."

Scott smiled, shaking his head. "How times change. The TV guys are doing it solo these days too, and so are reporters.

At least we are Rocky Mountain News refugees."

"Tell me about this book idea."

"There's a lot to this, Joe. You remember last January when a Regal Air jet hit a commuter?"

"Of course."

"That's the Regal Air captain they're bringing off the mountain right now."

"Really? What is he doing on my mountain at night?"

"That's...one of the things I need to find out," Scott replied. "Maybe he had an accident and couldn't climb down. Maybe, I don't know, maybe he was up there for the night communing with the universe. I imagine it's an incredible view of the starfield."

"You have no idea!"

"Joe, I've been studying the NTSB raw material, the reports from each of the investigatory groups, and there are a number of strange things I'm trying to understand. I'm sure the NTSB is working on the same puzzles, but they haven't held the hearing yet or even gotten close to issuing their final report."

"Seems diabolically simple. They had a midair, the little airplane's stuck on their wing with live people, and the captain refuses to follow his company orders and as a result, lives were lost, and now he's been charged with murder for insubordination. Right?"

"Well...somewhat. Those are the basics. But there's so much more here. First, I can't even imagine the pressure this guy was under to either sacrifice the people he'd rammed in that smaller plane in order to make a safe landing, or keep *them* safe and imperil the passengers on the big jet."

"Have you talked to this fellow? The captain?"

"Only his lawyer...that woman right over there. She's built a brick wall with concertina wire around him until the trial. And, of course, that's the other thing. It's unsettling when you try to crucify someone for a human mistake. You know, a professional makes a totally unintentional mistake and then tries his best to do his job and make decisions under pressure and some district attorney decides to convict him for it. That's third world shit, it doesn't belong in the U.S. But the public doesn't seem the least upset about it, while to me it's clearly malicious prosecution."

A broad smile spread across the big ranger's face as he regarded his friend of at least two decades.

"Scott, you remember that long-ago tv detective played by Peter Falk?"

"Columbo? Lord, that's been off the air forever."

"Well, you do know you're a bit like Columbo when you latch onto something, right? I mean, you don't have the seedy trench coat or the weird accent, but little things get your attention."

"Hey, I'm not a bit like Columbo!"

"You drive an old Volvo, right?"

"He didn't drive a Volvo...did he?"

"I really don't recall." Joe chuckled. "It was an old beater, though." He paused, both of them watching the sky.

"So, what, in this case, is keeping you up at night, Mister Scott?"

"Unexplained lights."

"Excuse me?"

"On final approach that night, after everything that had happened in the middle of the blizzard, the captain said in his hospital interview with the NTSB that suddenly bright lights snapped on just to the right of the centerline, and he reacted instinctively to avoid hitting whatever it was. He figured it was a snowplow in the wrong place, but the airport flatly denies any snowplows were anywhere near that runway and they're got video of their equipment parking garage which seems to support the point."

"Is the man lying?"

"I doubt it. He could have just imagined it afterwards, a trauma-induced false memory, but his history just isn't that of someone who tries to lie his way out of things. But you asked…and that's what's bothering me."

The landing lights of the approaching Blackhawk were suddenly visible and the two men watched as the thunderous roar of the blades and engine approached and the National Guardsman set the chopper back down in the landing zone. The door slid open and the two paramedics who had been waiting in their ambulance now scrambled aboard , and out again within a minute. They retreated to respectful distance as the pilot lifted the Blackhawk into the night sky once more and headed east.

Scott shadowed Joe Johnson as the ranger approached the two paramedics.

"What's going on, fellas?"

"No time to take the patient by road, sir," one of them said, folding an unused blanket and preparing to leave empty.

"Why's that?" Joe pressed.

"Excuse me, sir, you are…?" the paramedic asked.

"I'm the chief ranger here. I summoned you."

"Okay, sir, just…checking before I breach confidentiality."

The medic was looking at Scott but Joe didn't flinch and it was enough to declassify him as an interloper.

"So, why did he need air evacuation?"

"Well, when you have a suspected overdose, especially a barbiturate, there's no direct antidote, and they've got a bunch of things that have to be done fast. We don't have everything we'd need aboard."

"Overdose? You mean as in attempted suicide?"

"Off the record, probably. The crew chief said he recovered a prescription bottle and other stuff up there indicating the patient didn't intend to come down alive. They'll have him at a trauma center in fifteen minutes. It would take us an hour."

"What are his chances?" Scott interjected.

The medic shrugged. "Honestly, I have no idea."

CHAPTER TWENTY-SIX

Present Day — *August 15ᵗʰ, 10:00 am*
St. Michael's Hospital, North Denver

National Guard helicopters cannot successfully pluck
stranded climbers from a major mountain peak in a national
park at night without the story leaking like a failing dam.
When reporters glommed onto the fact that the rescue was
none other than the indicted captain of Flight 12, the chase
was on.

Acutely aware of the value to TV news reporters of an
on-the-scene backdrop to any interview, Judith arranged to
meet camera crews from three of the local stations on the
steps of the hospital. Determined to keep it brief, she had
already warned the media force that the 'conference' would
be confined to a prepared statement.

*"Hello. I am Judith Winston, attorney for Captain
Marty Mitchell of Regal Airlines. I appreciate everyone's
concern and presence here this morning wondering about
Captain Mitchell's condition. Captain Mitchell made an
ascent of Long's Peak yesterday, and was unable to descend
from the summit safely after dark. As a precaution against
hypothermia, a helicopter unit of the Colorado Air National
Guard volunteered to make a difficult landing on the
summit and bring him down to safety, and they performed
magnificently. Captain Mitchell is resting comfortably and
in good condition."*

Predictably, hands went up, and Judith turned back, pointing to one of the reporters – a planned maneuver.

"Ms. Winston, there are rumors that Captain Mitchell is despondent over his prosecution for murder in Denver. Did that play a role in his being on the peak last night?"

She smiled a practiced, indulgent smile before answering.

"I think any of us would be despondent over being wrongly and scandalously accused of committing a crime by doing nothing more than trying to save people in a major emergency. And when any of us are feeling such pain, we do different things to take our minds of the raging injustice – run marathons, do extreme sports, ski too fast, climb mountains...you name it."

Another reporter tag teamed the first.

"Did Captain Mitchell intend to come down but couldn't, or was there some other reason?"

"What are you asking?" Judith countered, knowing the word 'suicide' would not be openly asked.

The reporter started to respond but Judith interrupted.

"Folks, when the captain is released from the hospital's care, we'll hold a presser and let him describe the problems he encountered last night."

The same reporter raised her hand again.

"Ms. Winston, you're his defense attorney and it would be expected that you would denounce the prosecution of your client. But, do you truly believe Captain Mitchell is going to be found innocent of the specific charges, considering that he was warned by his airline not to attempt to do exactly what he ended up doing?"

Perfect set up, Judith thought to herself, taking a small step forward toward the cameras.

"The short answer is yes, he will be found innocent because the charges are ridiculous and this is a gross misuse of the criminal statutes of Colorado. But there's a far more important question that everyone out there who is aware of the national outrage over District Attorney Grant

Richardson's attempt to put a decent and even heroic pilot and Air Force veteran in prison needs to ask. In his public comments, he has been uncharacteristically unrestrained. Why is the district attorney so furious?"

There were more questions, but she waved like a veteran politician and sidestepped them all, disappearing quickly into the hospital's main entry.

Room 314

With a sudden involuntary convulsion, Marty Mitchell jerked back to consciousness, twisting his body as he sat bolt upright in the hospital bed, eyes wide, a feral look on his face as he tried to make sense of the images his eyes were transmitting. This was the second time in seven months he'd found himself in a hospital bed, decorated with plastic tubes and IV bags.

The unexpected movement had equally startled the only other person in the room, and once she got her heart rate under control, Judith Winston was on her feet, moving to the bedside, her hand on the side rail as he squinted at her in marginal recognition.

"Judith?"

"Yes."

"So…so I'm alive?"

"Not by much. You have enough charcoal in you to fuel a grill for a week."

"Charcoal?"

"They say you took a form of Seconal. That's one of the treatments."

"How…how did I get here?"

"Courtesy of our State National Guard and a great helicopter crew who plucked you off Long's Peak, despite the fact you were making obscene gestures at them."

He shook his head, taking a raged breath, and forced his eyes shut.

"I've got a hell of a headache…and I don't recall any of that. Obscene?"

"Yep. You apparently put on quite a show as they were approaching."

"God. I wasn't supposed to be here. Alive, I mean."

"I know. I broke into your house when you stood me up. Found your goodbye letters. You don't have to kill yourself to avoid an appointment, y'know. You could just call."

"You broke into my house?"

"Sure did. It's another form of attorney-client privilege."

"Okay. Right. Go away, Judith."

"Let's get at least one thing straight," she said, smiling ruefully. "I get really ticked off at criminal law clients who leave me prematurely, okay?"

"But, I thought I was your *only* criminal law client."

"That's right. You are. And I've rearranged my entire professional life to defend you, and, I have to say, I've become almost as angry as you over this stupid prosecution, so I'm not going to let you deprive me of the experience. Don't try this again or I'll do the job for you."

"Defending me, you mean?"

"No, killing you as painfully as possible."

He fell silent, eyes downward, rubbing his head as he lay back.

"I'm sorry, Judith. I was…I'm still…being tortured." He paused, looking up. "Does anybody know about the whole thing on the peak…other than the rescuers?"

"Oh, just the majority of the population of Colorado, plus a few tens of millions who watch national television, all thanks to a very clever and persistent Denver Post reporter. Same guy I've told you is trying to write a book on the crash."

Marty cringed.

"They *don't* have your suicide notes," she continued, "… and so far, no videos have surfaced of you flipping the bird at the bird, but the sudden notoriety is enough to make jury selection problematic for the DA, so…well done for that!"

"What's the point?" Marty turned away. "You said I was guilty."

She released the bed rail and paced around to the other side. "There's an immediate legal argument about the propriety of even bringing these charges that will make solid grounds for appeal if it came to that. But it's much more important to show a jury that what this idiot DA calls premeditation in no way fits the criminal definition. You were exercising captain's emergency authority. I need you on the stand to drive that point home. But you can't flip off the judge or the DA."

He was shaking his head again, gingerly. "My decision would have worked if..."

"I know, I know," she said, hand extended to stop him. "and no one can disprove what you thought you saw, and what you calculated. It doesn't matter one whit what the company ordered you to do. You were the legal authority. They weren't in that cockpit with you. You were doing your best and that story's got to be told. And you are *not* on trial for the midair collision, regardless of whether the NTSB ultimately tries to pin it on you."

Marty nodded as he looked quizzically at her. "I...was thinking the very same thing last night up there on Long's. I remember being distraught and furious that no one, including you, understood. At least I thought you didn't...maybe you do."

"You're going to stay with me through the trial, right?" Judith asked abruptly. "No more early sneaking out via suicide?"

There was a long moment of silence as Marty turned to stare out of the window, then turned back to her, nodding, his tone resigned.

"Yes. I'll stay."

"Okay. I am the *only* one licensed to terminate your existence before this is over."

"I got it. I got it."

"Anyone I should call to come see you? I know there's no immediate family..."

He laughed, a singular, explosive sound.

"Nope. No one cares. Except you." He looked at her in mild horror, as if he'd accidentally said something sexist. "I don't mean you *care*, care, just...that you have an interest."

"Well, actually I do," Judith said, almost if she were trying to bite off the words before they found air.

"Have an interest, you mean."

"No, dammit, *care* care, as you put it. I...also want the torture to stop for you, but with you still on the planet. Okay?"

Marty looked shocked. "I'm...not sure what to say?"

"Then don't say anything. That's not some weird declaration of love, all right? I just happen to care. End of sentence."

"Thank you."

"You're welcome."

"And thank you for not giving up on me...for saving me. When was that? Last night?"

"Just about fourteen hours ago. Life and death move faster these days."

She started to turn toward the door, then turned back. "I'll look in on you tomorrow. I expect they'll be ready to kick you out of here by then."

"I hope it's not sooner," he said. "I feel like crap."

"But you look alive, and act alive, which is what counts."

"Judith, is what happened going to affect the trial?"

"Other than pissing off a judge who loves to overreact? Actually, I don't think so. You didn't violate any court orders, and attempted suicide isn't illegal – though in ancient Rome it was a capital offense punishable by, wait for it, death. But in this case, in short, I don't think it hurts or helps us, but I could be missing something."

"Missing something?" he asked, genuinely puzzled.

"Yes. That actually happened once. Meantime, I have

an assignment for you. Think of it a trial prep."

"Okay."

"Seriously, Marty, I am not unaware or unsympathetic to how much this is torturing you, each time you have to re-live the crash and everything that led up to it, but I really need you to go over the last twenty minutes of the flight sequence with great care…meticulously, in fact. Write notes. Use bullet points. Leave out nothing."

"Why?"

"Let's just say something's missing from the logic of the story, and I have to know what. Don't misunderstand. I'm not saying that you're purposefully leaving something out, but some dots just refuse to connect. Also, I need you in my office in one week for a boot camp on surviving a criminal prosecution, and then we go to trial in three weeks."

"And after that?" he asked, meaning the question to be sarcastic but surprised at the hunted look that suddenly crossed his lawyer's face like the shadow of a fast building cumulonimbus.

Judith stepped toward him, her eyes on the floor for a second, her lips pursed, before she looked up.

"Marty, I'm going to presume that by then you will be a free man who can re-start his life. I can't guarantee anything. I can't guarantee someone doesn't bomb the courtroom and kill us all, or that we aren't obliterated by an asteroid, or that you won't have a massive coronary, or for that matter that I won't have one during opening arguments. But in the meantime, I simply refuse to see you as anything but free."

"Thank you."

In the dead of night an innocuous noise somewhere down the hospital corridor caused Marty to jolt awake as if jabbed in the ass with a red hot poker. Once awake, the only apparent pathway back to a tortured nightmare-ridden sleep was through the nurses and the hospital's pharmacy, and there was nothing to be gained with that approach. Besides,

Judith wanted an excruciatingly detailed review from him of the last twenty minutes of Regal Flight 12, and now was as good a time as any.

He felt a heavy shroud of sadness settle around him as he sat there in the bed, torn between despair over having been robbed of his final exit from all this pain, and yet entertaining a faint flicker of hope that he would be heard; and that maybe he was no longer alone in this fight.

But fight for what? To prove he'd been right that night? Or just to beg license to consider himself a decent, if deeply flawed, human.

As the image of the 757 cockpit coalesced again around him, Marty took a deep breath and submerged once more into the prison of his personal memory.

CHAPTER TWENTY-SEVEN

Seven Months before – *January 21st*
Regal 12

The temptation to accelerate the process and get the stricken 757 on the ground had grown to an internal imperative as primal as the human need to run from a monster. Marty recognized the syndrome. That form of "get-home-itis" had killed better airmen than him.

The controls had been given over to Ryan so Marty could force himself to think clearly and as free of panic as possible. It was a logical idea, but it wasn't working. His thoughts – propelled by the cascading urgency of everything real and imagined – were a confused cacophony clamoring for attention like a classroom of agitated 3rd graders.

I've done the final briefing with Ryan, but he has to back me up on the spoilers...wait, remember, there won't be any! Okay, reverse thrust is going to be our only friend after the brakes, and the braking factor down there is poor in the last report. Do I need to make another PA to the passengers? No...Nancy and the crew have it under control.

The very real monster, he understood, was the dropoff at the end of Runway 7, and it was time he faced it. The numbers and the graphs were not subjective. There was no flexibility in the cold hard prediction that there wasn't enough slippery runway in a blizzard for a big jet traveling a hundred knots faster than normal. Even if he slammed the 757 on right at the beginning of Runway 7, 230 knots of momentum was a huge amount of extra energy to dissipate, and the only tools he would have probably weren't enough – especially if the tires blew or the brakes were more ineffective than figured. What then?

If I can't stop her, should I run off the left side of the runway onto the taxiway?   There's a drop there, too, alongside, but maybe it wouldn't be that lethal.

Face it, he told himself, everything was stacked against them if he didn't reduce his approach speed significantly under 230 knots. He'd known it for the last forty minutes and been doing everything possible to treat the reality like the iconic three monkeys refusing to perceive evil. But there was a brutal binary choice, and it was as unyielding as granite: Slow down and make a safe landing and in the process sacrifice those people on the wing that were only there because of his mistake; or, stay at 230 knots to touchdown to save the occupants of Mountaineer while rolling the dice that skidding off the end of Runway 7 and down the slope at the eastern end would not seriously injure anyone.

After nearly losing the Beech 1900 fuselage in his experimentation with a slower airspeed, there was no longer any doubt that lower airspeed meant certain death for the occupants of Mountaineer 2612. It wasn't a gamble, it was a certainty.

Railing against the siren in his soul that screamed that there had to be another way, Marty locked down his decision: If it was a contest between certain death on one hand and a chance of everyone coming through on the other, he'd take the chance.

His thoughts were interrupted by the warbling of the satellite phone, and in the vain hope that it might bring unexpected deliverance, he answered it even though it had to be Paul Butterfield on the other end from Minneapolis – and was.

"Captain, we need to know your decision and your plan."

"Sir, we tried slowing and we almost lost the Beech at two hundred twenty knots. I'm maintaining two thirty knots and I'll land at two thirty knots with flaps at eleven, which is as far out as we could get them before asymmetry. That's the best we can do."

"I understand we're talking about Runway Seven, and you do understand it has almost no overrun, correct?"

"Yes, sir."

"And braking is reported nil?"

"No, braking is reported poor."

"How's your fuel?"

"We'll have ten to fifteen thousand at touchdown, most in the left main."

A long sigh and a long silence from Minneapolis marked the calm before the storm, and Butterfield didn't disappoint.

"Captain Mitchell, you're in charge…it's your decision…but we own the airplane and the liability, and, Captain, I have no choice but to relay to you what this company all the way to the chairman of the board desperately wants, and that's to take no chances with the lives of the passengers on our airplane. That may sound incredibly harsh, but nothing here is an easy judgment. And, in the final analysis, who's to say that fuselage won't stay attached? After all, the intensity of the airflow will be diminishing as you slow at the same rate you'd have to increase your angle of attack." _THE_

"Who's to say? I'm _the_ one to say…me and the other captain over there who would be dead now if I'd slowed any more. Bottom line? I will not kill those people, sir. I'm remaining at 230."

"Captain, I'm telling you…"

"No, Mr. Butterfield. You're not telling me anything of use. What you're trying to do is intimidate me to slow down. Perhaps you, and I guess the CEO, and everyone else, think that if I follow your orders, I can wash my hands of the moral responsibility for the results. But we all know that's bullshit! You're trying to make this horrible choice for me, and I cannot let you do it, because I know what will happen. Okay?"

"I can't legally order you..."

"No, you can't. But you can relay all you've said as a de facto order, and that's what you've made crystal clear: do what we tell you! It's pretty much the way Regal treats all its pilots. So okay, I understand your position. But it's my call."

"I'm not going to refute or endorse your characterization, Captain. Look, I'm not the bad guy here. None of us are. But you need to understand that your actions will have consequences."

Marty forced a sarcastic laugh into the receiver, making sure it was loud enough to register on the other end.

"How about that! My actions have already had consequences! So will this conversation if things go poorly. Keep your fingers crossed, Mr. Butterfield, because in truth what I'm going to do up here is go with a calculated risk, versus an execution. Goodbye, sir. I assume you're wishing me luck, but I'm disconnecting now in order to land."

He jabbed the disconnect button and felt a surprisingly unexpected calm, the decisional agony resolved. So now, even before the deed was done, it was done – and his career undoubtedly would go with it.

Marty turned to the copilot, wondering why Ryan was balancing his smartphone with a calculator displayed on the screen.

"How're you doing, Ryan?" he asked suspiciously.

"We've got a problem," Ryan answered, far too focused to be aware of the irony.

"Just one?" Marty replied with a snort.

"We must be burning fuel faster than I calculated."

"What are you seeing?"

With his left hand firmly on the control yoke, Ryan looked at the captain..

"We should have eight thousand pounds total remaining in the center tank, but we only have five!"

"How is that possible?" Marty asked. "I know we're

burning a hell of a lot more fuel down low and with the appendage on the right wing, but you had that figured, right?"

Ryan looked at him with deep concern bordering on true panic. "The center tank may be leaking, too."

"Okay, we have five, but how much in the left main?"

"We can't use that fuel! It's counterbalancing the Beech fuselage."

Marty was leaning forward and examining the tank readings himself.

"We have nine thousand in the left main. So, we're not going to flame out."

"No, but we have no idea how much we can burn out of the left main tank before we get in major control issues keeping the wings level. I mean, nine thousand pounds on the right along with all the drag and yaw, I don't want to eat too far into the nine thousand on the left."

"It'll be okay."

"Captain! We really need to get her on the ground inside fifteen minutes. And that's assuming whatever additional leak there is – if there is one – doesn't suddenly get worse."

"I got it, Ryan. But if we have to feed from the left tank, we will."

"Captain…" he began, sighing loudly and tilting his head down as he bit his lip deciding what to do. He snapped his head in Marty's direction with the suddenness of a rifle shot. "I'm not comfortable being in that position! We don't know where the point might be of loss of lateral control, and the limitation is twenty-five hundred pounds max imbalance. Two thousand five hundred pounds! We'll suck up that much halfway through a missed approach."

Marty sat in thought for a few beats, wondering why he felt such a flash of anger at being countered. That was precisely what a copilot was *supposed* to do. But what he *wasn't* supposed to do, Marty thought, was screw up the altitude and cause a midair! Maybe that was the source of the anger…the copilot's role in this disaster.

No, Marty realized. *It's my resentment over Butterfield's call. Ryan is right. The window for getting the 757 on the ground is shrinking fast.*

He turned to the copilot. "You're correct and I apologize. And I think we're about as ready for the approach as we're going to be." Marty let the words roll of his tongue as casually as he could, but he felt like a fraud. He was anything but the big, calm, thoroughly in command captain with ice water in his veins. He was thinking erratically, acting on impulse, and frightened beyond the nightmares of the meek.

Marty closed his eyes for a second, reaching for as much inner strength as he could find. He had to concentrate on what had to be done, not the mistakes already made.

Okay. It's time.

His finger found the transmit button on the control yoke.

"Denver Approach, Regal twelve. We're ready for vectors a long, twenty mile turn in to the ILS for Runway Seven."

"Roger, Regal Twelve.," the controller responded. "Turn right now to a heading of three five zero, maintain seven thousand."

"Right to three five zero and seven thousand."

In the Cabin of Mountaineer 2612

It had been a hard decision to send Luke Marshall to the back of the cabin with a crash axe to get to the cargo compartment, but with her shoulder at the very least dislocated, Michelle couldn't do it herself. It was painful enough to keep forward pressure on the control yoke to keep raising the tail and holding the nose down on the 757's wing.

It could be nothing more than her imagination, she thought, but the bouncing of the Beech fuselage seemed to have dissipated as it's center of gravity slowly shifted forward with every bag thrown out or emptied.

There had been no protests from the passengers over the impending loss of their checked baggage and all the contents, and three of them had jumped up to help Luke either shove the bags through the opened emergency exit hatch, or open each one and throw the contents out into the brutal slipstream roaring past the open portal. The main problem had been the reaction of passengers across the wing in the 757 who had completely misinterpreted what was happening when the exit hatch was pulled on the Beech fuselage. Regal 12's passengers had watched in panic, wondering if the Mountaineer passengers were going to try to cross the no man's land of the wing anyway, braving 230 knots of wind with no handholds.

Regal 12 Cabin

How much time had passed was a mystery Lucy Alvarez had no interest in solving. Every second was a living hell of praying, hoping, begging and pleading with any deity who might listen to take pity and save her lover. He was so close, and yet so very far away, and no matter how many times she waved her lighted cell phone screen in the window, Greg hadn't understood or responded. His phone remained off and unresponsive to her continuous stream of messages and texts. It hadn't occurred to her to ask the pilots to relay a message to him, but suddenly there was a flurry of moving flashlights in the cabin of the stricken Beech and to her utter shock, some sort of emergency exit hatch she hadn't noticed was suddenly opened, the hatch itself pulled back into the aircraft.

Logic played no role in Lucy snapping off the seatbelt and launching her body half way over the seatback of the empty window and middle seats ahead of her, her hands grasping for the same door latch the now restrained Roger had used. She fumbled with it frantically, her leverage all wrong for operating a latch meant to be pulled down by someone kneeling in front of the door, not leaning horizontally, but her hands finally solved the mystery and she felt the latching mechanism retract. But, she still couldn't pull the hatch out of its seal against the residual cabin pressure left in the 757.

Others were reacting now, both to her and to the open hatch on the Beech. Lucy could hear seat belts being snapped off and several yells as unseen people closed in on her even as she struggled to pull the hatch open. Finally, she let her body roll over the seatback, landing her torso painfully on one of the armrests, her feet in the lap of the aisle seat passenger, her body draped over the middle seat. The aisle passenger jumped up to get safely out of the way of yet a second mad person as Lucy scrambled to her feet and then knelt in front of the hatch to pull it out.

Cries of "No!" and "Stop!" made no sense to her...the hatch clearly had to be opened for Greg and the others when they came piling out of the Beech. Couldn't they see that? Giving the door the most powerful backward jerk she could manage, it finally came away in her hands as she fell back into the arms of a male passenger, the now familiar roar of the slipstream filling the cabin as once more somebody grabbed the hatch and re-seated it, re-locking the window.

"No! No, no, no!" She was shouting at them now. Why couldn't they understand? "Do you want to leave them out there on the wing? They're coming!" she screeched, trying to free her right arm to point to the hatch. He was coming across and they had to be ready to pull him in!

But the young man pinning her arms to her side and holding her from behind was speaking steadily in her ear, and she couldn't mute his voice.

"Stop! Stop, ma'am! Stop struggling. No one's coming across out there. It's not possible."

She tried to turn to see his face. "DIDN'T YOU SEE?"

"See what, ma'am."

"THEY'VE OPENED A DOOR OVER THERE. My...

my fiancé is over there! He's..."

Other voices filled in the gap in knowledge and the man tightened his hold on her.

"Ma'am, I'm sorry, but they're throwing out bags over there. That's all. They're not trying to come across. They're just lightening the load."

Frantic to make them understand she looked to the right in time to catch the sight of a lime green roll-aboard bag being pushed into the slipstream, and she was startled by the speed of its departure aft. She strained to lean down and look closer, but there were only bags and clothes and things coming through. No people.

No fiancé.

And with that, Lucy Alvarez went limp.

Cockpit of Mountaineer 2612

Michelle had failed to tell Marty Mitchell what they were doing until Luke's cell phone rang.

"Michelle, what the hell's going on over there?" the Regal captain asked. "My flight attendants are reporting that you've opened the left side emergency exit. For God's sake, don't let anyone try to cross!"

"No, no! We're throwing out the baggage to shift the center of gravity.."

"Jesus! You should have warned me. We had a guy open our exit hatch a while ago and got him under control, but when one woman back there saw what was happening, she went for it too! Her husband or fiancé or someone is on your bird."

"I'm sorry, Marty! I didn't think to tell you..."

"Is it helping?"

"Yes. At least we think so."

"Enough that I could slow down some more?"

The silence on Michelle's end was telling.

"Michelle?" he tried again.

She sighed loudly. "I guess that's why I stupidly thought I shouldn't tell you, because you're busy and…and because we're not brave enough to go through a moment like that again. Testing how slow, I mean."

"I understand. We won't try."

"At maximum, I think now it will only make a five knot difference. But it's helped our center of gravity."

"Don't worry. We won't try to slow again."

She paused. "Who's the passenger? I'll pass a message if there's time."

"There isn't," he said. "We're starting the approach in five minutes."

Michelle disconnected the call and handed the cell phone back to Luke, who was standing between the pilot seats.

"Thanks, Luke. Tell everyone to make sure their seat belts are tight…brief the brace position, to the extent they have an extra inch or two to learn forward."

"I will."

"We're about to start the approach."

He nodded, his face grim, and turned. She could hear him talking to their freezing passengers, trying to be heard over the slipstream's roar as she sat in the calm of her own internal privacy thinking briefly about this life that might be ending in minutes.

I've had a good run, Michelle thought. *I probably could have made it to Delta or maybe Alaska Airlines, but…this has been a real privilege, to get to captain anywhere.*

Outwardly, she had been irritated with her mother about the pictures of herself in her captain's uniform posted all over Facebook. But inwardly, she had felt so very proud. It had been a long haul.

Even the memory of an acidic and hurtful rejection years earlier – a sneering "Little girls can't handle airliners!" put down from a misogynist senior 747 captain she had approached to ask a few questions – faded in importance.

She'd already shown his kind what this determined "little girl" could accomplish.

Luke returned and strapped himself in before remembering Michelle's injured shoulder. There was no way she was going to be able to pull down her shoulder harness on the right side, so he leaned over and did it for her before securing himself in the copilot's seat.

"Thanks, Luke! And thanks for the exemplary teamwork.'

He looked over at her, his strained youth showing as a jumble of expressions rippled across his face, and he nodded with a judge-like seriousness.

"Thank *you*...for your exemplary leadership, captain. "You're...ah...a real inspiration." His eyes went to the floor and she could see that the question of whether this life had a tomorrow was suddenly consuming him. She heard the small catch in his voice.

"Luke?"

He looked up and over at her again. "Yeah?"

"We make our own reality, and mine is that we're going to live through this. Okay?"

He nodded mechanically in response, clearly unconvinced.

Michelle fumbled with her left hand for her small flashlight and toggled it on. In the cold, feeble light of the LED she could see the whiskey compass reporting a slow turn to the right. So, this was it. The 757's pilots were being vectored now to intercept the instrument landing system beacon for Runway 7.

"Keep forward pressure on the yoke, Luke."

"Will do."

"And, if it feels like we're trying to lift off, shove it forward all the way to the stops. Fly it to the end. We don't have ailerons. Well, we have one...but we've got full rudder and elevator. Don't assume they can't influence things."

"Regal Twelve, Approach. Airport ops is advising they still have men and equipment on Runway Seven trying to clear off the two thousand feet of the approach end they had abandoned before. They'll need ten minutes more to get them off."

Marty exhaled loudly and glanced at Ryan, who was looking back with a genuinely startled expression.

"Can we do ten minutes more, Ryan?"

"I guess we have to, but it cuts our fuel and balance margins even more."

Marty nodded. "The hits just keep on coming," he said pressing the transmit button.

"Approach, Twelve. Okay, but no more than ten minutes. Can you keep us in a series of gentle right turns until we can rejoin the approach localizer in ten minutes?"

"Roger, Twelve. Turn right now to two five zero, turn rate your discretion, and maintain seven thousand."

"Two five zero and seven thousand. And…are they sure of that time estimate?"

"Twelve, they're trying to get the equipment off the runway right now."

"You're using the word 'trying.' Are they having a problem doing so?"

A telling hesitation from the approach controller raised alarms in Marty's mind. "Don't tell me something's broken down on the runway?"

"Twelve, Approach. I haven't heard about any breakdown, but those plows don't move too fast. I'm not sugarcoating anything for you, sir. The estimate should hold."

"Roger, Approach. It has to, or fuel is going to become critical almost immediately."

CHAPTER TWENTY-EIGHT

Seven Months before – January 21ˢᵗ
Aircraft Rescue and Firefighters' Station #1, Denver
International Airport

Clad in his yellow protective coveralls and already wearing his boots, Josh Simmons lowered his cell phone and turned back to Scott Bogosian.

"You've got a decent reputation with us, Scotty. The chief says he remembers that great article you did on us years back, so, you may ride along, Glad to have you."

"Thanks."

"Get in that gear I laid out on the chair there, and we'll roll in about five minutes."

Scott struggled to don the oversized overalls and boots and clambered up the side of the behemoth fire fighting machine built especially for airports, plopping himself in the back seat of the cab. He'd never been inside a so-called Crash Tender before, but the specialized machines had been described as a fire truck on steroids – capable of speeding over rugged terrain with a huge load of water and fire suppressant, the floor of the cab some four feet off the ground. Within minutes, the other members of the crew were aboard and the diesel engine roared to life as the firehouse door lifted on what could have been Prudhoe Bay in the dead of a winter storm.

Scott turned to the firefighter seated beside him.

"You know the details of what's apparently happened here?"

"Yes, sir. A midair collision and somehow the little airplane is on their wing, or something. We're calling this a red alert. Most of our precautionary landings are called amber alerts – not to be confused with saving kidnapped kids – but we call them as red when there's a real possibility of death or injury. We're stationing ourselves and three other trucks along Runway Seven."

"Is all the plowing complete? At least whatever they're going to do?"

"I think they're bringing the plows in now. They gave up on all but Runway Seven almost an hour ago."

Scott watched as the huge fire truck crunched resolutely through the fresh powder, negotiating several turns onto now-abandoned taxiways on the way to the southernmost east-west runway. For some unfathomable reason, Scott's eyes fixated on a pair of fresh tire tracks leading off to the north as they passed the end of Runway 34R. The tracks immediately disappeared into the whiteness, heading off in the rough direction of where the approach end of the closed runway should be.

Scott turned to the young firefighter. "Do they send airport cars and trucks around checking on all parts of the airfield on a night like this?"

He shook his head. "No, sir. When they abandon an area to a major snowfall, they turn off the runway lights and kind of keep it what I would call sterile. What you're seeing now is an all-but-shuttered airport."

The taxiway along the only remaining runway at Denver International was ahead of them now, but the visibility through the blowing curtains of snow was less than a few hundred feet.

"All units, the flight is ten minutes out for Runway Seven. Engine Three, you're on the eastern end, but stay back on the north edge of the parallel taxiway, and be prepared to go into the ravine at the east end if necessary."

"Ravine?" Scott asked.

Josh handed back a map, his finger on the dropoff from the eastern end.

"Too bad they didn't keep the sixteen thousand foot runway open. You roll off the end of that, all you're going to tear up are prairie dog towns and a few fences."

CHAPTER TWENTY-NINE

<u>*Seven Months before*</u> — *January 21st*
Regal 12

With the good news that the conga line of snow plows was now off the runway, Denver Approach passed the unwelcome information that the visibility conditions for Runway 7 were now well below legal minimums and hovering at 300 feet.

"Denver, we're going to make this a Category 3B approach," Marty replied, referring to the high-precision approach procedure that would let a crew fly to fifty feet above the concrete before seeing the runway and landing.

"Regal, that runway is not certified for a Cat-3."

"We have no choice, Denver. Please ask tower to turn up all the lights to the highest step but be ready to bring them down if we ask at the last minute."

"Roger, Twelve. Turn right now to zero four five degrees, intercept the localizer at seven thousand, and you're cleared for the approach. Tower is coming up this frequency so just stay with me."

Mountaineer 2612

Living with the seismic bouncing of the Beech fuselage and the occasion screech of torn metal was becoming familiar, or perhaps she was just going numb. Michelle kept forward pressure on the control yoke and had become used to her feet on the rudder pedals as they vibrated and shook, the still-intact rudder of the regional aircraft's fuselage being battered by the roiled airflow over the 757's wing.

There was something new, however, and she had tried to convince herself that it was just hypersensitivity…but it was real. Almost a rotating moment, as if the aircraft was trying to rotate left just a bit.

As an almost unconscious remedy Michelle held her feet firmly on the vibrating rudder pedals.

With no warning a deafening screech was accompanied by a severe swing to the left, and in the space of a split second Michelle realized the Beech had lost the connection of torn metal to torn metal on the left side, and was now being held on by only the main gear strut on the right. She jammed her right foot on the right rudder pedal instantly, meeting the rotating force with a counter rotation back to the right, and realized with a sinking feeling that she was now reduced to flying the wreckage of her plane to stay on the wing.

"What was that?" Luke asked, his voice squeezed by fear.

"I'm…hard right rudder, Luke. Get your feet down there…feel it with me."

"I don't understand!" he answered, wide-eyed.

"Only thing holding us now is the right gear strut and holding her straight with the rudder. Nose down on the elevator, full right rudder. Help me, Luke! Keep flying her…we have to keep her attached."

Luke felt for the rudder pedals on the right, feeling the right pedal severely displace. He could feel Michelle literally flying the fuselage nose down, and now nose right, in a continuously desperate attempt to hang on.

How long, he wondered, before the strut failed and they were in free fall?

Of course, if that happened, both of them would try to fly it all the way to the ground, but it would be no use, and suddenly, that exact fate seemed inevitable.

Ryan was shifting in his seat, his hand waving slightly for Marty's attention.

"Yeah?"

"We're down to two thousand five hundred pounds in the center tank," Ryan said.

"Understood. But she'll automatically start feeding both engines from the left tank when we run dry, correct?"

"Yes, the way I have it set up."

'Okay. Let's keep the landing lights off until the last second. I'll call for them if I need them. Here we go," Marty said. "I'm going to hold the gear until one mile out. You concur?"

"I do."

Marty had pulled into position the clear slab of blue-green glass called a combiner, adjusting it in front of his eyes. The so-called heads-up display allowed a pilot to focus outside and essentially have the airspeed and altitude and instrument landing system information all projected on the glass as if it were parading across the distant horizon. The HUD had become the essential piece of equipment for landing in near zero-zero conditions.

"The combiner is working perfectly, Ryan, but I'm changing the normal procedure."

"Okay."

"Below two hundred feet I want your eyes out, too. Call a go around if we're dangerously misaligned, otherwise just...help make sure we can see the concrete."

"Wilco."

"Lowering the gear shouldn't change the pitch in any way. I'm holding two hundred thirty knots and I'm planning to just barely flare to keep the sink rate from being excessive. I'm also going to duck under the glide slope by one dot to get us on the runway as close to the approach end as possible."

"Marty, we're seven miles out, two miles from glide slope intercept."

"Roger. I'll start down…one dot low."

"Did we tell the other captain we're landing?" Ryan asked.

"She knows. She can feel it."

The approach controller's voice cut the silence.

"Regal, we show you one mile from intercept,"

"Roger," Ryan replied. "And you said cleared approach?"

"Yes, sir," the approach controller replied, "… and the tower has cleared you to land."

Marty took a deep breath and tried his best to concentrate. Something that had been bothering him was now raising the hairs on the back of his neck. Whatever it was, it was something overlooked, or something they hadn't considered – but definitely the sort of thing he would be called to account for. He tried again to push the rising feeling out of his mind, but it kept circling his consciousness, like a defiant horsefly.

"Glide slope intercept, one dot low," Ryan intoned. Marty had pulled the thrust levers back slightly, watching the airspeed with laser-like intensity as they started exchanging altitude for reduced power to keep the same speed.

"Should we ask for the current RVR?" Ryan asked.

"It's immaterial. We're landing regardless," Marty answered, pulling the thrust levers a bit more as the airspeed tried to increase."

"Four miles out, Marty."

"Got it."

What the hell am I forgetting? Marty's brain again demanded, and once more there were no answers, just the clucking of some distant part of his mind that he would deeply regret ignoring.

"Three miles, holding one dot low, on speed," Ryan intoned.

"Stand by for the gear at one mile."

"Standing by. Five hundred feet to go, Marty. No decision height."

"Roger."

"Coming up on two miles to the runway, on speed, on glide slope minus one."

"Roger."

"Four hundred above and one mile," Ryan was saying.

"Gear down," Marty commanded, as Ryan's hand moved the lever downward, starting the hydraulic sequence that lowered the huge main gear trucks and the nose gear into place.

Whatever had been eating at him loomed suddenly as one of the most profound warnings he had ever ignored, and this time it refused to go away. A very insistent part of his mind screamed "Go Around!" and finally, at a radar altimeter reading of 190 feet above the terrain, the last tumbler between nuance and reality fell into place.

"GEAR UP!" Marty commanded.

"What?"

"Going around. Gear Up! Tell the tower."

Marty nursed the throttles forward while pulling gently to arrest the descent of the big jet at 120 feet, starting a shallow climb.

"WHAT ARE YOU DOING?" Ryan demanded, eyes wide.

"Tell them we're on the go!"

Ryan froze for a few microseconds before realizing that a protest over how little fuel they had was now too late. The runway was zipping by unseen beneath them, and with it, it felt like their last chance was slipping away.

"Denver, Regal Twelve is…ah…on the go," Ryan said as ordered.

"Roger, Twelve. Climb straight ahead to seven thousand. What are your intentions?"

Unaware that his finger had once again pressed the transmit button, Ryan's thoughts found voice: "I wish the hell I knew!"

CHAPTER THIRTY

The neatly dressed man in a crisp white shirt and well-cut blue suit was a far cry from the disheveled and disillusioned pilot who had plopped down in the firm's main conference room months before with radioactive toxicity. *That* version of Marty Mitchell had been a study in smoldering anger and determined, martyred defeat. *This* version was ready for battle and, if not full of confidence, at least focused on what must be done. His fist-shaking rage atop the mountain had been a primal scream at the loss of his integrity, but without really wanting to admit it to himself, it had been Judith's caring and determination that had restored the possibility of vindication...however remote. *"When everything is black and you see a flicker of light, you follow it – no matter how far and faint it is,"* he had explained.

And that, Judith Winston thought, looking at her client, was a significant victory, and something she could be proud of, however this mess turned out.

She hesitated for a second, watching him from across the office through the glassed walls of the conference room as she organized her thoughts. Since the Long's Peak incident and the visits to his hospital room, the contentious barriers between them had slowly dissolved. Even last week's meeting at the same conference table – a grueling all-day affair to go over every minute detail of the case, the crash, and the critical aspects of the upcoming trial – had been devoid of the fulminating anger at the system that had marked their early meetings. He was still unable to laugh easily – to shed the appearance of a man quietly spooked and ready to run. But at times she had managed to elicit a few genuine smiles.

Judith moved easily into the room, quietly pleased that Marty's gentlemanly upbringing brought him to his feet as she motioned him back down.

"I...dusted off an old suit," he said, a bit self-consciously.

"Doesn't look old to me!" she replied, taking a more detailed look. "Perfect. Quite professional and right for the courtroom."

"I thought about wearing my airline uniform," he added.

"So did I," she said, tilting her head. "I'm still mulling over whether that could be interpreted as somehow arrogant or inflammatory. Or it might just focus the jury on the gravity of the situation. You know, you're not just someone they call a pilot. Here sits a uniformed airline captain with all his experience and gravitas. And, after all, Regal has yet to fire you, therefore it's not misrepresentation."

"Regal would be apoplectic."

"Fuck 'em."

He hesitated, smiling slowly at her response. "So... bottom line... you're not sure about me wearing the formal uniform?" Marty asked.

She sat down next to him in one of the high-backed leather swivel chairs.

"Frankly, no. Before we decide, though, I want to consult a friend who does big criminal cases. Actually, I've been consulting with her quite a bit to make sure I... don't screw this up in any way." A ripple of apprehension twittered down Judith's spine at the thought that she'd just admitted what every aspect of her prior demeanor had been designed to refute: That criminal defense was neither her familiar territory nor an area in which her confidence level was unassailably high. Self-doubt was one thing they both had in common.

"I appreciate that," he said, looking down at the table

where his fingers were drumming softly. He looked back up. "Judith, I know this is a stretch for you…not your native turf. And I know the damned judge wouldn't let you withdraw from the case. "

She started to protest that she was well prepared now, but something in his eyes told her it was unnecessary, and he'd already raised the palm of his hand to stop her.

"You're a damn good corporate lawyer, which means you're a damn good lawyer, period. You don't need to say any more. I truly appreciate what you're doing for me."

"Thank you."

He cleared his throat, as if to disavow the heartfelt nature of the statement.

"Speaking of the stupid judge, what happened this morning to our motions?"

She glanced past him for a second as if taking in what was happening in the reception area, then looked back.

"It's more the damned DA than the judge, and of course Grant Richardson was there himself, full of restrained outrage at the mere idea that I would dare file a motion to quash the indictment, let alone a motion to dismiss."

"I take it both were rejected?"

"Yes, but…the judge said something interesting, something that makes me think he isn't rubber stamping the idea that criminal charges are legal in a case like this."

Marty was leaning forward. "Tell me."

"He said that, without reference to any future appeal, there was a societal interest in determining whether a purposeful act by a captain in discharging official duty constituted even a prima facie case of premeditation sufficient to support a murder charge. In other words, he gave voice to one of my main arguments, that the legislature never meant for the premeditated aspect of murder to include a captain's decision. Richardson tried to bat it down, but it was there and on the record. It won't stop the trial, but it's very well written."

"Is my union doing anything?"

Judith shook her head. "Just monitoring. Someone will be in the courtroom, and they'll file a friend of the court brief, an "amicus" brief – if we lose and have to appeal. But they're confused. This isn't a case of prosecuting a pilot for making a mistake, which always lights a torch under their tails. This is alleging criminal responsibility because you knew the consequences if you didn't slow down, and you decided not to slow down anyway. Where the union guys jump the track and glaze over is when we talk about Regal's attempt to intimidate you. The DA says it doesn't matter, and that this case is not about you following orders, because as a captain in an emergency you don't have to. It's about you having been provided the indisputable information of what would happen if you did Plan A versus Plan B, and, knowing the consequences, you still decided to go with Plan A. Since Plan A included a high probability of killing someone, that's where the theory of premeditated or purposeful murder comes in."

"But, Judith, that screws the whole principle of captain's authority! I mean, that's worldwide international law!"

She chuckled ruefully and shook her head. "You know, in law school, one of the universal legal answers to any question – we learned this almost in the first month – was: 'Well, yes and no!' and I've got to use that phrase to answer you now. Yes and no. Yes, this case involves second guessing a captain's authority, but no, it is not necessarily inappropriate to require accountability after the fact. If you decided to shoot and kill a passenger, you would be called after the flight to defend yourself as to why that killing shouldn't be ruled a homicide. Similarly, you can legally decide to land overspeed, but if you do so, you can be held accountable for the correctness or appropriateness of your decision."

"Jesus! So, it's perfectly okay for society to prosecute someone like me for making the best decision I could possibly make for the best interests of all? What a wonderful society!

Remember, Judith, it wasn't a case of choice A versus choice B, and only one might result in death. *Both* choices – *either* choice in this case – bore a high probability of death. There was no Plan C."

"And, Marty, that's exactly the point, that this is a ridiculous case when viewed in the greater framework of what society wants and needs. We need decisive captains who can do their best in a dire emergency, captains, *and* first officers, who are unafraid to use their best judgment. And they need to feel the support of our legal system beneath their wings. This case is going to set a vital precedent, one way or another, and losing it directly harpoons flight safety worldwide."

If you ended up convicted for doing your best, can you imagine the chilling effect on virtually every pilot out there who might face an emergency some day? "

"I don't want the union involved. They can file friend of the court briefs later if this ends up the wrong way, but no... not now."

"Okay. They do have an interest. We don't need captains trying to act as lawyers in the middle of a major emergency because they're afraid they might be prosecuted for an honest decision that went wrong! Criminal law was never supposed to be applied this way, and hopefully the jury will see that with clarity and spend five minutes finding you innocent."

"And if not?"

"Don't go there!"

"I'm not plea bargaining, you know that, right?"

"Absolutely! I was only going to sneer at any offer from the DA, but he never opened the door!"

Marty stopped and looked at her with a puzzled expression. "What does that mean, Judith? Why wouldn't he try to sell me a plea bargain and assure a conviction, versus, as you call it, rolling the dice that I might be exonerated and he'd look stupid... not that he isn't?"

"Not offering a plea means one of two things. First

possibility, that this whole prosecution nonsense and all his grandstanding and the unnecessary submission to the grand jury is some sort of theatrical production for him, and he doesn't give a rat's ass whether he convicts you or not as long as he gets a chance to strut indignantly around the courtroom and show the world how much he resembles F. Lee Bailey, Jeanine Pirro, or Perry Mason from an earlier age."

"What's the second possibility?"

"That he *is* genuinely outraged at your decision not to slow down, and he *does* care about convicting you. If that's the case, where does that outrage come from? That's a prosecution born of passion, and it feels to me like malicious intent. Not only does that usually subvert justice, but if I could find out what it is, and if it was significant enough, it might be sufficiently embarrassing to him to sour the jury in your favor on what we call prosecutorial misconduct. You know, get the jury angry over the idea that this whole thing is based on some personal axe he wants to grind."

"You can tell a jury that?"

"Not directly, and I may have to be really sneaky to get it in front of them. I may have to risk censure from the judge or even contempt, and risk a mistrial. Of course, if it was *really* a major personal conflict, I could attack the indictment as having been issued under undue influence. But, before I can tell the jury or do anything, I have to discover myself what the hell that motivation is… and right now I haven't a clue. It may just be that he's getting older and meaner."

"Anyone we can ask?"

"We've had a private investigator on this for weeks… one we use often. Hopefully he'll dig up something. We've got another PI firm doing everything they can to find out whether there was a snow plow on that runway, or what those lights were that distracted you. As far as Richardson's anger? I don't know…maybe Regal Airlines lost his bags sometime in the past or refused to give him a free first class upgrade, or worse, didn't recognize who he was at the gate!"

Marty looked puzzled. "What would any of that have to do with coming after me?"

"I'm trying to be funny…and not obviously not succeeding. Sorry."

"Oh."

"The investigators are supposed to report back this afternoon."

Marty shook his head. "The trial starts in two days."

"Believe me, I know."

"Judith, I want to testify. I know I don't have to, but…"

She had her hand out to stop him as she nodded an assent. "I want you to. But I want you to be very, very aware of the fact that you have to stay extremely calm, because Richardson will try to gore your goat and get you to show anger or arrogance. The jury needs to see you as the consummate captain – the unflappable guy with icy steadiness they would want flying their loved ones around, and a guy who is being persecuted by a bully of a DA. You can't whine about being prosecuted, and you can't go into some diatribe about the injustice of it all. That will lose the jury in a heartbeat. You absolutely must be calm and professional and serious and as certain that you made the right choice as you are broken over the results. Can you do all that?"

"A month ago, hell no. A week ago, maybe. Now… yes."

"Good. Remember that classic movie, "A Few Good Men," with Jack Nicholson playing a flint-hard Marine, Colonel Jessup?"

"Absolutely."

"Can you quote Nicholson's best line?"

"That's a strange request. But, yes, so happens I can."

"Go ahead," she said, crossing her arms and sitting back for the performance.

He took a deep breath and leaned forward, adopting a furious expression, eyebrows flaring and index finger wagging the air, his voice thick with sarcasm.

"You want the truth? *YOU WANT THE TRUTH?* **YOU CAN'T HANDLE THE TRUTH!**"

She clapped slowly and smiled. "Very good!"

Marty relaxed back into his chair, his face returning to normal. "That was kinda fun, but I don't get the point."

Judith leaned forward then, looking him steadily in the eye for an uncomfortable few moments before speaking.

"The point is, you can't be Colonel Jessup, Marty. Colonel Jessup goes to prison."

Denver – Brown Palace Hotel Churchill Lounge

Entering the plush, leather-bound, cigar-friendly Churchill Lounge in the historic Brown Palace Hotel was always a mixed pleasure for Scott Bogosian. He loved the hotel with its central atrium and 1890's history, and he also loved the wafting aroma of rich, varietal cigars which enveloped the lounge's patrons on entry. But any visit had its price: as an ex-smoker of cigarettes already worried about the damage he might have done to his lungs in the past, the temptation to smoke a cigar or to just give in and re-start the two-pack-a-day cigarette habit always reverberated for about a week.

The old friend who'd recommended the Churchill as their meeting place waved to him from the far corner, near the bookcase, and Scott moved to greet him.

"Hope you don't mind, Scotty," he said, "…but I haven't had one of these in months." He held up the lit Rocky Patel. "And, I suppose it's not too early for a scotch. What'll you have?"

A waitress materialized and Scott ordered coffee as he sat down.

"How long has it been since we've seen each other?" Scott asked.

"Well…since the paper folded, probably. We started

working together back in the 80's if you'll recall."

Scott laughed. "Yeah, I do. Others do, too! A friend… in fact, the chief ranger up in Rocky Mountain National… remembered you recently as the guy carrying a sack of Nikons."

"About right," he laughed. "But that was back when dinosaurs walked the earth and we used something called film. Nowadays I dance with the pixels!"

"Which is why I wanted to see you," Scott replied.

"Uh, oh. Not a social occasion, huh? Business?"

Scott pulled an 8x10 photo from a thin folder and slid it over the table.

"This is one of yours, right?"

The veteran news photographer studied the shot for a second. "Yep. That's one of mine. I don't know the exact date, but sometime in late January."

"That was taken at the funeral of one of the Regal Airlines crash victims, as I recall?"

"Yes. I remember, her name was Martha Resnick. The teenage girl killed in the crash. Why are you interested?"

Scott sighed. "I'm trying to figure out why our district attorney is so damned determined to put this airline captain in prison. The captain of the Regal Air crash in January."

"Right. Just doing his job, I guess, right?"

"Well, Richardson is making a lot of people in aviation very angry by charging the guy with murder and really stretching the law to do so, but the odd thing is, he's all but snarled about it in news clips, like he really hates that pilot. Why the intensity? I can't find any evidence or even rumors that he and the captain knew each other or had ever met. I checked school records, newspaper morgues, a world of databases, military records…you name it. Nothing. So, I have to wonder, was there was someone he knew in that accident? Someone who's death upset him? I haven't found any connection yet, but I thought it might be a big clue if he had attended any of the funerals."

"Did he?"

"I don't know, but that's where you and this shot come in. I looked at the newspaper and online coverage and saw your shot and when I looked closely, there's this one guy standing just behind the main family group who might, just might, be Grant Richardson. I just can't see his face."

"So...you're hoping I have more shots in the file, and maybe one or two of them might show him?"

"Exactly."

"I don't know, Scotty, but I'll look. You mentioned you're doing a book on that crash, right?"

"I'm really close to making a launch decision, yes. But there's no real hurry."

"A lot of very shaken people came off both those planes."

Scott sighed. "Probably none more so than a woman on the 757 who thought her fiancé was in the cabin of the Beech on their wing. Lucy Alvarez. She was sitting right across from them and was convinced she'd seen him in one of the windows."

"If he was aboard the commuter, though, he lived. Right?"

"Well," Scott began, "...after she lived through hell, it turns out he was at her place in Denver with a dead phone wondering where the hell she was. He'd ditched his business trip to be with her, and she was angry at him and fleeing to Florida."

"So they're probably married now?"

"Nope. Broke up," Scott replied. "Survivor's guilt was part of it."

"You do know the trial is coming up in two days, right?"

"This has nothing to do with the timing of the trial, and in fact, the captain's lawyers probably already have this question about Richardson answered. I just can't stop wondering."

"Tell you what," the photographer said. "Rather than emailing, I'll dump everything I shot at that funeral on a flashdrive and get it to you. It won't be many pictures...I was taking pains to be very discreet and respectful."

"I appreciate it."

"You're welcome. Who knows. One of the frames might show Richardson passing money to a Russian prostitute or something else deliciously salacious."

CHAPTER THIRTY ONE

Office of the Managing Partner – Walters, Wilson, and Crandall, Denver

One of the primary reasons Judith Winston had accepted the post-law school job offer from Walters, Wilson, and Crandall so many years ago was the warmth of Jenks Walters, one of the cofounders. With a fearsome reputation as a corporate litigator, personally he was as jovial and friendly as he was a truly excellent lawyer. Compared to the only other living senior partner, Roger Crandall – who was cold, humorless, and always gave the impression of being royally pissed off about something – Jenks was somewhere between a grandfatherly entity and a very sharp colleague.

Now, Judith needed the latter.

She had spent the previous fifteen minutes briefing the senior partner on the Mitchell prosecution, and he had reviewed the pleadings as well as a particularly brilliant paper she had commissioned from an outside expert on the law pertaining to sea captains and airline captains and their emergency authority.

"Judith, great preparation as always. I said you'd have no trouble rising to the challenge of a criminal case, but... you've got to understand the basic equation here. Judge Gonzalez is an angry little man with a couple of huge chips on his shoulder who has little use for arcane legal theory. I tried a fairly simple corporate case before him several years ago and he, honest to God, actually told me to cut out all the 'legal schmeegal' arguments and just state the law. I *was* stating the law, but he didn't have the patience, or perhaps the understanding, to follow."

"He is a lawyer, right?"

"Yes, and I checked up on him. He was fairly high in his law class at UNM in Albuquerque. But he just doesn't have the patience. And…that's why I'm bringing this up. That paper you commissioned may only be useful on appeal. All it's likely to do for Gonzalez is irritate him."

Judith had been standing, more or less gazing out of the window toward the front range of the Rockies while Jenks sat back in his plush desk chair and studied her. With the last statement, Judith turned to face him, her stomach tightening as the slight bravado she'd felt evaporated.

"Jenks, you…you think we're going to *lose* this?"

Jenks Walters looked at her for a long time before answering.

"Well, Gonzalez is going to let Richardson put on as much of a show as he wants, and Grant is more actor than lawyer so he'll play to the jury, and you already expect him to read the criminal statute word for word which, as you know, clearly says that if the defendant knowingly caused a death he's guilty of second degree. Judge Gonzales is not going to allow anything in regarding the broader law of the air and sea, and…on top of all that…while I don't necessarily disagree about putting your captain on the stand…"

"Bottom line, Jenks?" she interrupted.

"They'll convict him," he shot back without a pause. "They won't freaking have a choice, unless you can pull an entire warren of rabbits out of your hat…and you don't normally wear hats, to torture the metaphor."

"How about the success of an appeal?"

"You'll have a better shot with an appeal, but it's not a slam dunk. What's really needed is a legislative change to prevent this kind of miscarriage of justice from ever happening again. Oh, and Judith, one more item. After you boy's little mortality-threatening stunt on Long's Peak? Expect Gonzalez to vacate bail and jail him immediately after the verdict as a flight risk, no pun intended."

She sighed deeply, eyes averted downward as she thought about the agony of having to prepare Marty Mitchell for the worst.

"Judith, you breeding any rabbits?"

She jerked her head up suddenly. "Excuse me? Oh! Sorry. I...well, I've been puzzled by Grant Richardson's conduct." She outlined the refusal to offer a plea bargain and the apparent anger driving his prosecution and having unleashed the firm's private investigator as early as possible to find reasons. "I just thought there might be some personal animus that I could use as a basis to seriously question the indictment on grounds of misconduct. I even stated that to the news people the day after Mitchell tried to kill himself."

"Yes. I saw that performance, Judith. Very polished, very professional – and very dangerous. You know my thinking on trying cases in public."

"I do, but I'm very worried and maybe a bit desperate to crack this. Jenks, you know him personally, don't you?" she asked.

"We're talking Richardson, right? Not the judge?"

"Grant Richardson, yes."

"I know him, but I don't like the little pontificating weasel. I even caught him cheating at golf."

"Can you think of any connection he'd have with any of the victims of the crash? I ran every name through every possible connection or family link I could think of, but found nothing."

"Grant's an arrogant climber who wants to be president and doesn't care who he steps on along the way. I don't think the man has any principles, and of course we don't need any more people like that in government. But I tell, you, Judith, it's hard for me to imagine Richardson caring for anyone deeply enough to want to avenge their death. It's just not like him. I wish I had a better forecast for you.. I think the jury will have no choice but to convict, because you can be certain the jury instructions Gonzalez will approve are going to be simple and tough. You know, if there are clouds in the sky, you must convict. No latitude."

"And no justice."

"Hey, young lady," he said with a grin. "Where do you get off thinking this is a system of true justice? We're just working at it. That's why we call it a practice."

Near Denver International Airport

Perhaps it was the darkened interior of the large hangar-like warehouse, or maybe he was losing the ability to come up with creative adjectives. But the only word Scott Bogosian could think of to describe the atmosphere in the warehouse was 'spooky.'

The Boeing 757 had not been torn to shreds in the crash, but the fuselage had broken along what was commonly called a 'production splice,' and the two major parts of the fuselage sat grotesquely twisted and forlorn on the concrete floor, the wings and engines removed, surrounded with a jumble of various tagged parts that had come off the bird.

The landing gear and the tires in particular were Scott's main focus, and his escort – the head of the local office of the National Transportation Safety Board – had been more than accommodating when Scott called.

"I hate to bother you," he'd begun, "…but there's a part of the raw accident report on Regal Twelve that's bothering me."

In fact, it was two things: an unusual lateral cut on one side of a main gear tire mentioned in the factual report and almost visible in one of the color photos of the wreckage; and, the insistence of the captain that lights had suddenly appeared on the runway just ahead. The common assumption seemed to be that he'd mistaken a glimpse of the approach lights and misunderstood, thinking they came from a misplaced snowplow still on the runway. There must have been something unusual to explain why a competent captain would attempt a dangerous go-around on fumes and with a broken airframe on his right wing.

But where had that cut on the tire come from? Was it pre-existing, or had the 757 hit something other than the runway that night?

And then there was that one additional detail from his own memory that kept nudging Scott: Fresh tire tracks in the deepening snow that couldn't have been made by a behemoth fire truck. He remembered them with crystal clarity. They had been small tracks, like those a car or pickup would make, going in one direction as the fire truck he'd been riding in turned in another. Admittedly, Scott thought, his sense of both direction and location that night were markedly poor. The tracks he saw could be easy to explain, and yet, considering the fact that the captain was adamant that lights had appeared on the runway ahead, the question was inevitable: was there any substantive proof that a vehicle had, in fact, been on the runway? What vehicle had made the tracks he saw, and why?

The NTSB rep had asked if Scott would like to take a closer look at the wreckage, and offered a field trip to the warehouse near Denver International where they were storing it pending the completion of the investigation.

"It's all been tagged and photographed extensively so, I don't want you touching or moving anything, but you can look at anything you like."

"Where are the main gear tires?" Scott asked, following his host's guidance to a jumble of twisted landing gear parts and tires. He moved carefully around each one, trying to recall which tire of the four on the right main landing gear had a lateral cut, but found it quickly.

Scott looked up at the investigator.

"Let me just sit here for a second and look at this and think, if you don't mind," Scott said.

"Sure," was the response, and the NTSB rep paced slowly away, trying not to appear bored as Scott took out a pocket flashlight and began examining the cut.

CHAPTER THIRTY-TWO

Present Day – Afternoon of September 5, the *day before the start of trial*

The so-called 'war room' of Walters, Wilson, and Crandall's gleaming main offices in downtown Denver had never been used for a criminal trial. Judith had commandeered both the war room and the firm's treasury to pay for whatever help was needed to defend the Mitchell prosecution – and also to fund comfortable hotel rooms a block from the offices. With Marty living in Boulder and Judith only a few miles closer to Denver, avoiding an exhausting daily commute and the chance of being late for court was more than worth the expense. From the Hilton, the Lindsey-Flanigan Courthouse was a mere five blocks away.

One of the senior partners, Roger Crandall, had started pushing back weeks before against the growing expenses. But Judith's none-too-subtle reminder that he, himself had been largely responsible for bullying her into taking the assignment rapidly ended the conversation.

"Whatever you need, Judith," became the watchword.

Unlike the glass-walls of the main conference room, the war room was larger and fully enclosed, with walls of fine oak paneling dominated by a highly polished walnut conference table covered in an avant-garde tablecloth of legal papers, exhibits, and pleadings. Judith was the commanding general of this army of evidence, assisted by two paralegals, an outside criminal defense attorney, and two in-house legal associates – young eighty hour-a-week partner wannabes intrigued that their stiff, white collar, corporate law firm was hip deep in a criminal case.

Sitting at one corner of the huge table was the subject of it all: Captain Marty Mitchell. His feelings ranged from puzzlement, to engagement, to animated participation as they meticulously reviewed plans to deal with and counter anything the district attorney and his team could possibly throw at them.

"I can see why you call this a war room," Marty said quietly sometime around the 9th hour.

At 6 pm, her review agenda complete, Judith called a halt and scheduled everyone to be back in the room at 7 am sharp.

"Court begins at nine, and we must be prepared and ready to go."

As the others filed out, Marty got to his feet and began pacing.

"Wow. The complexity of this is mind-boggling."

Judith looked up and smiled as she scooped papers into a briefcase.

"Well, looking at the switches and dials and screens and things in a Boeing cockpit is equally mind boggling. In our case, in law, being exhaustively prepared is virtually everything. Same as planning logistics in a war."

"You use the doctrine of Sun Tzu? You know, the '*Art of War*.'"

"Not quite that colorfully, Marty. I've read the book, of course. Do the opposite of what your opponent expects. Some of those principles help in a legal battle in court, but the best method in litigation is to understand everything the opposition can throw at you so well, that you're never surprised, and be able to argue the law and the facts better than anyone else there…which means research, research, and more research. And…" she added, raising an index finger as she snapped the cover of the leather briefcase closed, "…on that note, the one thing I did not talk about today is that legal brief I commissioned on the role of captain's authority in law and society."

"Can we file it with the judge?"

"Probably not, but…we'll get it in somehow."

Judith winced internally, the words feeling like a premeditated lie. Just as Jenks had said, it was probably useless in Gonzalez' court. But telling Marty that would only serve to depress him, and a depressed client could be dangerous to his own case. That thought, in turn, started gnawing at her. How much in the dark was she going to keep Marty about the almost certain outcome of this trial? She could see he was relatively relaxed and reasonably confident and that was exactly where he needed to be. But the crash at the other end of the verdict would be magnified, and she was not, in her heart, capable of dishonesty beyond a point.

"Judith, one other question."

"Sure."

"You've said all along this case was legally wrong. Can't the judge see that? Can't we ask for dismissal on those grounds?"

She sighed. "We already have, Marty. Two weeks back we moved for dismissal on the law and as I fully expected, he denied it. But it's what we do to lay the foundation for an appeal."

"Okay."

"Okay," she echoed, with a forced smile and as much sincerity as she could muster. "We both need to relax and get a good night's sleep. I'd like to buy you a really expensive dinner and go over a few things."

Meaning, she thought to herself, *I need to keep him focused and ready for court, and I'm worried about letting him out of my sight. Maybe I should just sleep with him!*

"Dinner sounds good," he replied. "You seem preoccupied, Judith?"

If you only knew, she thought, carefully hiding any indication that she'd just scandalized herself with that private joke. Using sex to control one's client was not exactly ethical.

"My favorite steakhouse is three blocks away. Meet you in the hotel lobby in twenty minutes, and we can walk there."

He caught her arm gently as they were stepping out of the war room.

"Judith, all this…" he gestured to the room and the day, "…what are my chances?"

"Of getting an acquittal?" she asked, instantly on guard.

"Of actually being sent to prison. Honest assessment."

She sighed and pursed her lips, meeting his gaze. "You want me to quantify a percentage of probability?"

He half chuckled. "I guess that's what I mean. I just don't speak lawyer."

She nodded. "Okay. I don't gamble on my cases…in other words I don't have a bookie. But if I did, and he forced me to lay odds, I'd say they're two to one against you ending up for an extended period in jail or a prison, because even if we lose the trial, I think the case for a successful appeal is very strong. And, I never said this, okay? But even if we lost an appeal, I'd badger the governor mercilessly until he pardoned you, or exiled me"

"Two to one?" he said, looking shocked. "Not for acquittal but against extensive jail time?"

"Roughly, " she added.

"So…if I understand you correctly as to what you're *not* saying…the odds are against an acquittal?"

Judith sighed, feeling trapped by her own hatred of lawyers telling lies. "Marty, my law partners think an acquittal is unlikely. I do not agree, but you're right, the odds are no better than fifty-fifty. But, two to one odds against, as I said, any extensive time in a lockup."

"Oh, Lord," he said, his face betraying the loss of confidence like a falling barometer.

She took his arm and turned him back toward her. "But, Marty, how you conduct yourself as a calm and competent captain in that courtroom is going to make all the difference."

"I understand that," he replied, a sad but deeply thoughtful look on his face as he sighed and chewed his lip. "Thank you for leveling with me, Judith. I imagine that was a tough decision...especially considering how volatile I've been."

"I'll admit," she said, "...I've been a bit frightened of how you'll handle the courtroom environment."

"Two to one. That's just short of terrifying! Frankly, I'm beginning to wish the air national guard guys had turned you down."

"Marty, look at me!" Judith commanded. "You deserve the opportunity to set the record straight, and that would never have happened if you'd died up there. I'm absolutely..."

Marty held up his hand to stop her.

"It's okay, Judith. The die is cast. I'm here and I promised you I'd stick it out, and I will, on the outside chance..."

"Those odds aren't apocalyptic, Marty!"

"I know...I get that. I...can still sleep with those odds."

She held his gaze for a few more beats, her expression slowly dissolving into a relieved smile.

"The real question is," Judith began, "...can you *drink* with those odds? Right now, I mean?"

"Hell, yes," he said.

CHAPTER THIRTY-THREE

Present Day — *September 7 — Day Two of the trial*

Sleep had come rapidly, and escaped just as suddenly, leaving Marty in the plush hotel bed with his mind racing. The repetitious dream sequence of the headlights popping on in front of him in the blizzard just before touchdown was actually becoming a bore. It never changed, and there was never an answer.

Marty checked his watch, dismayed to see it was only two-fifteen. He knew his wakeful profile all too well: there would be no way of returning to REM sleep before daybreak.

Show time in the lobby is 6:30 am he reminded himself. With two very long and very tedious days of jury selection already behind him, the real trial would get underway at 8 am, and the first agony would be listening to that scumbag Richardson as he oiled his way around the subject of why Marty Mitchell was a mad dog killer who needed to be locked away from society.

I must have wronged him in another life, Marty had joked. What other possible motive did Richardson have?

That same dark and deep panic that had propelled him to the top of the mountain weeks back returned without warning. There was a coherent point to it, and it was a scream that no way could he survive the ultimate shame of being a convict, or the uselessness and endless agony of vegetating in a sterile cell while the world quickly forgot about him. Yes, he would stay until the verdict as he promised, but if the verdict was guilty, he'd impose his own death sentence to be carried out immediately. He didn't have the stomach or the endurance for an appeal, and this time he wouldn't need a mountain. There were at least a dozen ways to leave the planet he'd considered, and the most bizarre and demeaning involved the courthouse steps in front of cameras.

Marty rolled out of bed in one fluid motion, landing on his feet before heading for the shower with intent to use the hotel's hot water supply as a watery escape pod of white noise. But the shower was a massive fail at masking the pain and the panic, and after a half hour he dried off, liberated a tiny bottle of bourbon from the mini-bar, and plopped back on the bed, working hard to talk away from the ledge the panicked little boy inside him.

There had to have been, he thought, a reason for surviving his suicide attempt. There had to be a bigger purpose, right? Judith had essentially preached that to him at dinner the night before, but she could barely convince herself.

He called up a mental image of her and the thought returned a smile – not because she was beautiful or alluring, which she was, but because she had done something very simple that now brought tears to his eyes. She'd decided he was worth saving.

Judith had promised him an expensive pretrial steak dinner, and she had delivered, both of them feeling comfortable and calm enough to spend those hours joking about last suppers and other snippets of twisted gallows humor. He'd found himself enjoying the tones of her voice – the polished and professional words spoken with near-perfect diction that betrayed none of her Oklahoma roots – although she'd cracked him up by lapsing in to what she called her original Okie accent. Aided by too much of an obscure brand of smoky bourbon which had loosened his tongue, he'd taken her verbally back to the top of Long's Peak to show her how much, at that moment, he had longed to leap to the next reality. He fumbled the description of those moments and the fear of nothingness, but she understood.

On a far deeper level than just nodding, she got it.

Judith, it turned out, was as much a cynic as he, especially when it came to religion and faith and what she characterized as the "Sit down, shut up, and believe what we tell you!" terrorism of rigid dogma. He'd caught a glimpse in that discussion of the smart little girl who had taken a huge risk in rejecting the hypocrisy that had consumed her family. She had survived, but the cost had been high, and even now, she told him, her siblings – two sisters – communicated reluctantly and only on holidays, as if sending carefully worded messages to the enemy.

A few moments of silence passed between them as Judith decided she was being too frank and Marty felt himself thinking protectively, as if he could scoot back in time and protect that little girl.

He shook himself off the subject.

"How did you get from there to the law?" he asked.

A warm smile had spread across her face in response, broad, profound, and slightly embarrassed, all of it coming through with clarity.

"I desperately wanted a structure I could trust, Marty. Some...*human* institution built on honesty, or at least a continuous struggle to find honesty and, that elusive concept, justice. I fled home, enrolled in college, and threw myself at a much older guy who was a lawyer. I loved the way he looked at the world! I loved what he taught me about the law...and, a few other more intimate subjects. Yes, he was using me shamelessly as a willing girlfriend, but what I got from him was a fast track to law school, and it turned out I was really good at it – good enough to get admitted to Yale. See, in the practice of law, it's not what you believe. It's how you can prove something or convince someone based on facts and the structure of the law. Yes, we have horrid hypocrites running around with law licenses, the DA being one of the worst. But we also have a profession that retains a sense of propriety, and, I think, a real sense of honor. At least when we screw it up and act unethically, *we* know we're over the line."

Marty recalled with painful clarity averting his gaze at her words and nodding.

"I did admit that I screwed up, Judith, and climbed to the wrong altitude."

She had come forward, alarm showing in her eyes.

"No, no, no, Marty! I didn't mean that in reference to you. I meant…we have a disciplinary structure to go after ethics violations."

But it was too late. The shame of making such an epic mistake overwhelmed him again, and there was simply no more to say. The dinner ended quickly, and sitting in his bed now, Marty realized they had come very close to a moment of shared insight, or maybe even intimacy. But that intimacy had receded like a rifle shot – ripped from the artificial reality of an absorbing movie by a filmbreak in the projection booth.

It was now 3 am, and the only recourse was the TV remote.

CHAPTER THIRTY-FOUR

The small procession of lawyers surrounding the defendant moved quickly down the corridor outside Courtroom 5D to a small conference room. TV and print media marked their progress with rolling cameras as Judith Winston leaned toward the uniformed airline captain to whisper something out of range of the reporters.

"Say absolutely nothing and keep an even expression and don't engage anyone's eyes!"

When the door had closed behind them, Marty Mitchell whirled and pointed to the courtroom.

"What...what the hell was *that?* When did my goddamned copilot decide to turn on me?"

"Marty," Judith began.

"No! Seriously. Whiskey tango fox! I thought he was on my side, not out to help the fucking DA!"

"He IS on our side" she snapped, fitting the retort in between his angry sputterings.

"What do you mean, 'he is'? He just sold me down the river!"

"Marty, please sit down. This is not a problem. This is not what it seems. The prosecution has presented their case-in-chief, and they called Borkowsky as a prosecution witness and only got the raw truth out of him. This is just the opening round of our defense, which is why I asked to preserve our right to reexamine him on cross, and why I recalled him now."

The other three lawyers in the room were keeping their distance, their mouths shut, two of them wide-eyed as they, too, tried to see as a good thing any aspect of the previous ten minutes in which First Officer Ryan Borkowsky had testified that his captain knew people would die if Flight 12 wasn't slowed before landing.

Marty slowly slid down in one of the chairs, his eyes on his lawyer in disbelief.

"Am I not getting this correctly, Judith? Isn't that F'ing bastard of a DA trying to convince the jury that I knew people would die if I didn't slow down, and isn't that the basic criteria for conviction, and correct me if I'm wrong, but didn't that sniveling little scone-chomping weasel just say precisely what Richardson wanted to hear? Basically, I'm screwed!"

She bit her lip and fixed him with a steady gaze and the hint of a smile.

"No, you're not. Marty, do you trust me?"

His eyes flared, but the quick and angry retort that would have flown at her like a shotgun blast a month before was a hang-fire, and his jaw moved up and down a few times before he shook his head 'no,' while saying 'yes'.

"Yes...I do trust you. But...what the hell am I missing?"

"I can't tell you why just yet, but this is unfolding precisely as I would have designed it."

"Judith...*how?* Didn't he just throw me under the bus, for want of a better cliché?"

"He answered my questions correctly and honestly and, thank God, didn't embellish. I asked if you were aware of the company's statement that if you two didn't slow down significantly for landing on Runway Seven, people would be killed. He said yes. I asked him to explain how he knew this, and he told us about the satellite phone call, how he had the sat phone button up on his interphone panel so he was hearing both sides. He testified about Butterfield pushing you hard, and he said it was crystal clear to both of you what Butterfield and the company were saying and what it meant."

"That if I didn't slow down…"

"That if you didn't slow down during a landing approach for a fully plowed Runway Seven…"

"Yeah, Butterfield himself said that yesterday, but I didn't expect a rubber stamp from Borkowsky!"

"It's okay, Marty."

"And this helps me how?"

Judith could see two of the other three lawyers leaning forward ever so slightly to hear the same explanation Marty was seeking. The third, a veteran criminal defense lawyer, was keeping an even expression but as Judith expected, not in need of an answer he already knew.

"It helps us, Marty, because in the end, the fact that you understood what Butterfield was saying is immaterial, and Richardson's entire case hinges on it being material."

Marty's head went down as he exhaled loudly, his hands thrown up in frustration.

"I…shouldn't even try to follow this insanity."

"Again, Marty, trust me! Seriously!"

He was nodding, his expression grim. "I do, I will, but good Lord I don't understand this. I thought criminal defense was supposed to be straightforward, and here I am with my life hanging in the balance and I find out it's nothing but a fucking game!"

"I know it seems that way, and maybe it is to a certain extent, but it's the best method we've come up with to try to get at the truth."

He looked up, a sarcastic expression painting his features. "Yeah, and they can't handle the truth, right?"

"Marty, they can't handle the truth because they don't know what it is. We do."

Judith sighed as she checked her watch. "Okay, everyone hit the restrooms and let's get back in there. Poker faces in place. Borkowsky is still my witness for cross. No talking on the way in. Everyone...especially Marty...did good walking down here. Please give me a repeat performance."

The senior partners had promised Judith Winston the best support possible to defend a major criminal case, and the lynchpin of that support had come early in the trial preparation in the welcome form of a veteran criminal defense lawyer who also happened to be an old friend from her early days of practice.

Joel Kravitz, in his seventies, gave the visual impression of being ten years older, his craggy features, gravelly voice, and slightly stooped posture masking a razor-sharp mind that had navigated a half-century of criminal law. When Joel Kravitz and Judith were alone in the room, she looked at him the way an advanced student checks a beloved professor after a presentation.

"What do you think?" she asked.

He exhaled and inclined his head. "The basic plan, Judith is reasonably sound. But what you must do, without question, is convince that jury – or at least one of them – that in fact the airline was wrong about slowing down being the only way. You're right, of course. Richardson is going for a straightforward kill on the statute. He's not expecting this tactic. He's so disgustingly angry...I can tell...he's left himself open to a mistake like this."

"His mistake?"

"Yes. Of course. But don't get cocky. This is still a long shot and that jury will be more inclined to buy Richardson's binary argument than follow your more complex reasoning."

"God, I wish we knew, and could explain, how Marty lost control and dug a wingtip."

"Speed had nothing to do with causing that. Well, I mean, I'm no flyboy, but the research does show that despite Butterfield's statements, there *was,* in fact, a credible chance he could have made it, primarily because two thousand feet of Runway Seven had not been plowed further and would have provided back-door braking. That changed the equation. That uncertainty is a tiny thread, admittedly, but it's sound."

"So, you're happy?"

He snorted, a twisted smile on his craggy face.

"HELL no! I'm never happy until double jeopardy attaches and my defendant is acquitted. Then I'm not happy 'til I'm paid."

"You're a curmudgeon, Joel!" she teased.

"And that's why you love me!" he replied.

CHAPTER THIRTY-FIVE

Present Day — *September 10*
Police Department, Denver International Airport

Being summoned away from the courtroom at the height of a murder trial was both a relief and a worry; an uneasy balance between the targets of his curiosity.

Scott Bogosian glanced at his watch, which proclaimed him ten minutes early for the appointment that the chief of police of Denver International Airport had requested. Scott sat back and let his thoughts slalom freely around the last two days of Marty Mitchell's trial, noting that his dislike of Grant Richardson had increased markedly. Maybe it was disgust that a pilot was being forced to fight for his freedom for doing his job imperfectly, a perception that triggered a feeling Scott did not want: a sense of common cause with the pilot. Or perhaps it was the smarmy intensity of the practiced litigator and the constant feeling that Richardson was sneering at anyone who did not believe Mitchell should be drawn and quartered without further ceremony.

Those, of course, were not the words Richardson had unleashed at the jury. His opening statement had been full of righteous indignation about a paid servant of a company with smarter people at the helm who had issued the gospel according to Regal Airlines, and the unbelievable, unforgivable act of the renegade captain to reject that wisdom. It was, Richardson said, open and shut, and the jury would find it very easy to dispense with the case by voting quickly for a guilty verdict. The rest, he warned, would be smoke and mirror verbiage from the defense solely designed to pull the jury off target. After all, he told them, the defense has no defense.

"It's terribly simple, folks," Richardson had said, as if talking to a tight team of intellectual equals about to be egregiously bored by morons, "…the law…*The Law*…okay? The law says, with crystal clarity, that when someone in this state knowingly causes the death of another, that person is guilty of second degree murder. 'Knowingly' means that you are informed that if you do a particular thing, it will cause a death, but you do it anyway, and, indeed, a death occurs. You're then a murderer. No if's, and's, or but's. No qualification. And that is precisely what the state will show: that pilot in command Martin Mitchell did something he was informed in no uncertain terms would, in fact, cause the death of at least one other human. He rejected that wisdom and did what he was told not to do, and sure enough, people died. End of case. Guilty is your only possible verdict."

"Mr. Bogosian?" a uniformed officer was leaning over him.

"Oh! Yes. Sorry."

"The chief wants to know if you can wait about fifteen minutes while he deals with a routine emergency?"

"Sure," Scott replied, wondering exactly what emergencies could be considered routine at a major airport.

He settled back in the waiting room chair, recalling the look and the smell of the huge tire he had been inspecting so carefully in the nearby warehouse days before. Whatever had gouged the extremely tough rubber had gone from front to back along the left side of the tread. It was no more than a quarter of an inch deep, but the question that was bothering him most was whether the tire had touched something prior to the launching of Flight 12, or something moments before the crash.

Scott had leaned in to get as close a look as his eyes would allow and by playing the flashlight around the cut, began to realize what he was staring at: a small amount of colored substance along and embedded inside the cut. It looked for all the world like flecks of yellow paint, but just a small track of it.

Scott had glanced around furtively, verifying that the NTSB investigator who had been his willing host was elsewhere for the moment. He pulled an envelope from the inside of his jacket...another overdue bill, but the envelope would do. Using a penknife, he scraped as much of the yellow substance as he could into the envelope and quickly stowed it and the penknife before standing.

"Really fascinating," Scott said, his voice causing his host to turn around some thirty feet away where he'd been inspecting a part of the broken fuselage.

"I'd like to see the top of the right wing over there, if I could," Scott added.

"Sure," the investigator replied, turning and waving him into motion. "It's an incredible sight, how that Beech fuselage rammed itself into the wing structure without taking out the wing spar and collapsing the wing. There's no way they should have stayed attached with them flying for over a half hour at such a speed. In fact, there's no way anyone should have survived such a midair collision to begin with."

Twenty minutes later, emerging into bright daylight, Scott had thanked the man profusely before lofting a final question.

"There's no yellow paint used on the runways here, right? No surface signage?"

"Not that I know of. That's a rather odd question."

"Just curious. I get these little dangling facts sometime that don't fit the mosaic."

To Scott's relief, the investigator considered the remark too far out to pursue. He decided to let it go, probably wondering if anyone could explain how reporters think.

Scott remembered not a moment of the drive back to town, but he recalled clearly obsessing over the incongruities.

He knew the airport and its equipment well. No yellow paint was used on the snowplows, or the airport supervisory trucks. Yellow *was* used on all the fire trucks and fire command cars, but according to Josh Simmons, absolutely all of the fire and rescue equipment had been well accounted for as Regal 12 flew over.

So, where was the source of the gouge and the yellow paint? What could that tire have grazed? Maybe this, too, was nothing – but the loose-end aspect of it wouldn't leave him alone, especially since he'd read at least five times the transcript of the NTSB's interview with the captain:

NTSB: Captain Mitchell, you say a bright light appeared just in front and to the right, startling you."

MM: Yes. I couldn't tell if it was like headlights or a single light but something clearly was in the way, on the runway, at the last second. I figured it was a snow plow in the wrong location and to understate things, I did not want to hit it.

NTSB: The First Officer has reported to us that he did not recall seeing such a light.

MM: Maybe he didn't. I did. Things were happening very, very fast at that speed.

NTSB: But Captain, if a vehicle was on the runway and its lights on sufficient for you to see, and if the copilot was looking out as well, why would you have been the only crewmember to see it?

MM: You guys calling me a liar?

NTSB: Certainly not, Captain Mitchell. We're trying to…

MM: There was a light from something down there right in front of us and it would have been potential suicide to continue descending into it.

NTSB: You are aware that the airport authority reports that there were no vehicles on that runway, and that all airport and fire vehicles were accounted for.

MM: Yes. That's what they say. But something was there.

NTSB: Did you tell your copilot you were seeing a light?
MM: No. There was only time to react. Did I tell him?
We're talking a split second!"
NTSB: Could you have mistaken a runway edge light or
one of the approach lights for a vehicle?
MM: Absolutely not. I know what I saw, and it was not
an approach or runway light!

Scott's assumption that he could pull a very big favor from the head of the Colorado State Patrol's crime lab had almost been proven wrong, but an impassioned plea won the day. It was obvious, however, that there would be no future concessions. He'd dropped the yellow scrapings off at the lab and hoped for a call back that hadn't come for six days. But at last, with the trial of Captain Marty Mitchell in its fifth day, Scott's phone rang with the lab director on the other end.

"Scott, your substance is automotive paint, used only on Chevrolets manufactured between the years of 2004 and 2006. Called Wheatland Yellow. Does that help?"

"Immensely. Thank you!"

"I can't send you a formal report, but I can send the basics to you via email, and I'll preserve the sample that's left."

Just as the trial had adjourned for the day, a quick call to the Denver Airport Police had snagged the chief on his way out of the door. Scott had met the veteran cop months before and dutifully followed his habit of taking business cards or asking for phone numbers.

"May I ask you a question…partially a legal question?"

"Sure."

"All of this is off the record, if that's okay with you."

There was a chuckle from the chief. "Wait, aren't I supposed to ask that?"

"Works both ways, sir. Okay, here's the question. If an airport worker drove his appropriately tagged private vehicle onto a closed runway during the January blizzard, without authorization or clearance, about the time of the Regal crash, would that be a police matter?"

There was a calculating hesitation on the other end.

"Well, that would definitely be a disciplinary matter but…yes, we would want to know about it."

"Chief, there is a small streak of yellow paint confirmed to be from a Chevrolet product manufactured between 2004 and 2006 found in a lateral gouge on the bottom of the right rear tire on the right main gear of Regal 12. The captain maintained to the NTSB that a pair of headlights suddenly came on in front of him that night on final approach and directly influenced his actions, but there has been no proof, and essentially, the story has been discounted. Now, there are no official yellow Chevrolet cars or trucks as far as I can tell in the airport inventory. Additionally, of the fire and rescue equipment on the field – all of which is painted a different, almost greenish shade of yellow – none is made by General Motors. So, would it be possible for you to run a check of all the private vehicles which have permits to be on the air side of the airport to see which ones might be yellow Chevy products manufactured between those years?"

"We have the ability to do that, of course. Probably dozens of cars would fit that bill, if you're talking about personal cars which can be driven into the appropriate parking areas."

"Yes. Exactly. If we did a search like that, we could then cross-check that list against whoever might have been working on the airfield that night, to see if we could narrow it down to one person and one car, and then see if there has been any disturbance to the paint on that car."

"You're using the word 'we' rather liberally, Mr. Bogosian."

"Yes, Chief, I know. But I'm just a curious journalist trying to nail down an explanation for something really bothersome, and I figured it would be bothersome to you, too."

"Spell it out for me."

Scott described in greater detail the captain's claim and how it could easily be a key to his last second manipulations of the 757's controls.

"Hold on. Are you ignoring the reality that no wrecked car was found on that runway that night or later?"

"What if the car was merely grazed, and not wrecked? What if the driver had driven it off the airfield afterwards?"

"Okay…possible, I suppose. And this, I assume, would be material to the investigation?'

Scott had decided to throw a wild card.

"Chief, it might answer a very important question, and it may even be a definitive piece of evidence in the murder trial of the pilot. I have no dog in that fight, but I'm thinking of writing a book on the crash, and I've been attending the trial every day."

"Did someone reputable do the formal forensics on that paint?"

Scott debriefed the information from the state lab.

"And where did the sample come from?"

"Me, and the tire itself. I took the sample. The chain of custody is protected."

"Did you have the authority to do that?"

"I was accompanied by an NTSB investigator," he replied, sidestepping the question's real import.

There was a thoughtful sigh audible from the chief's end. "You know, Mr. Bogosian, you're thinking like a cop."

"I'll take that as a compliment, Chief."

"It is. Most of the time. Okay, give me your number and I'll get back to you…maybe. I appreciate the information, but I may not deem it appropriate to tell you the results."

"Yes, sir. Understood."

"That would be pretty bizarre, someone on a runway in their own car in the worst blizzard in ten years. I don't think that's a viable possibility. But…I have to admit, I've seen crazier behavior."

As have I, Scott thought.

Scott came back to the present and looked around, refocusing on the fact he was in the police chief's waiting room. The assistant was standing in front of him again.

"The chief is ready if you are, Mr. Bogosian."

It was noteworthy, Scott thought as he sat down, that the chief requested his door be closed before coming around the modest desk to sit opposite a utilitarian couch.

"Well," he began, holding a file of papers, "it turns out there are two Chevrolet products with permits to be on the airside of the field, but one of them was in a shop in Aurora for maintenance the night of the crash, with the wheels off."

"And the other?"

"The other, Scott, belongs to a gentleman who works for the airport authority. In their command center."

"And...was he here that night?"

The chief nodded, a guarded smile on his face as he watched the reporter.

"Have you interviewed him?"

"Tell me what we should ask him?"

"Well...I guess the first thing is, could we see your car?"

"And then, if he says yes and there's no damage?"

"Did you have it in the shop at any point between then and now?"

"Keep going."

"And, the big one, I suppose, was this car anywhere near the runways the night of the Regal crash?"

The chief nodded and stood up. "I agree. And we've got the gentleman waiting in an office down the hall. This is not a by-the-book procedure to bring in a civilian to observe a police interrogation, but I'm making an exception because we would have had no suspicions without your input."

"You haven't asked him anything yet?"

"No, other than to bring his car with him. It's a 2005 Chevy Tahoe."

"Yellow, right?"

"Oh, yeah. Wheatland yellow. You want to look at the truck first?"

"Absolutely!"

He followed the chief to the parking lot just outside and several stalls down to the unmistakable shade of yellow. The SUV seemed well kept and clean, and devoid of a roof rack. Scott stepped up on the running board and peered over the edge, taking in the roof.

"See anything, Scott?" the chief asked, clearly leading him.

"There's a square patch in the middle without paint, like something's been taken off."

"That's right. Something like this," the chief added, triggering a picture on his smartphone and handing it to Scott. In the image, a small antenna with a square base was presented as a factory replacement part for the Chevy Tahoe. Scott worked the screen for a moment, looking for specifications that included dimensions.

"One and a half inches tall by a base of two inches by four."

This chief nodded. "So, you saw the cut on the tire, Scott. Could that cut have been made by an antenna like this?"

Scott looked at the police chief as he handed back the phone.

"With embedded pieces of the same paint in the grove it cut as a piece of rubber impacted it at two hundred thirty knots, yes. I mean, I'm not an engineer, but this could be exactly what caused that mark."

"Then let's go talk to the boy."

CHAPTER THIRTY-SIX

Present Day – *September 10 – Day Five of the trial*
Courtroom 5D, Lindsey-Flanigan Courthouse, Denver

"All rise."

The familiar tones of the bailiff presaged the entrance of Judge Gonzalez who mounted the bench somewhat ponderously and then scanned the courtroom to assure himself everyone was in place.

"All right, Counsel, before I bring the jury back, any motions, objections, or temper tantrums?"

A few people in the galley chuckled and Gonzales smiled at them before ordering the twelve jurors readmitted.

Judith watched with an even expression, ever so slightly relieved. She had expected a rancid attitude toward her from Gonzales after his boorish conduct earlier in the year, but he had been a gentleman in the courtroom, and seemed openly respectful of her as well as the district attorney. Judith, however, was not about to drop her guard.

"Call the witness please, Counsel," Gonzalez directed, looking at Judith.

"I re-call First Officer Ryan Borkowsky."

Borkowsky got to his feet, looking as rattled as before, and climbed back into the witness box carefully avoiding Marty's gaze.

"You realize you are still under oath, Mr. Borkowsky?" Judge Gonzalez asked.

"Yes, sir."

Judith took her time approaching the witness stand, a

sheaf of papers in her hand as she consulted first one, then another.

"Mr. Borkowsky, after overhearing the conversation by satellite phone between Mr. Butterfield and Captain Mitchell, did you provide any advice to the captain regarding the speed to use on landing?"

Richardson was on his feet instantly.

"Objection, your honor. She's testifying."

Judith was shaking her head. "No, your honor, I am not suggesting an answer or testifying through that question. He was the first officer, the second in command. He overheard a conversation in which his company was essentially ordering their flight crew to do certain things regarding airspeed. The captain had clearly been resistant to those suggestions from the company. It would be appropriate for a first officer to offer an opinion or advice to the captain following such an exchange. I am merely asking if such a communication occurred. And, may I remind Mr. Richardson that Mr. Borkowsky is his witness, and this is cross-examination, which means I can ask leading questions."

Grant Richardson was standing beside her now, making his case with equal force that the question the defense attorney was asking presupposed that advice was required. Judge Gonzalez raised his hand in a stop gesture, his ruling surprising Judith who was already working on an alternate query. Richardson seemed equally surprised.

"Objection overruled. Ms. Winston, you may proceed."

"Thank you, Your Honor," she replied, turning back to the witness. "First Officer Borkowsky, did you offer the captain any advice or recommendation regarding the speed to be used on landing subsequent to the satellite phone call between the captain and the company?"

"Yes."

"Would you tell the court and the jury what that advice or recommendation was?"

"I told the captain we should slow for landing."

"And it is your testimony that you provided that advice after the satellite call between Mr. Butterfield and Captain Mitchell?"

"Yes."

"Not before, but after?"

Richardson was standing again. "Objection! Asked and answered."

"Withdrawn," Judith replied smoothly, stepping closer to Ryan, her eyes going over the papers in her hand and a puzzled expression on her face.

"Sir, I don't see any such advice on the NTSB transcript."

Grant Richardson leapt to his feet again, his voice pained.

"Your honor, I object! Now she *is* testifying!"

Judith had her hand in the air. "I'll rephrase the question."

"Continue," Gonzales added.

"Let the record read that I am now showing opposing counsel, and the witness, defense exhibit E, the transcript released as public information by the National Transportation Safety Board of the cockpit voice recorder. Mr. Borkowsky, this is from the top of page fifty-three, lines 18 through 21, I am going to read out loud for the jury and I'd like you to follow along. Okay?"

"Yes, ma'am."

"Captain: You okay for a few more minutes, Ryan? I need to talk to the company. First Officer: Yeah. I'm getting used to her now. We're gonna slow for landing, right?"

Judith paced for a few seconds before looking back at the first officer.

"Mr. Borkowsky, you testified that you advised the captain to slow down after the satellite phone call between Mr. Butterfield and your captain. Does the exchange I just read from the cockpit voice recorder contain advice?"

"I'm…sorry?" Borkowsky was looking trapped, and his expression morphed into frustration.

"I'm trying to understand if the question, 'We're gonna slow for landing, right?' is advice you provided the captain."

"Yes."

"But that was not the advice you testified you gave after the satellite call, is it?"

"Yes, it is! That was the advice!" his voice was rising in volume and tone, his right hand flailing the air. "I didn't have to…to give him a formal statement! We know what each other means in the cockpit."

"So, Mr. Borkowsky, the only advice you gave the captain was the phrase I just read from the CVR transcript?"

"Yes, I think so," Borkowsky sighed, shrugging his shoulders.

"But you testified, did you not, that you gave advice on slowing down after the satellite call, correct?"

"Objection, Your Honor! She's badgering the witness."

"Overruled, counselor!"

"Mr. Borkowsky?" Judith said.

"That WAS the advice! I said so. This is ridiculous!"

Judith suppressed the smile she would normally have displayed at the very outburst she was hoping for.

The first officer looked like he was going to bolt in terror. At the defense table, Marty had turned to one of the lawyers with an incredulous look which deepened when the younger attorney shrugged his shoulders.

Judith was approaching the first officer again, her eyes boring into his.

"The statement I read is merely a question and not an advisement?"

"No! It was advice. I mean it was obvious I meant he should slow."

"Were you afraid of Captain Mitchell?"

"No! Not at all."

"Do you consider him a tough captain?"

"No."

"Was he difficult to talk to?"

"No! I mean, he's a bit stiff and disapproving sometimes, but we got along just fine."

"Did you elect, that day, in that emergency, to give advice in the form of a question because you were concerned he might not like what you had to say?"

"No. I could tell him anything."

"Was it important that he slow down for landing?"

"Yes."

"If the speed on landing was important, and if you were not afraid of Captain Mitchell, and if he was not hard to talk to, and if you could 'tell him anything,' and if the both of you got along 'just fine,' why, Mr. Borkowsky, have you been unable to direct the court's attention to any evidence attributed to you that would have constituted a recommendation to slow down for landing, instead of a question?"

"I...knew he was thinking it through."

"Mr. Borkowsky, I am handing you the aforementioned defense exhibit E, and I call opposing counsel's attention to page 116, line 25. At that point in the CVR transcript, as I have tabbed it, the satellite conversation between Mr. Butterfield and Captain Mitchell begins. Do you see that?"

"Yes, ma'am."

"Yet the phrase I read, and which you testified constituted your advice to the captain to slow down, appears on the same CVR transcript at page 53, as I previously indicated."

"Your Honor," Richardson interjected, "Objection! Is there a question in there somewhere?"

"Ask your question, Ms. Winston."

"Yes, Your Honor."

Judith's mind was racing through the tutorials Joel had given her, and chief among them was to never start a question with 'isn't it true,' although that was what she dearly wanted to lead with next. She sighed internally and turned back to the witness.

"Mr. Borkowsky, it was your testimony that you did provide such advice subsequent...in other words, after...the satellite call?"

A worried expression passed over Ryan Borkowsky's

features as he sensed a trap he couldn't find. "Yes."

"Then, could you explain, sir, why the transcription of the question that you asked of the captain – the question that you say constituted advice subsequent to the satellite call – can you explain why that begins on page fifty-three of the same transcript, some sixty-three pages and a considerable amount of time *before* the satellite call?"

"I…ah…I thought it was before but…I guess I was wrong."

"In fact, you did not advise the captain to slow down for landing subsequent to Butterfield's satellite call."

"No ma'am. I'm sorry…I mixed up the sequence."

"Mr. Borkowsky, maybe I haven't been as clear as I could have been with my questions. I apologize. I'll try my best to be more specific. It's your testimony today that you provided advice to the captain in the form of a single question that was asked before the satellite call."

"Yes."

"Why did you not advise the captain to slow down after that call?"

"I…I don't know. I mean, there were other choices."

"Other choices for how to land and where to land?"

"Yes."

"Did the company's advice regarding speed cover all possibilities that you and Captain Mitchell considered?"

The shadow of relief appeared on Ryan Borkowsky's face as he appeared to re-inflate, squaring his shoulders slightly and coming out of the defensive slouch that had characterized his last fifteen minutes on the stand.

"No. Butterfield was concentrating on just Runway Seven, and I was too, but Marty…Captain Mitchell…was thinking beyond that."

"So, the company's advice between slowing down for Runway Seven, or risking death and serious injury on Runway Seven in particular if you didn't slow down, that binary choice did not include any other runways?"

Borkowsky's head was suddenly on a swivel as he looked at the judge, looked at Judith, and then, for the first time, looked at Marty before answering.

"Yes. That's exactly right. We had other choices."

"Choices that might *not* automatically result in anyone's death?"

"Yes."

"Choices that your company had not considered?"

"Yes."

"So, Mr. Borkowsky, the choices that Captain Mitchell ultimately made about where to land and what speed to use on landing were different from the singular scenario that Regal Airlines was warning against when they tried to direct the two of you to slow the aircraft if you landed on a fully plowed Runway 7?"

Once more Grant Richardson was on his feet, looking pained and shaking his head. "Your Honor, PLEASE! Who is testifying here? This is beyond leading the witness and I object and ask that this entire exchange be stricken from the..."

"Overruled, Counselor!" Gonzales snapped. "I want to hear his answer! "

The judge turned his full attention toward Ryan Borkowsky, who was taking a long drink of water, his hand clearly shaking.

"Would you like the question repeated, Mr. Borkowsky?"

He shook his head no in staccato fashion.

"I can answer it. It was a very fluid situation, and I knew that Marty...Captain Mitchell...was weighing a dozen options a second. I didn't know exactly what he was thinking other than what he told Butterfield on the sat phone because things were unfolding far too fast. I didn't even have a clue why he broke off the approach to Runway Seven until a minute or so later. Yes, the company told us not to land at that speed on Runway Seven, and I don't think they ever realized several thousand feet had been left unplowed.

So, were there other options other than what the company was worried about? Yes. Absolutely. And he didn't have time to explain them to Butterfield or to me."

"And, in your opinion, Mr. Borkowsky, of those other potential options the company did not know about, do you believe that at least one of them might reasonably be expected to result in no deaths at all?"

"Yes. Definitely. I do."

"No further questions," Judith said, turning to walk back to the defense table with a side glance at Grant Richardson. "Your witness."

CHAPTER THIRTY-SEVEN

"Judith, conviction or acquittal will turn on the final instructions to the jury," Joel Kravitz said as the two lawyers sat in the bar of the Hyatt-Regency an hour after leaving court. "It isn't always that way, but in this case, it may make the difference."

"I know it," she replied.

"Grant Richardson seems to have only limited credit with Judge Gonzales, which portends well for your getting the best language you can in the instructions, but in the end, Richardson is going for simple and stupid."

"What are you telling me, Joel?"

The older attorney sighed. "Shit, I hate things like this. All right. It is my duty to tell you that despite what has been a brilliant attempt on your part to undercut this sleezebag DA, I think he still has you cornered."

"I'm not following that."

"He's reaching the jurors better than you are. This jury is worrisome. Our jury consultants have been watching each of them as you know, and they're convinced, despite your best efforts to select the best panel you could get, these folks don't seem terribly bright.

"That seems harsh."

"It is, but my point is that in the end, they're going to go for simple because the big DA told them to look for simple and primed them to expect you to do a smoke, mirrors, and sparkly-thing shuffle to confuse and distract them. He's warning them not to fall for complexity, or compound thoughts. I don't know if there's any way you can defuse that prejudice in your closing, but that will be your last, best chance. They're already sitting there glazed over with their arms folded. Very bad sign."

"Jesus, you're a barrel of fun tonight!" she said, gesturing absently to the bartender for a refill.

He laughed.

"I suppose I should point out to you that citing Jesus to a Jew bears some risk of lowered credibility?"

She sighed. "Sorry. I'm just...what's the word the kids use? Bummed?"

He smiled, and shook his head as if his student just wasn't getting it. "You really should update your repertoire, Judith. That phrase died in the nineties. Hang out with some certifiably insane teens. Smoke a joint. Listen to some crap music."

"You mean rap?"

"One and the same."

She took a sip of the Manhattan she hadn't really wanted and studied nothing for a few seconds, working hard to keep any feelings of panic at bay. Finally, she turned back to Joel.

"You and the jury consultants really believe this jury is dumb?"

"High probability. Maybe not quite as stone-cold stupid as the OJ jury, but not the sharpest cheese on the cracker. You did your best in voire dire, but...the jury pool was pathetic. No one with a real job ever seems to show up for jury duty anymore."

She nodded.

"Are you putting your boy on the stand in the morning?" Joel asked.

"I am. I was. Should I?"

"If you're sure he can stay controlled, yes. His voice is great, a captain's voice filled with tones of reassurance, and it just might work."

"Thanks." She shifted uncomfortable on the bar stool and turned back to him.

"Did Gonzales stipulate that no one could bring up the cause of the midair collision?"

"Yes. That was quite a pretrial battle, but since the NTSB has not ruled, I used the principles of federal preemption and the fact that it had virtually nothing to do with the crime charged, and he agreed. Months ago I wanted to kill that disgusting toad."

"Richardson?"

"No…Judge Gonzales. But he's been very fair so far."

"Oh, by the way, Judith, do you remember that of the five killed in the crash, one was a young socialite named Victoria Moscone?

"Yes, I saw her name. I don't know anything about her."

"This may not be worth mentioning, but her husband has been in the courtroom every day so far, sitting quietly and watching. This guy is worth billions – all from venture capital shenanigans and good gambles over time – name is Carl Moscone. Victoria was his much younger trophy wife. Moscone owns a private jet, of course, but it was grounded and she was racing to visit her sick mother in Orlando."

"Is his presence significant?"

"I don't know. He's a very private person…I've met him in prior venues…but he's politically powerful and usually gives the maximum donation to politicos he likes."

"Such as Grant Richardson?"

"Don't know, but I'll check on it. Of course, he has every right to be torn up enough over his wife's loss to come watch the trial. Maybe it's just part of closure for him. He hasn't said a word to anyone."

She sat in thought for a second wondering where to file this new shard of relatively disconnected information. Was there any chance Richardson's emotional attack on Marty was a surrogate action propelled by a rich widower calling in a political favor? It wasn't a question she could answer, and it probably wasn't worth the effort to even try. The PI she'd hired had reported back empty handed, too.

She shook it off and looked back at the senior lawyer.

"So, Joel, other than fighting like hell over the wording of the jury instructions and preparing a closing argument that will have all twelve of them physically attacking Richardson with pitchforks, what else would you advise?"

"The ultimate fallback in a criminal case, Judith. Go for reasonable doubt. It was always my north star through decades of these types of battles. Plant reasonable doubt like a kudzu vine. Kudzu grows about a foot a day, by the way, and that's how fast inserting real lingering doubt into their thinking will grow, if Richardson doesn't kill it with simplicity."

"Kudzu? Really?"

"It's a good example. Convince them that Richardson has failed to meet his burden. Convince them he's failed to prove every element of the charge beyond a reasonable doubt. Reasonable doubt can also be compared to a virus. If it can grow past a juror's mental immune system and outlast any anti-viral attack by the prosecution, when it comes time to vote in that jury room, it can save the day. One vote to acquit is the last line of defense."

"I love your analogies."

"In more traditional terms, my dear, pivot everything on the fact that there is no way that anyone could accept, beyond a reasonable doubt, Richardson's argument that to knowingly cause the death of another includes an airline pilot who tried everything he knew to save his passengers, and lost a few nevertheless. Couple that with the universality of captain's authority in an emergency and Richardson will have a steep hill to climb to overcome it and get all twelve past reasonable doubt. He wants to use simplicity? Give it right back to him. The very nature of the captain's decisional process instills not just reasonable, but severe doubt that his actions could ever meet the language and the intent of that damned law that defines second degree murder."

"That's it?" she asked, standing.

"In the final analysis, that's all you've got, kiddo."

CHAPTER THIRTY-EIGHT

Present Day – *September 13 –Day Six of the trial*
Courtroom 5D, Lindsey-Flanigan Courthouse, Denver

"Ready, Captain?"

For the previous hour, in a commandeered hotel meeting room, Judith had been carefully and calmly running through the basics of what Marty could expect on the stand when court resumed in less than an hour. There had been one more on the defense list but it was going to be impossible to get that witness to court in time, and Judith had made the unusual decision to go ahead with Marty's testimony. It was a risk, Joel had warned, to let a defendant testify in the first place, and more so when his voice wasn't the last one heard from the witness stand. But the risk was not without calculation. Marty's calm demeanor was both reassuring and disturbing, and the question kept echoing through her mind of whether he was really that composed, or doing a great job of acting? The weekend recess had been taken up with constant study for Judith, and mostly sleep and a few workouts in the hotel gym for Marty.

"Am I ready?" Marty echoed. He nodded with a tight smile, and a big hand reached out to gently touch her shoulder.

"Thank you, Judith. However this debacle turns out."

She resisted the urge to repeat her warnings about how totally critical it was for him not to get angry or agitated. He might perceive the repeated warning as a lack of confidence.

"You're welcome! Now let's go do this."

With the rest of his legal team reassembled in the

courtroom an hour later, Judith called him to the stand, and Marty walked forward with calm confidence, his uniform pressed and sharp, his captain's hat with the gold braid on the visor left on the defense table, yet clearly visible to the jurors.

Judith glanced at the twelve jurors once again, wondering if they were really as unsophisticated as the jury consultants believed. She had struggled in her opening statement to find the right words to plant in their minds how outrageous was the injustice being visited on this good man. Time would tell if they had heard her. And, as Joel had warned, the statute seemed deceptively clear, and she would have to meet Richardson's strategy head-on.

Marty Mitchell was right, she mused. *It's a shameful game. But occasionally justice is the imperfect byproduct.*

From the witness stand, Marty had fully anticipated that seeing Grant Richardson at the prosecution table front and center was going to be a struggle; and he knew that watching the smarmy bastard sitting back casually with such a smug and self-confident look could upset him. But at Judith's urging, he'd been preparing himself for this moment for weeks, and an inner calm had genuinely replaced his intense hatred of the man. He looked at Richardson now as somewhat pathetic, especially since the DA had nothing more important to do than personally torture a surviving airline pilot.

Marty could recall almost word for word Richardson's opening statement, as well as all his questions of his witnesses during the first days of the trial. The DA had been smart in avoiding the vilification of the captain of Regal 12. Instead, he'd cast the accident as a sad series of tragic mistakes, one of which had to be answered with punishment lest people die in the future from another pilot's negligent and disobedient decisions. Marty knew the jury was curious and not preprogrammed to hate him, and they *were* being preprogrammed to consider this a simple matter – if A fits

B, the only verdict is guilty. He would have to connect with each of them on a profoundly human level to get them to look beyond. In pilots' lexicon, it was the ultimate checkride with his freedom in the balance. The good part of that, he concluded, was that Marty Mitchell had always been ice-water steady in checkrides, even when the check pilot was an unspeakable ass working relentlessly to rattle him.

For the entire morning and after the lunch recess, Judith followed the usual introduction to the jury by guiding Marty through the details of the flight, the preflight discussion with the dispatcher, the collision and airborne calls with Butterfield, the rapid-fire decisions that had to be made in an unprecedented emergency, and the agony of pushing back against voices that were telling him to condemn the sixteen people on his wing to death.

And finally, as promised, she had turned and asked the questions he had been dying to answer all day, giving him the opening to explain without interruption the last act of the flight."

"Captain, your first officer testified that when you started a missed approach to Runway Seven, you were low on fuel and the runway was in sight?"

"Yes."

"Why did you elect to go around?"

"Because," he said, "I suddenly had a better idea, one that had been staring me in the face as we came down final for Runway Seven, but one I hadn't figured out until about two hundred feet above."

"By a 'better idea,' what do you mean?"

"One that wouldn't kill anyone. A way of getting all of us down safely, not just the passengers aboard my Boeing."

"Would you please describe to the jury what happened from the moment you decided to go around, to the crash?"

Marty Mitchell nodded and took a long look around before beginning, and, to his amazement, the courtroom and all the sounds and sights within began to recede as he commenced speaking, until once again it was the snowy night of January 21st and he was in the cockpit again, the snow streaking past the windscreen, the same fear roiling his stomach as they streaked down final approach far too fast, the remains of Mountaineer Flight 2612 still hanging onto the right wing. He could hear Ryan's voice, just as before, when Marty ordered him to standby for landing gear extension.

"Five hundred feet to go, Marty. No decision height."

"Roger."

"Coming up on two miles to the runway, on speed, one half dot above the glide slope."

"Roger."

"Four hundred above and one mile," Ryan was saying.

"Gear down," Marty commanded, as Ryan's hand moved the lever downward, starting the hydraulic sequence that lowered the huge main gear trucks and the nose gear into place.

What had been eating Marty Mitchell finally coalesced, like a blindingly bright flash of crystalline insight. He'd been dutifully following a single idea down a narrow tube and failing to consider or even see any other possibility, but just because a runway was formally declared closed and full of snow didn't mean it had ceased to exist! What they needed was runway length and some means of slowing down and the absence of a dropoff at the far end.

Jesus! he'd thought, *that's Runway 36 right!*

"GEAR UP!" Marty commanded.

"What?" Ryan had asked.

"Going around. Gear Up! Tell the tower."

For perhaps sixty seconds he held his breath that the change from the shallow descent to a climb hadn't disturbed the wreckage on the right wing, but he made the pull up very, very smoothly, bringing the power in extremely slowly arresting the descent and gingerly beginning to climb as he held the exact same speed. There was more than enough energy stored in the 230 knot velocity to trade for altitude before the engines came up to full power, but keeping it smooth and the angle of attack constant was absolutely imperative.

He heard Ryan's expression of befuddlement to the controller but there wasn't time to worry about it.

"Ryan, tell them we need vectors to the south and then a Category 3 ILS to Runway 36 right."

"Captain, that runway is closed!"

"Yes, because it's full of snow, and what do we need? A way of slowing down on the runway, and that's exactly what a few feet or more of snow will give us! And it's sixteen thousand feet long with a flat plain beyond."

"We can't land on an unplowed runway...can we?"

"We can and we will! At the same speed."

"But there's a twenty-knot crosswind on that runway!"

"This aircraft can take it. Tell the tower!"

The obviously stressed voice of the controller acknowledged the request and repeated the same information that the runway was closed and the ILS turned off.

Marty pressed the PA button on the interphone panel.

Folks, this is the captain. We went around because we think there's a better and far safer way to get us on the ground. We're going to use a much longer north-south runway. I still need you in brace position, your seatbelts tightly fastened, and to follow the instructions of your flight attendants."

He pressed the #1 VHF radio button again and hit the transmit button himself.

"Approach, whoever I'm talking to...there's no time for debate. I need the unplowed snow to slow me down and I need the length, and I need that ILS turned on right this second."

"Ah, Twelve, roger, we're doing it. It takes the ILS time to come on line."

"Approach, it will take about five minutes I figure, for us to come around for a stabilized approach. Give me maximum on the runway lights, approach lights, the rabbit, and the VASI's, all of it."

"They may be snow covered, sir."

"I know that. Please do it. All equipment clear?"

A brief pause marked the controller's relay of the question which resulted in a quick response.

"Roger, Twelve, the tower advises the runway is clear of everything but snow. Turn right now, one eight zero, climb to and maintain eight thousand."

"We'll stay at seven thousand, Approach."

"Roger...seven thousand. I'll turn you for the intercept in about five miles."

Ryan was looking at him with a feral expression and Marty glanced to his right long enough to acknowledge it.

"What, Ryan?"

"We're burning fuel now from the left main, Marty. Our balance is going to be affected quickly."

"We need five minutes. Do we have five minutes?"

"God, I hope so. You really think this will work?"

"Same answer. God, I hope so! But, yes, it's what we both were missing. Who gives a rat's ass what runway is formally open? We have emergency authority to land anywhere."

"Can the gear take it? This is big landing gear! Maybe we should land gear up?"

"No. If the gear can't handle it, we'll still be decelerating on a very long runway with no dropoff at the end. Dammit, why didn't I think of this before?"

"Regal Twelve, turn right now to a heading of three one zero, maintain seven thousand feet to intercept the localizer, and you're of course cleared for the Cat 3 approach to Runway 36 R as requested. Be advised our ILS monitors are not indicating a stable signal yet."

"We have it up here, and we've got GPS backup. We're

good."

"The emergency equipment will be relocating from Runway Seven."

"Roger."

Marty carefully banked the 757 fifteen degrees to the right, holding the turn until on a 45 degree intercept for the final approach course. He could see the localizer coming alive and beginning to move across the screen, the artificially created horizontal situation indicator showing them rapidly approaching the centerline of the runway as projected out many miles by the instrument landing system transmitter. He began another bank to the right, and rolled out on centerline.

"Intercepting localizer."

"How do you want to do this, Marty? As a monitored approach?"

"No time. I'll hand fly. Read the radio altimeter all the way down and help me find the runway. We'll lower the gear in three miles. Give me landing lights at two hundred feet."

"Speed is two thirty, on the nose," Ryan announced. "Flaps are still where we left them."

"Got it. Bringing the combiner back down," he said as he pulled the heads up display back into position in front of his eyes. With both pilots used to approach speeds being somewhere between eighty to a hundred knots slower, the rapid approach of the normal descent point was startling, as if they were flying a high speed jet fighter instead of a lumbering transport.

"Give me the gear, now!" Marty called, realizing he was about to overrun the descent point. "Gear down, before landing checklist."

Ryan responded immediately, the gear handle snapping down and the sound of the huge main landing gear and nose gear rumbling into place, followed by three green lights on the panel.

"Down and three green,"

"Before landing checklist," Marty ordered, and Ryan began rapidly going through the sequence.

"Checklist complete, one thousand feet above, speed two thirty."

"Roger."

"You're a bit above the glide slope!"

'I know it. I'm going to stay in a right crab against this right crosswind until just over the runway, then I'll kick it out and align us." Marty's hand pulled the two throttles back a bit more, his eyes darting between the attitude indicator, HSI, and airspeed as he gently lowered the nose to increase the rate of descent.

"Still one dot high on the glide slope," Ryan called out.

"I know it."

"Seven hundred above, two miles to go."

"Gear and flaps rechecked down?" Marty asked.

"Gear down and locked, flaps just beyond ten degrees."

Marty was working diligently to keep the speed on target at 230 while checking to make sure the deck angle of the 757 was at least two degrees nose up. The main gear had to touch first, but any flaring of the aircraft, and raising of the nose just over the runway, with such excessive speed would simply fly them back into the air. Yet the descent rate was just over twelve hundred feet per minute which would mean a very hard landing that the gear could probably take, but it would be a crunching arrival at best, and if too hard, the Beech fuselage would undoubtedly be broken loose.

"Five hundred feet, just over a mile. I've got some fuzzy lights ahead and the snowfall is decreasing."

"Roger."

"Three hundred feet. Half a dot high on the glide slope. Two hundred feet above, landing lights coming on." Ryan left hand had been resting on the landing lights and he snapped them on now, revealing a torrent of snow streaming past the windscreen.

"Approach lights in sight," Ryan added, "…slightly to

the left! One hundred feet"

Marty's focus had been on the projected green numbers and lines in the combiner, but with the landing lights came the streaking snow and the faint glow of a sequenced line of strobes called the rabbit, as well as the white runway lights which were broadening and moving toward them like outstretched arms, the dark of the runway between them, suddenly illuminated by something that made no sense at first.

Two lights, just ahead, right in the middle of his intended touchdown and nowhere near the runway lights or any other rational explanation except that maybe there was still a snow plow on the runway and they were aiming right for it at over two hundred thirty knots!

Marty was still crabbing to the right and had just begun to push the left rudder while holding the right wing down, but suddenly the entire picture changed.

"Fifty feet, over the threshold," Ryan said.

Time dilated in Marty's mind, his left hand translating the only rational action which was to roll the aircraft back to the left enough to let the right main gear pass over what he could see now was slightly to the right of the runway centerline. He pulsed the yoke back slightly as he rolled left, with no time to explain to anyone, and when the lights of whatever was below had flashed beneath them with no feeling of impact, he began to move the yoke back, unprepared for the heavy gust of wind that was suddenly raising the right wing and rolling him much further left than he'd panned. A quick pulse to the right with the yoke wasn't enough, and with growing horror he felt the left wingtip drag onto the runway surface, the drag pivoting the 757's fuselage left as the left main gear crunched onto the runway partly sideways, followed by the right main gear, and now it was a frantic attempt to kick the aircraft back to the right and keep the right wing from contacting the runway, but every attempt to regain control was too little too late as the aircraft went fully sideways, rolling to the right, the right wing now skidding along the surface, the sound of tearing metal and impossibly confusing gyrations lasting for an eternity and exceeding anything he could influence as his world skidded along the snow covered surface shedding parts.

Marty's consciousness returned to the courtroom. There were no sounds around him, all eyes looking in his direction, and his words still effectively echoing around the heads of everyone present.

He could see his attorney standing quietly by the defense table, watching him with a slightly stunned expression, and he was greatly relieved when she shook herself into motion and stepped forward.

"Thank you, Captain. I have a few more questions."

He swallowed hard and nodded at her.

"When all the motion had ceased, what do you recall?"

He exhaled and shook his head. "It was pitch black and very cold and I heard sirens everywhere. We were on our right side…the cockpit section…and I didn't know the fuselage had broken in two. Ryan was knocked out, but I could see he was breathing. I had no idea who was still with us, where anyone was, and I guess I blacked out before they pulled us out of the wreckage."

"Captain, if no headlights had appeared in front of you, would the crash have happened?"

Richardson had shaken himself into action as well and was on his feet to object.

"Objection. Speculation."

"Overruled, counsellor," the judge replied. "I think this man is perhaps the most qualified individual in all Christendom to answer that. The witness may answer."

"No, we would not have crashed. It was going to be a hard landing, but I could have kept it under control, and even if the Beech fuselage had detached at that point, they had a long, flat surface ahead in which to safely decelerate. So we would all have been okay."

"So, Captain, the presence of those headlights was a material factor?"

"Yes. If I hadn't needed to avoid that snowplow, or whatever it was, I would have been able to safely align the aircraft with the runway as I had started doing, and then using the snowpack to decelerate us."

"Did your selection of 36 Right mean that there was an alternative to the two choices Mr. Butterfield had considered?"

"I'm sorry?"

"Mr. Butterfield, according to his testimony, said that there were essentially two choices that he had heard from you. One was to slow the aircraft to normal or near normal landing speed so as to be able to land on Runway Seven and stop before the drop-off to the east, and the second choice was to maintain your speed in the hope that the Beech fuselage and the occupants would not fall off the wing."

"Yes."

"So, in both your sat phone conversations with Mr. Butterfield, your choice was either to slow or maintain speed, but landing on Runway 7 was the only choice, correct?"

"That's right. My idea about landing on Runway Three Six Right provided a third potential solution, and I knew it was the key to getting all of us down without anyone dying. I had been fixated…bore-sighted, so to speak…about landing on Runway Seven. So…yes, I made the decision to reject the course of action Butterfield wanted me to reject, if that makes sense.

"So you did *not*, in fact, knowingly do anything to cause the death of anyone."

Richardson was on his feet again, this time sounding almost wounded.

"Objection, Your Honor, if that isn't leading the witness, I don't know what is!"

"Sustained. Counselor, rephrase the question."

"Yes, Your Honor. Okay, Captain Mitchell, in choosing to land on Runway Three Six Right, did you knowingly do anything to cause the death of another human being?"

"Absolutely not!"

"No further questions."

It was disturbing, Judith thought that Grant Richardson asked to delay his cross examination of Marty Mitchell. Obviously the defendant was going to be available the remainder of the trial, but it was the unknown strategy behind his request that concerned her.

Gonzales had approved a fifteen minute recess as Marty left the stand, yet it seemed like a mere heartbeat before everyone was back. There was only one remaining witness on Judith's list, but this one, she figured, would be a considerable surprise to the jury, and indeed, the eyes of every juror went to the door of the courtroom as an attractive woman walking hesitantly with a cane moved with obvious pain and deliberation toward the front.

"Your Honor," Judith said, "the defense calls Captain Michelle Whittier to the stand."

Hyatt Regency Lounge

The small gathering in the hotel bar just after 6 pm consisted of Marty Mitchell and his legal team, and was supposed to have included the captain of Mountaineer 2612. But after testifying, Michelle Whittier had been thoroughly exhausted and begged off, her ride home provided by a chauffeured town car with Judith's heartfelt appreciation.

"She's in the middle of physical therapy, and as you saw, she's struggling."

"I thought she was wonderful," Marty said.

Judith nodded in agreement. "She may not have contributed anything to the legal analysis, but she connected with the jurors big time. You agree, Joel?"

"Completely," he responded. "All sixteen humans on that Beech were saved by this man's refusal to just follow orders, and there was one of them in the flesh in that courtroom, a brave woman who would be dead and buried except for Captain Mitchell's perseverance. In essence, what this jury needs to feel is that a vote to convict Marty here is a statement to that young woman that she should have been abandoned and killed. That's powerful. Richardson took a hit with her, and you noticed his cross examination was respectful and essentially useless. To ask the jurors to reward Marty for saving her life and that of all the others by throwing him in prison is unspeakably horrific. By the way, was she the worst injured?"

"Yes," Judith replied. "There was a neck injury to a male passenger caused by the collision, but the amazing thing was, when the 757 began to go sideways at that blazing speed, the Beech fuselage skidded off pretty much cleanly and rocketed right down the runway and it didn't tumble. The Boeing actually went tumbling ahead of it. The Beech fuselage collided with part of the disintegrating right wing of the 757, or that would have been the only injury. Michelle would have walked away."

"But she'll make a complete recovery?" Joel asked.

"She was in a coma for two months. There was a massive concussion and a closed skull injury, and when she awoke, she couldn't walk or talk coherently, so she's made incredible progress and I'm told will eventually fly again."

Judith could sense Joel was holding back a less optimistic analysis of the day for a private conversation later. She could see it in his eyes, despite the broad smile. But providing some much needed relief for Marty right now was more important, and she repeated her earlier compliments about his self-control, and the cool authority he had projected throughout the time on the stand."

"So how are you feeling?" she asked Marty.

"I'm good. But how are we doing?"

Judith forced herself not to hesitate or glance at Joel. "I think we're on target. Richardson will get a shot at you tomorrow or the next day, and he'll have his whole team working on how to get a rise out of you, but just repeat today's outstanding cool and we're fine."

When they had called it an evening and dispersed, Judith shoved the card key in her hotel room door and gratefully closed it behind her. Her smartphone had been buzzing with increasing urgency, but she'd suppressed the urge to pull it out until now. She kicked off the pumps that had begun to cause her real pain by the end of the afternoon, and read the screen. Three missed calls and an urgent text from her assistant.

Judith, I've been trying to reach you! I know you've got to be exhausted but there's a reporter for the Denver Post about to break a very important story on Regal 12 and he's been battering our door down to get to you.

A weary sigh accompanied her callback to her assistant's cell phone.

He answered on the first ring with the name of the reporter.

"Okay," she said, pushing her hair back and thinking about a hot bath and delighted there was a jetted tub even though she had yet to use it. "Please call Mr. Bogosian and inform him that I will not give any interviews on or off the record until...what?"

It was uncharacteristic for her assistant to interrupt her, but his voice was urgent.

"No, Judith. He doesn't want an interview. He wants to give you information he says is vital to Captain Mitchel's case."

"Did he say what that information was? Could be a ploy."

"Only that he's been in the courtroom every day and although he's not taking sides, whatever it is will be extremely important to a just decision."

She snorted. "Who the hell talks about just decisions anymore?"

"His words, Judith. Not mine."

She copied down Bogosian's cell number and punched it in, noting the fact that he, too, answered on the first ring.

"I understand you want to talk to me, urgently, Mr. Bogosian? This is Judith Winston."

"Where can we meet?"

She sighed. "Whoa, hold your horses! I'm…it's been a very long day, and I'm already in my hotel room…"

"It's not quite eight and I'm sure there's a bar."

"Yes…of course there's a bar. There's always a bar, and I just left it, but..."

"Please tell me the hotel and I'll meet you in that bar in fifteen minutes."

"Seriously? I have no idea who you really are or why you're even calling."

"Google me. I absolutely promise you it's vitally important, what I have to tell you."

"Okay, but…is this really necessary? Tonight, I mean? Can't you tell me over the phone?"

"Yes, it's very necessary and no, I need to talk to you in person, and tomorrow my story will be front page above the fold and I would feel very bad if you were blindsided."

"Front page, huh? And this concerns Captain Mitchell's prosecution?"

"Materially."

"You understand I will *not* be giving you any information or interviews on or off the record?"

"Absolutely. I accept that ground rule. I'm the one doing the talking."

"Alright, Mr. Bogosian. Hyatt Regency bar, then. Fifteen minutes."

CHAPTER THIRTY-NINE

"Your Honor, I request a sidebar," Judith announced.

"Approach!" Judge Gonzales said with a weary wave to both lawyers.

"I have an emergency addition to the defense's witness list," she offered.

Judith watched Judge Gonzales take the information in stride but instantly look at Grant Richardson, who looked at her incredulously. .

"Your Honor, I object. We haven't been notified of any motion for inclusion of a new witness. The state is surprised."

"Of course, you're surprised, Counsellor," Judith said, smiling as sardonically as she could manage. "So are we. That's the very nature of a material witness who emerges at the last minute about whom nothing was known previously."

As she expected, Richardson's argument was heated and built around the concept that even if the offered witness confirmed the existence of a car on the runway, that had nothing to do with the primary question of whether or not Captain Mitchell knowingly caused the death of anyone.

"Judge," Judith began, "if there was no vehicle on Runway Three Six Right , then the fact that Regal Flight Twelve crashed does not disprove prosecution's contention that whether the defendant chose Runway Seven or Runway Three Six or any other, it was his refusal to slow down that in essence constituted knowingly causing a death. In other words, there was no runway he could have landed on at two hundred thirty knots without killing someone. But, if he could have landed safely on Three Six Right even at two hundred thirty knots, that means his ultimate decision, the one on which he acted, did NOT constitute knowingly causing a death. Therefore, the presence or absence of the alleged vehicle is material and incredibly important in determining whether a safe landing could have been made if no car was there. Therefore, this witness must be heard."

From there, the ruling for inclusion was all but unavoidable for Gonzales, especially since Judith's hands were clean regarding any prior knowledge of a witness named William Jantzen.

It had been obvious to Judith that Marty would be concerned to the point of near panic over why she had broken with the usual pattern and, instead of briefing him and the team, had closeted herself with someone Marty had never seen before. There had been no time for Judith to explain, and he had the distinct impression that she had intentionally engineered it that way.

Now as the unfamiliar name of the new witness was called, a slim, sandy haired young man in his twenties, wearing a slightly bushy mustache, walked unsteadily down the aisle, his features and his color ashen, his shoulders stooped as if he was carrying an unseen burden. He was wearing an open-collar shirt over black slacks, and Marty watched him in deep puzzlement.

When the witness was sworn and all the usual opening questions of name and employment had been completed, Judith walked toward the witness box.

"Mr. Jantzen, what exactly is your job at Denver International Airport?"

"I...ah...I work in the central control building and coordinate the various
ground equipment." His somewhat nasal voice betrayed a southern origin.

"Does that include snow plows during winter storms?"

"Yes, ma'am."

"Were you on duty the night of January 21st, when the crash of Regal Air 12 occurred?"

"I was on that night, but…I finished my shift and was relieved before the accident."

"How long before the accident?"

"Ah…about thirty minutes."

"What was the situation from your work perspective that night?"

"Well, we had had everyone deployed trying to keep the airport open, and we were slowly being overwhelmed, so I was constantly moving the plows and supervisors around. It was decided we would abandon everything except Runway Seven, but we had to leave the last two thousand feet unplowed because we didn't have time with the inbound emergency to do the whole thing one last time."

"So, you removed the plows from Runway Seven?"

"I was gone by then."

"Please explain what you mean by 'gone,'" Judith asked.

Jantzen looked nervously around the room, catching the judge's eye as well, as he sat fidgeting in the witness chair, leaning over the microphone and looking at it repeatedly as if worried it might bite him.

"Well, my supervisor told me the battle was over and I should clock out and get home if I could. You know, because the snow was just incredible. So I got my parka and scraped the snow drift off my car, and…it was so beautiful out there, and frankly I was so exhausted, I just wanted to sit and veg for a while, you know?"

"What did you do then?" she asked.

"Well…I…you gotta understand, the entire airport other than Runway Seven was closed down. They had turned the lights off and the instrument landing system off on Runway Three Six Right, and there was too much ramp traffic around where our parking lot is, so…so I drove over to find a safe place to just park and watch the snow."

"Where, exactly, did you go?"

"I have a little GPS with the runway diagram? Since you couldn't tell any more where the concrete and grass come together, I just followed the gps out on one of the closed runways, because it was wide enough I wasn't running the risk of driving off the side, you know?"

"Mr. Jantzen, did you have an aviation frequency radio in your car, or anything with which to monitor the control tower or talk to them?"

"No, ma'am."

"Was it required that anyone driving on the runways or taxiways be in two-way radio contact with the tower?"

Jantzen looked down, nodding, his head continuing to bob as he looked up at her.

"Yes, ma'am, when the airport runways and such are open. I mean, they were closed, so I didn't think I needed to be in contact."

"Are you authorized to drive airport equipment on the airside areas with a radio?"

"Yes, ma'am. I'm trained."

"But not in your personal vehicle?"

"No, because I don't have a radio, but, see, there's no way I would ever have driven my car over there if the airport had been operating."

"Why did you choose Runway Three Six Right?"

"Because we had lost control of the snow on that runway later in the evening, and I knew the drifts wouldn't be too high to drive in." Judith paced back for a moment, taking in Marty's wide-eyed expression of disbelief as he put together the meaning of the words Jantzen had just spoken. Grant Richardson's face was also broadcasting massive dynamic tension as he tried to find something to object to.

"Was it exciting to you, being in the middle of the runway?"

"A little."

Richardson was already standing. "Objection. Relevance."

"Sustained."

"Mr. Jantzen, once you drove onto the surface of Runway Three Six Right, what did you do?"

"I parked. I turned around to the south facing the way I had just come in, 'cause I figured if I saw my tracks disappear it would be time to go."

"And then what did you do?"

"I turned up the heat, turned on a CD I had…Jimmy Buffet, you know…to counter the winter. And then I lit a joint. I mean, it is Colorado. It's not illegal. And I was just trying to unwind from a really intense day."

"So, you were relaxing and smoking and listening to music. What kind of car were you in?"

"My Chevy Tahoe."

"What color is it?"

"Kind of a yellow."

"Does it have a roof rack?"

"Ah, no ma'am."

"Was the engine running?"

"Yes, ma'am."

"And were the headlights on?"

"No, ma'am."

"Had you driven out there with the headlights on?"

"No, ma'am."

"Why not?"

"Well…the snow was still coming down…and I was following the GPS…"

"Could you see the terminal from where you were on Runway Three Six Right?"

"Yes…barely."

"So, if you had used your headlights, someone might have seen you?"

Finally, Richardson was on his feet. "Objection! Calls

246 | JOHN J. NANCE

for a conclusion."

Judge Gonzales broke his gaze from the witness and moved it to the DA, a scowl on his face at having been interrupted.

"Overruled."

"But, Your Honor, there's no foundation for this testimony. We don't have a clue where this is going!"

"Well, if you'll stop objecting, maybe we could find out. In fact, there is a foundation. Sit!" The judge looked back at the witness. "You may continue, Mr. Jantzen."

"Okay."

"I'll rephrase the question," Judith said, keeping her expression devoid of the smile she desperately wanted to display. "Tell me all the reasons you kept the headlights off when driving onto Runway Three Six Right?"

"Well...as I said...I was really driving by the GPS and didn't need to see ahead, but I guess I also didn't want anyone worried about why I was out there."

"So, you did not want anyone seeing that you were on the runway?"

"Yes, ma'am."

"Did you...at any point in time once you had parked and turned on your music, did you turn on your headlights?"

"Yes, ma'am."

"When and why?"

Jantzen took a deep breath and looked down, still doing his uncomfortable dance around the microphone before looking up.

"Lights suddenly came on. Landing lights. In my face! I mean, the runway was closed, and suddenly I've got what looked like a big airplane coming right at me!"

"What did you do?"

"I panicked! I was fumbling for the headlight switch, y'know, and I was trying to put the car in gear at the same time and figure out where to run to and finally I got the headlights on but I'd forgotten the parking brake and the car wouldn't move and suddenly this thing goes right over my head and rocks the car, and when he's passed me, I finally figured out the damned parking brake was still on, and I got it off and got the hell out of there."

Marty had come forward in his chair at the defense table, his heart pounding. This was his corroboration! Those headlights had *not* been a figment of his imagination, or some sort of manufactured or trauma-induced memory. Even though Ryan had not seen or remembered headlights for the brief time they were in view, they had really been there.

"You left the runway then?" Judith was asking.

"Yes," Jantzen said. "…and the airport, as quietly as I could. I mean, I was shaking scared, and then all the emergency equipment starts rolling past me with sirens and lights everywhere and I had no idea…"

The young man looked up, tears now streaming down his face. "I…I had no idea there had been a crash, and that same plane that was going to land on Runway Seven had crashed right over me!"

"Did you know that any part of that aircraft had touched your vehicle as it flew over?"

He was all but hyperventilating now and Judith looked at the judge before asking if he needed a moment to compose himself, but Jantzen forced himself to sit up and continue.

"The whole car shook when he passed over but I didn't think it had touched me," he continued, "…but it was a lot later, maybe weeks, when I was up on a ladder in my garage and I looked at the top of my car and saw a little antenna was missing. I never knew what that thing did but it was kinda cool, so I remembered it. I didn't think about it being hit by the plane, because, y'know, I didn't feel any impact. But then later I began to wonder."

"Did your employer know you had been on the runway that night?"

"No, ma'am. Well, not until this week."

"Did you know for a fact your antenna had been removed by the tire of the passing jet?"

"No, ma'am. Not for sure. Not until yesterday, or, I mean, the evening before."

"Had you read in newspapers or online or heard via radio or television or from any other source that the captain of Regal Flight 12 claimed that headlights had distracted him during his emergency landing?"

Jantzen's face betrayed something beyond utter confusion – it was the primal look of someone being chased by a grizzly realizing he's backed up to the edge of a cliff with nowhere to go.

"Yes, ma'am."

"And you didn't come forward or notify anyone that you might have been the source of those headlights?"

In all the corporate litigation Judith Winston had handled, never once had a witness broken into body shaking sobs on the stand, but William Jantzen was instantly beyond the ability to force words out of his mouth, and he sat there, quaking and sobbing as the judge wondered what to do and the jury took it all in.

"I have no further questions," Judith said at last, as the bailiff gently moved the microphone away from Jantzen's face, quieting the ungodly sounds that had filled the courtroom.

Judge Gonzales ordered a ten minute recess, which was barely enough time for Jantzen to get himself under control and face a cross-examination

Despite the best efforts of the DA to shake his story, William Jantzen remained consistent, and Richardson finally decided the witness had done enough damage.

"I have no further questions, Your Honor."

"Mr. Jantzen, you are excused."

He looked at the judge in confusion."

"I'm sorry?"

"You may leave the stand and leave the courtroom, Mr.

Jantzen."

It had been, Judith explained to Marty at the next recess, the visit of Scott Bogosian, the evidence he'd collected, and the presence of the airport police chief in Jantzen's living room that had convinced him that his car had been impacted however slightly by Regal 12. But finding out that without question the flare of his headlights being turned on had actually been a major factor in the crash caused the man to all but collapse. He had offered any help he could, including agreeing to Scott Bogosian's shoot-from-the-hip question of whether he'd be willing to tell the truth in open court to save a man's professional life. Jantzen's immediate "Yes!" had caught Scott by surprise, as had the difficulty of getting Judith Winston to listen to him.

Scott had agreed to take the stand as well to verify the yellow paint in the groove in the 757's tire, and Grant Richardson had apparently given up fighting the point, permitting the presentation to go forward without a real objection. It was that reaction that further worried Judith. Was he just giving up, or more likely, was he preparing to convince the jury that none of that mattered?

CHAPTER FORTY

Present Day – *September 14* – *Day Seven of the trial*
Courtroom 5D, Lindsey-Flanigan Courthouse, Denver

Aside from the very real possibility that his exclusive story about William Jantzen and the crash of Regal 12 might result in the offer of a full-time position with the Post, Scott Bogosian realized he had developed a proprietary attachment to the trial of Captain Mitchell. Try as he might to avoid taking sides, he was sliding into Mitchell's camp and developing a serious dislike for the district attorney. Treating an inadvertent airline tragedy as a criminal act was, to him at least, patently ridiculous.

Scott sat now in the gallery of the courtroom, watching preparations for what might be one of the last days of the trial as Grant Richardson got to his feet to re-call Captain Mitchell to the stand.

It had been a shock, Scott recalled, to see the airline captain in full uniform on the first day of the proceedings. He had thought it pretentious at first, but now the idea that Marty Mitchell the man could be separated from Captain Mitchell, the pilot in command of Regal 12, made little sense. In effect, they were trying the captain of a ship, not an individual, and that was the pivot point for the furious response of most airline people.

Marty adjusted himself in the witness chair again, feeling far more settled than he expected as the enemy walked toward him.

"Captain Mitchell, I just have a few followup questions," Richardson began, an unctuous smile on his face.

Rather like an open-mouthed rattlesnake getting ready to strike, Marty thought. The image was amusing and also somewhat calming.

"Why, Mr. Mitchell, did you abort the landing on Runway 7?"

Judith was on her feet.

"Objection. Asked and answered."

"Sustained," the judge replied.

Richardson was unfazed.

"Very well, let me ask it this way. Is it true, Mr. Mitchell, that a primary reason you elected to abort the landing on Runway Seven was because of your concern over the combination of a two hundred and thirty knot landing speed against the useable length of that runway and with consideration of the severe drop-off at the eastern end?"

"That was...those were major considerations, yes."

"Were you worried about damaging the airplane?"

"I don't understand the question."

"Well, was your primary concern about the speed and the length and the drop-off that if things didn't go just right, the airplane might be damaged? Was that your primary concern?"

"Of course not."

"A yes or no will suffice."

"No."

"Very well. Was your primary concern in aborting the landing on Runway Seven the safety of your passengers, including the people on your right wing?"

"Yes."

"Did you then decide to land on Runway Three Six Right because it would run a lower risk of injury to your passengers, including the sixteen on the right wing?"

"Yes."

"The primary component of your concern...the reason

this wouldn't be a normal landing...was the excessive airspeed?"

"Well, I was trying not to kill the people on the right wing."

"Understood, Mr. Mitchell, but..."

"Objection, Your Honor," Judith interjected. "May we have a sidebar and approach?"

Richardson shrugged and the judge motioned them forward.

"Go ahead, Ms. Winston."

"Judge, there is a level of purposeful disrespect for the witness in refusing to address him by his title of 'captain.' This trial, and the charges leveled by this district attorney, wholly concern his official conduct as a captain, and Mr. Richardson's tactic of addressing him as 'mister' is a calculated ploy to negatively influence the jury by heaping scorn on the witness. I move that the court forbid it."

"Judge," Richardson answered, shaking his head, "Mr. Mitchell is a citizen like all of us. His rank is not military, nor governmental, such as would be the case if he were an ambassador or senator statutorily entitled to the use of a title. 'captain' is merely a commercial title. Indeed, even the FAA does not use the term 'captain,' they use 'pilot in command.' He is not charged with a crime his airline committed, he is charged with personally committing a crime. Ms. Winston's motion should be denied."

Gonzales sighed and rolled his eyes. "Counselors, this amounts to squabbling and I don't appreciate squabbles in my court. But, Ms. Winston is correct. Mr. Richardson, have you ever used the suffix "esq" after your name to designate that you're a lawyer?"

"Ah...yes, Your Honor, but what does..."

"So have I, and that is not a statutorily imposed requirement. You will address Captain Mitchell as Captain Mitchell, because this action is inextricably intertwined with the essence of this professional position. Proceed."

"Captain Mitchell, is it true that with or without the fuselage on your right wing, the primary element which made any landing more risky was the excessive airspeed of two hundred thirty knots?"

"Yes."

"And you chose Runway Three Six Right to lessen the detrimental effect of that airspeed?"

"Yes."

"Could you guarantee that even on Runway Three Six Right that excessive airspeed would not magnify, or make far more lethal, anything else that might go wrong?"

"No."

"So, whether there was a car in front of you on Three Six Right or not, the excessive speed put everyone at greater risk?"

"Technically, yes."

"Wasn't the excessive speed the essence of what Mr. Butterfield and your airline were trying to warn you about?"

"Yes, for Runway Seven."

"But, you just stated, did you not, that it was the excessive speed that would be a problem for any runway?"

"It would raise the risk."

"For instance, it could cause tires to explode."

"Well, the tires are good to two hundred twenty-five knots and this was a cold surface, so, no, the tires were not a problem."

"But if anything went wrong, excessive speed raises the risks."

"Yes."

"And you said the risk you were worried about was not the risk of damaging the aircraft, but the risk of hurting someone, correct?"

"Yes."

"Including the risk of killing someone?"

"Yes."

"And although you speculated and were using your best

guesswork, you in fact had no way of knowing at what speed or angle of attack you might lose the fuselage of Mountaineer Twenty-Six Twelve, correct?"

"That's correct."

"So, therefore, you could not guarantee that slowing to a normal approach speed would or would not result in the loss of anyone in the Beech fuselage, correct?"

"No, but I had to use my best judgment that it would."

"But you didn't know for an aerodynamic and structural certainty, did you?"

"No."

"And approaching Runway Seven and then deciding to land on runway Three Six Right were volitional decisions?"

"Excuse me?"

"You made the decision to land on Runway Seven, and you made the decision to change and land on Three Six Right, is that correct?"

"Yes."

"Stated another way, you knowingly made the decision to land on both runways."

"Yes."

"You knowingly made the decision to land on Runway Three Six Right even though the excessive airspeed of two hundred thirty knots could result in deaths?"

"I made the decision to minimize the possibility of hurting or killing anyone."

"Yes, or no, Captain Mitchell?"

"I…what?"

"Let me re-state the question. Knowing full well that the key problem was the excessive airspeed of two hundred thirty knots and that such airspeed could result in the death of at least one passenger, you nevertheless knowingly decided to use that airspeed on landing on Runway Seven and then on Runway Three Six Right. Yes or no?"

"You're trying to twist this around…"

Richardson turned the judge, obviously having waited

for this moment.

"Your Honor, the witness is being unresponsive. Would you please direct him to answer the question?"

Judge Gonzales turned his head toward Marty and nodded. "Captain Mitchell, you will answer the question with either a yes or a no."

Marty met the judge's gaze, seeing a weariness there as he tried to make a decision on how far to push. He knew precisely what Richardson was trying to do, using the word "knowingly" right out of the statute. But how would the jury view a refusal to play the game? The complexity of the legal question surrounding that statute was beyond his understanding, so did it really matter?

Nevertheless, allowing himself to be cornered was simply not in his nature.

"My answer is 'no'," Marty said.

Richardson looked confused. "Captain, how can you answer no when you already told the court that you were aware that excessive speed was the primary concern regardless of where you landed and that excessive speed raised the possibility of killing someone?"

"The answer to your question is no," he tried again. "Would you like me to explain?"

"I ask the questions here, Captain, in a cross examination, and I did not ask you for an explanation."

Once again Judith sprang to her feet. "Objection, Your Honor. He just got through asking the witness for a subjective response as to his reasoning for answering 'no.' Now he's being argumentative, and he wants to stifle that explanation!"

"Sustained," Gonzalez replied. "Mr. Richardson, either withdraw the question or permit the witness to answer fully."

Richardson nodded, his face betraying annoyance as he paced a few steps to one side and then addressed Marty once more.

"I withdraw the question."

Grant Richardson paused, papers in hand, looking for the best method of salvaging what had been building to be a final self-incriminating 'yes' from the defendant. But after the 'no,' to spar with him further would merely defuse the effect and probably bore the jury.

"No further questions, Your Honor."

"Ms. Winston?" the judge began, "have you any further questions?"

She rose, glancing first at Joel then at Marty as she walked toward him.

"Just one re-direct, Your Honor."

"Proceed."

"Captain Mitchell, did you at any time, inclusive of your decision to land on any runway, knowingly take any action that would be reasonably expected to result in the death of anyone?"

"Absolutely not!" Marty answered, "I was doing everything I could to save all lives, not hurt anyone."

"Thank you, Captain." She turned to the bench. "No further questions."

Marty stepped down and returned to the defense table feeling painfully self-conscious and embarrassed, as if he'd been intellectually shown to be an idiot by a superior speaking a foreign language. He knew he'd been tripped up by Richardson, but the 'how' of it was eluding him.

Judith motioned him to stay quiet as she conferred with Joel for a few seconds, then got to her feet.

"Your Honor, the defense rests."

CHAPTER FORTY-ONE

The insistent banging on the hotel room door had fit uneasily into a complex dream involving byzantine collections of criminal defendants and a jury that had reacted to everything she said with derisive laughter. Judith's brain finally sorted out which reality to pay attention to, and she sat bolt upright in the plush bed, the banging instilling a flash of fear.

She slipped on one of the hotel robes and moved to the door, checking the peep hole before turning the doorknob, incredulous to find a haggard Marty Mitchell standing on the other side looking like a refugee.

"What on earth?"

"I'm sorry."

"You can't sleep?"

"It's beyond that."

She sighed. "Come in. Sit."

Somewhere in the back of her mind it occurred to her that letting a distraught male into her bedroom in the middle of the night when she was clad only in a robe was a risky decision, but she dismissed it with a silent laugh.

"Marty, I need my sleep. I was up until one working on the closing argument. What time..." she glanced around at the clock on the nightstand. "Jeez! Three fifteen."

There was a small round table between the bed and a bench seat under the window and he settled onto the window seat, his eyes red and wide.

"I figured it out, Judith."

"Figured what out?"

"Richardson has been laying a huge trap and I fell right into it."

She sat opposite him on the only chair, the table to one side, tempted to say that of course Richardson had been trying to lay a trap, but she could see that would be useless in calming him down.

"Tell me why you think that?"

"That criminal statute! The way the damn thing is written, it's a Catch 22! He got me to say that I knowingly decided to land, and tomorrow he'll tell them that it was the speed that means I condemned someone to death."

"Marty, you said very clearly that you did not make any such decision."

"No, no, no! Don't you see? He's already twisted everything up! The jury will believe that the only way I'd be innocent is if I followed the company's dictates and slowed down. I'm screwed!"

"I'm ready to fight that interpretation. Yes, he's going to make that argument, but all we need is one juror to think it through."

"I want you to put me back on the stand!"

"Marty, I can't do that."

"Can't you go to the judge? I have more to say…I can clear this up!"

Judith sighed, running her hand through her unruly hair after catching a glimpse of herself in the mirror looking like a Medusa. She stared at the rug, letting her mind deal with the interlocking geometric patterns woven into the carpet before meeting his eyes again.

"Marty, I think I know you well enough now to know you seldom if ever panic. Yet here you are, in the middle of the night, essentially panicking."

"I'm sorry…I'm really sorry, Judith, but..."

"I've got a very strong closing for morning, Marty."

"I thought if I could re-take the stand I could make them understand."

She got up and moved to the small refrigerator, tightening the loose tie on the robe before taking out a chilled bottle of water.

"You want one?"

He shook his head.

She unscrewed the top and sat again.

"Marty, no lawyer likes to admit this, but you were right when you called it a game. But it's a serious game, with serious rules, and in the end, it's designed to get as close to a correct decision as humanly possible."

"They don't understand, Judith!"

"I think they will! But I cannot put you back on the stand unless there is new evidence, and there isn't. We already proved the existence of the car on the runway…that was huge, Marty! Huge! It validated everything you said."

She took a swig of the water and put the bottle on the table, then moved the chair forward and reached out, taking both his hands in hers, looking him in the eye.

"You promised to stay with me, Captain. Remember?"

"I am. I'm here."

"But I need your courage as well."

A tear had begun to roll down his face, and he turned in an attempt to hide it as she gave his hands a small shake.

"It's going to be okay, Marty. I'm not supposed to say that…it's unprofessional to speculate…but it's going to be okay."

His eyes were pools of anguish and pain, a watery window into his tortured soul.

"I'm scared, Judith," he said at last, inhaling sharply as the admission left his lips, "…and I have no one else to tell." The words were spoken so softly they barely registered. He snorted suddenly and looked at the ceiling. "Getting ready to kill myself on Long's? I wasn't a bit scared. But now… I'm…terrified. Far worse than in the cockpit that night."

Mentally Judith stuffed a sock in the face of her better judgment and rose from the chair, sitting next to him then, pulling him to her, folding her arms around him until he leaned into her at last, his head resting on the fabric of the robe pulled tightly over her breasts as the silent tears morphed into body-racking sobs.

CHAPTER FORTY-TWO

Present Day — *September 15 — Day Eight of the trial*
Courtroom 5D, Lindsey-Flanigan Courthouse, Denver

The fact that Carl Moscone had once again slipped quietly into the courtroom registered on Joel Kravitz, who had glanced at the wealthy investor and saw the same absolute poker-faced expression that apparently never changed. The question of why he was here in the first place had begun to take greater precedence in Joel's mind, and the formula so far didn't balance. The man had lost his young and beautiful wife in the breakup of the Regal Air 757 on Runway 36R, yet there wasn't the slightest flash of anger, angst, or grief, and certainly none of the sneers that Grant Richardson had poorly hidden in his obvious anger toward Marty Mitchell.

As Richardson took the floor in his attempt to hit a homerun with the jury, Carl Moscone sat expressionless.

At the defense table, Judith Winston sat quietly, several pages of notes in front of her, each anticipating one of the points Richardson was bound to make. In his first fifteen minutes, he had missed nothing.

"So, ladies and gentlemen," Richardson continued, facing the jury box, "you've heard all the facts, and you've also heard Captain Mitchell's attempt at excuses, and in a little while you will hear an eloquent attempt by Ms. Winston to distract you so badly with smoke and mirrors that, she hopes, your confusion in the jury room will lead to a wrongful acquittal. So, let me insulate you against the dog and pony show to come. The law is stunningly simple. It says that if you, or I knowingly cause the death of someone, we're guilty of second degree murder here in the great state of Colorado. There are no if's, and's, or but's regarding the person's intentions other than one thing: Did they know that a particular action would most likely result in the death of someone, and yet they took that action anyway? If so, they're guilty of second degree murder. That's it! That's literally all you have to decide, and the decision has already been made for you. Captain Mitchell was warned that to keep two hundred and thirty knots of speed would result in a crash, and he disregarded that advice, maintained that speed, crashed his plane and killed five passengers. Nothing else matters. It does not matter legally whether the crash was on Runway Seven or Runway Three Six Right or anywhere else, or what might have contributed.

|| Now, Ms. Winston will try to mesmerize you with the fact – and it is a fact–that Captain Mitchell was attempting to save the lives of the poor passengers in the Beech fuselage. But, he did not have the right to condemn the passengers in the 757 in order to *maybe* save the Mountaineer folks. Remember, Captain Mitchell testified that he did not know whether the fuselage would come off or not. That fear was pure, panicked speculation. What he DID know was that landing overspeed on Runway Seven would kill someone, and the fact that he changed runways without slowing does not erase the fact that he made a 'knowing' decision that resulted in five deaths. Ms. Winston will ask you to have sympathy for him because he was trying his best. She will remind you that his last, best idea about landing on 36R would have worked except for a car on the runway. But all that is nonsense when you consider, as you must, that he knowingly made the decision to maintain a dangerous speed, and people died as a result. That leaves you no legal choice. You may have sympathy and pity and feel very bad for Captain Mitchell, but as a matter of law, you are required to fit the evidence to the statute which leaves no room for

any other verdict than a verdict of guilty. Thank you."

A short recess separated Richardson's rhetoric and Judith's by fifteen minutes, but as they reassembled in the courtroom, she leaned toward Marty and gave a reassuring pat on his hand.

"He didn't surprise me at all. I expected everything he said."

Marty nodded, his face a study in stoic apprehension. He took his seat again and listened as Judith moved for dismissal on the grounds that the state had failed to prove even a basic case, but as she had told him, the motion was just for the record and would be rejected, as it was.

The embarrassment he felt for coming apart in the middle of the night had been all but replaced by a quieter level of dread. But even that was diminished by the feeling that he was not alone. The yawning chasm of loneliness that had been his life for the last few years, long before January, had been breached, and that gap had admitted a vulnerability he had long denied. He was still scared to death, but there was something different about the way that felt.

Judith was on her feet now, the jury following her as she moved out from behind the table, wearing a carefully chosen, classy dress in a soothing shade of blue, set off with a simple strand of pearls. She smiled and greeted the jury and began to walk them through the facts from Marty's point of view rather than the cynicism of Richardson's re-telling. She painted a crystal-clear picture of a dilemma into which no human should be placed, laced with the unhelpful pressure from the airline and the shifting facts regarding runways and snowfall that all had to be dealt with by two pilots who also had to struggle to keep a crippled airplane aloft while balancing a precariously attached fuselage of another aircraft on its wing."

"Yes, I ask you to empathize and sympathize. We are, after all, human, and it would be completely inhuman not to put yourself in this man's position, in that cockpit, where we are now told that having the courage NOT to condemn those sixteen souls to certain death was a crime. Mr. Richardson would have you believe that because no one technically knew precisely what combination of angle of attack or airspeed would condemn those sixteen people to fall off the wing, Captain Mitchell's best estimate should be discounted. An airline captain fighting for survival in a dire emergency seldom has the luxury of dealing with certainties. By the way, that is precisely why we have humans and not computers flying our jetliners and making the tough calls in emergencies, as rare as they are, because machines can't deal with uncertainty the way we can. You heard the testimony about the near-disaster in Singapore a few years ago with a fully loaded Airbus A-380, Qantas Flight Thirty-Two, using the largest passenger airliner on the planet. It took five qualified pilots nearly three hours to figure out how to land safely. If the computers alone had made the decisions, the aircraft would have crashed with the loss of all aboard, over three hundred people. We *need* captains like Marty Mitchell who can quickly take in all the evidence, and working *with* the captain of a Mountaineer 2612, determine that slowing down would be fatal. You heard Michelle Whittier's testimony! She and her copilot had to fly… literally fly…their fuselage in order to stay on the wing of the 757 even at two hundred thirty knots. Can you really ignore all that testimony? Can you really say that Captain Mitchell should have just assumed they'd stay attached, suppressed his own training and experience and instincts and experimentation, thrown all that away and just trusted that his airline's spokesman had better information, and then slowed to normal approach speed? You see, far from smoke and mirrors, that's the key to this and to your deliberation. Mr. Richardson wants you to conclude that slowing down was a certain win for the occupants of the 757, *and* that since there was no certainty about when the Beech would fall away, deciding to slow down would *not* have constituted knowingly causing the deaths of those sixteen. But that's nonsense! In fact, if Captain Mitchell had slowed down, and if everyone aboard the 757 had lived, but the sixteen people on the wing had died, by his definition of the criminal statute we would still be right here with Mr. Richardson charging Captain Mitchell with second degree murder because he had knowingly slowed the aircraft…knowing that it would case the deaths of the Mountaineer passengers. Are we really ready to imprison someone who had an impossible choice? Are we that crass and hateful as a people to use the literal meaning of law to inflict an outrageous result?

"Again, that's the key. No matter what he did, by Mr. Richardson's definition of the law, we would be here trying the same case for a different set of deaths."

"The law against second degree murder is for punishing someone who knows that doing something completely voluntary, such a pulling the trigger on a gun they've cocked and aimed, would likely result in a death, and they did it anyway. This law was never intended to cover a dire emergency by reference only to its outcome. Captain Marty Mitchell, as he said himself, never did anything volitionally or knowingly to hurt another human. That has one conclusion and only one when you get into the jury room. You must acquit." "Please keep this in mind: If you do not acquit, you will be sending a major message to every airline pilot who flies into or through Colorado that should an emergency ever happen with life threatening potential, their only hope of avoiding criminal prosecution will be blindly following whatever their company tells them to do. Imagine being on such an airplane and the pilots are not allowed to use their own training and intelligence. Imagine your life hanging on the opinion of someone in a distant command center who isn't even there and who cannot have all the facts. If that's what you want to fly with, then convict Captain Mitchell. If you want thinking, caring humans doing their best, you must acquit."

Richardson was not about to let Judith have the last word, and since the prosecution gets the chance to make the final comment, he rose again to address the jury with as much simplicity as he could muster.

"Ladies and gentlemen, Ms. Winston certainly didn't disappoint in providing a great opportunity to distract you. But let me bring you back to reality. Captain Mitchell made the conscious decision to maintain a dangerous airspeed knowing that the potential for loss of human life was very great, and thus regardless of any other information about runways or headlights or any other distraction, the fact is unavoidable: Because of his refusal to slow down to a safe speed, he knowingly caused five deaths, and in accordance with Colorado law, you have no choice but to convict."

Two hours of intense wrangling between Judith and Grant Richardson in front of the judge finally distilled the court's final instructions to the jury, as she explained to Marty later, the best compromise they could engineer. With that, the case went to the jury, and the waiting began.

Sitting quietly at the defense table, Marty was aware of Judith and the team beginning to repack all the notebooks and legal pads and other supporting materials, but he remained without comment until she snapped her briefcase shut and turned to him.

"You okay?"

"I don't know. I've never wanted to snap anyone's neck before, but with Richardson...I..."

They were interrupted by someone handing a folded note to Judith

"What's this?" she asked.

"A gentleman in the back would like a word with you, if you have a moment."

She unfolded the note.

It is urgent I have a moment to speak with you. I believe a great injustice is about to be done, and there is a very material element to all this that you – and the court – should be aware of. Carl Moscone

"What is it?" Marty asked.

"I'm not sure. Would you go with Joel and the others back to that conference room and let me see."

"Sure. But what do you think?"

She touched his arm, "Marty, I think we hit all the points, and I don't think Richardson scored any home runs. But this is what we all hate about the jury system – having to wait and worry."

He knew that wasn't a real answer, but he was being kind enough and calm enough not to press.

She moved toward the courtroom door feeling a combination of exhaustion and dread, none of which she could articulate.

When the small conference room door closed behind her, Carl Moscone shook her hand formally and asked her to sit.

"What is this about, sir?" she asked.

He remained standing, a well-groomed man in his late sixties, gray at the temples but with a full head of dark hair and a sculpted, almost regal profile.

"Had you wondered, Ms. Winston, why Grant Richardson is so angry with your client?"

She sat forward. "Absolutely, but despite spading up heaven and earth with our PI's, we couldn't discover any connection, other than his attendance at two of the funerals."

"He would have attended the funeral for my wife, Victoria, but he feared someone would find out."

"I'm not following you."

"My wife, Ms. Winston, was much younger than

I. There was the usual clucking about a trophy wife, but when we married, we were both very much in love, and we remained so, although in certain areas…libido, for one… we became increasingly mismatched. She quietly set out to do something about it, and I essentially pretended not to notice."

"I…find this fascinating, but what does it have to do with…"

"Victoria had a longtime lover, Ms. Winston, and his name is Grant Richardson, our District Attorney."

"Oh my God!" Judith responded, her had involuntarily going to her mouth. "No wonder…"

"Victoria enjoyed him as a clandestine lover, but I happen to know that she wasn't prepared for him to fall head over heels in love with her, which happened years back."

"So, when she died in the crash…"

"He was devastated, angry, and determined to blame someone, and your client was in the crosshairs."

"Richardson has a wife and kids!"

"Yes, as he has reminded us all in his exploitive political ads. That didn't bother Victoria. As for my attitude? Frankly, I don't respect hypocrites, and the more Richardson puffed his chest out as a pseudo-lawyer politician and a defender of family values while banging my wife behind my back, the more I disliked him."

Judith sat and watched Moscone for a minute as he looked at the wall, his hands clasped behind him.

"How did her death affect you, Mr. Moscone?"

"Carl, please. I internalize my grief. I was deeply affected, and feel a great loneliness and loss which hasn't lessened. But I understand what happened, and I have great empathy for the impossible dilemma Mitchell faced. I do not blame Victoria's death on him. I did expect Grant Richardson would be emotionally devastated, because for all his buffoonery and dishonesty, I know he truly loved her. I also know the man wears his feelings on his sleeve, so to speak. But I did not expect vengeance. I feel very badly for your captain because I am very opposed to using criminal law to address honest human errors of any sort. It is a bastardization of the law."

"Of course, I couldn't agree more," Judith echoed.

"That's why I've been here every day watching, Judith. May I call you Judith?"

"Certainly."

"I would have preferred to stay silent about Grant and Victoria's relationship, but I can't allow this miscarriage of justice. I was simply hoping this case would be dismissed, or that by the time it went to the jury, it would be an inevitable acquittal and I could stay silent. But it didn't and I can't. You are very impressive, by the way."

"Thank you, but I'm really a corporate lawyer."

"Oh, I know. All the more impressive."

"But why now, at the eleventh hour?"

"Because you're going to lose."

"Why do you say that?"

"Technically, Richardson is right on the law, and it's the law that's wrong and far too broad and poorly written. But it's time the judge knows that this entire prosecution is a personal vendetta. I hope we're not too late. He may be willing to quash the indictment and dismiss this prosecution without forcing it into an appeal. Perhaps I should have come forward earlier, and I apologize for not doing so."

"Richardson will just file it again."

"Someone else will have to do it without his participation once the world knows why he did this to begin with, and there's the little fact about double jeopardy attaching when the jury is sworn in."

"You sound very familiar with the law?"

"I went to law school and passed the New York Bar a very long time ago, then quickly decided I'd rather hire lawyers on Wall Street than be one. But I do keep up. Now. How do we proceed?"

CHAPTER FORTY-THREE

Present Day — *September 15 — Day Eight of the trial*
Courtroom 5D, Lindsey-Flanigan Courthouse, Denver

The urgent request from the defense to bring Judge Gonzales back to the bench in open court had been met with an irritated order to assemble both legal teams in his chambers. The rancid memory of the last time she had entered Gonzales' small office flashed in high definition across her mind as Richardson came through the door angry to be summoned back to the courthouse without a verdict. Judith looked at the district attorney, surprised to feel a tinge of pity for the man, if not for his love and his loss and the impending destruction of his career, then for the seismic shock she was about to deliver.

Carl Moscone was waiting in the same conference room, out of sight, but available if needed.

"All right, Counsellors, what's so urgent?" the judge said, settling his considerable bulk behind his desk.

"Your Honor," Judith began, "…we are prepared to move in open court for the dismissal of the indictment against Captain Mitchell on the grounds of prosecutorial misconduct and prejudice."

Both Judge Gonzales and Grant Richardson looked at Judith as if she'd lost it.

"What are you talking about, Ms. Winston?" the judge asked.

"I would prefer to present this in open court on the record, Your Honor."

"That may be your wish, but I want to know what the hell you're talking about?"

Judith glanced at Richardson who still had no clue.

"Just after you sent the jury out to deliberate, Your Honor, I was approached by a prominent member of the community with information based on firsthand knowledge that explains Mr. Richardson's vehement and puzzling prosecution of Captain Mitchell. This information constitutes grounds for immediate dismissal of the indictment."

"And what, Ms. Winston, would that information be?"

"That the hidden and undisclosed impetus for this prosecution was the death aboard Regal Airlines Flight 12 of Ms. Victoria Moscone, and the fact that Mrs. Moscone and Grant Richardson had been involved in a long term and ongoing romantic and sexual relationship for many years."

'WHAT?" Richardson snapped, his eyes suddenly wide. "Who the hell made that allegation?"

She turned to bore her eyes into his, speaking slowly.

"Mr. Carl Moscone, who, by the way, is here in the courthouse waiting for an opportunity to testify under oath if necessary."

Gonzales sat back in his chair as if trying to widen the scope of his vision as he looked at Richardson, who was trying not to stammer.

"Is this true, Mr. District Attorney?"

"Judge," Richardson began, but Gonzales raised a hand to stop him, sitting forward suddenly, his eyes narrowing. "Be...very...careful, counselor, with your next statements and answers. I will jail you on criminal contempt if you lie to me, is that understood? Clearly?"

"Yes, Your Honor. Of course."

"Did you have a romantic and sexual relationship with Victoria Moscone, who perished in the crash of Regal Twelve?"

Grant Richardson's shoulders slumped ever so slightly as he exhaled and nodded. "Yes, but that did not..."

"That's enough!" the judge snapped. "We're re-convening in open court immediately."

Ten minutes later, with Marty and the defense team as well as the prosecution team back in court, and the court recorder in position, Judge Gonzales entered the courtroom and sat down, banging his gavel angrily.

"Court is now in session. Ms. Winston? I believe you have a motion to make?"

"Yes, Your Honor. I move for the immediate dismissal of the indictment for second degree murder true billed against Captain Mitchell on the grounds that the grand jury was misled and not informed about a fatal personal conflict of interest on the part of the District Attorney who brought the case. Specifically, malicious prosecution which constitutes prosecutorial misconduct during grand jury proceedings also constitutes valid grounds for attacking an indictment, and such indictment must be dismissed if the defendant has suffered actual prejudice or been the target of prosecutorial misconduct, which includes a prosecutor hiding a major personal conflict of interest. In this case..."

Grant Richardson was on his feet, his interruption totally unexpected.

"Your Honor, the State moves at this time for dismissal of the indictment and all charges against Captain Mitchell."

The bailiff entered quietly and passed a note to the judge, who looked at it and shook his head.

"Hold everything and everyone in place," the judge instructed. Nodding, the bailiff scurried from the courtroom as Gonzales returned his gaze to Richardson.

"Counselor, do I understand you to be moving on behalf of the State to do precisely what Ms. Winston is requesting?"

"Yes, Your Honor."

"And, I presume, your intention is to obviate the necessity of Ms. Winston presenting her evidence for quashing the indictment and dismissing this circus?"

"Ah...yes, Your Honor...in essence, her testimony is not

needed."

"To the contrary, Mr. District Attorney. I am taking your motion under advisement until I hear all applicable evidence from Ms. Winston and any witnesses she cares to present."

The expression on Grant Richardson's face was ashen. His last, best ploy to prevent the nightmare of public disclosure of his infidelities was taking precedent over any concern about malicious prosecution of a mere airline pilot, and he jerked around to see whether Carl Moscone was already in the courtroom, unaware Moscone was waiting just down the corridor.

"You may proceed, Ms. Winston," Gonzales ordered.

The temptation to point and screech at Richardson for all the hell he'd caused was not easy to resist, but Judith had always prided herself on a professional demeanor under fire. She calmly finished laying the legal grounds for dismissal of the indictment before proceeding to the very thing Grant Richardson was desperate to avoid: repetition of what had been said in the judge's chambers.

But there it was, at last, on the public record, and sure to be the lead story on the evening news.

"I therefore request immediate dismissal of the indictment, and of the charges against Captain Mitchell," Judith said.

Gonzales shifted his gaze to Richardson, who was standing by the prosecution table breathing hard.

"Do you have anything to say or add, Mr. Richardson?"

"No, Your Honor, other than...no. Just no."

"Well, Counselors, I have a bit of a dilemma, because the note I received several minutes back was from the jury foreman informing me that they have reached a unanimous verdict. I, of course, do not yet know what that verdict is, but I now have a difficult choice. I can agree with Ms. Winston and dismiss the indictment and run the risk for Captain Mitchell that someone in the DA's office who did *not* lose a girlfriend aboard Flight Twelve will re-file the charges. I can do so and run the risk of being overturned by the appeals court on the ground that the prosecutorial misconduct was not sufficiently severe or prejudicial. I can table both motions and reassemble the jury and hear their verdict, in which case if it's an acquittal there is no need to dismiss because double jeopardy protection eliminates any chance of re-trial. However, if they have reached a guilty verdict, then I am faced with whether to set aside the verdict and dismiss the indictment, or let the verdict stand and assume Ms. Winston will appeal."

"For the record, Your Honor, the defense would request a dismissal as moved," Judith added.

"Understood, Ms. Winston. And I also have the state's request for dismissal, which I will not allow to be withdrawn as of this moment. But first I have to say, Mr. Richardson, I am going to file charges against you in front of the state bar for grossly unethical conduct. You, sir, have utterly wasted the time of this court and twisted and violated your oath to faithfully discharge your duties to the public, and materially harmed the man you indicted out of obvious personal animus and anger. I can't recall a case of such unforgivable misconduct."

"I offer my humble apology, Your Honor."

"Well, sir, for the damned record, that is not accepted."

Judge Gonzales sighed heavily, his eyes going to Marty for a second.

"Very well. First, the State's motion to dismiss is granted with prejudice. I do not need to hear from Mr. Moscone since Mr. Richardson has already admitted to having had an intimate affair with Mrs. Moscone, who was killed in the subject crash, and whose death has propelled this ill-conceived prosecution. Secondly, this court agrees with the premise that the law relating to second degree murder has been illicitly used in this case, and I would hope the Colorado legislature will correct the ability of anyone in the future to misuse that statute in the way it was misused in this case.

Thirdly, this court formally apologizes to Captain Mitchell. All charges are hereby vacated, and you, sir, are free to go. Now, bailiff, please clear the courtroom so I can bring the jury back to thank and dismiss them."

It was Joel Kravitz who touched Judith's arm in the corridor outside the courtroom, alerting her that the bailiff was standing and waiting for an opening.

"Ms. Winston, the judge would like a word with you in chambers."

"Called to the principal's office again!" she said with a smile directed at Joel. "Marty? Joel? Please wait for me. We at least need a debrief at the nearest bar."

She followed the bailiff down the familiar hallway, surprised to find Judge Gonzales standing in an open doorway waiting.

"Judge?"

He reached out and took her hand. "Two things, counsellor. One, I want to apologize for my...shall we say less than gentlemanly demeanor when you visited me several months back wanting off this case. I...admit I had a bone in my throat and you walked into my gunsights. Second, though, I am very glad I was angry enough to refuse to let you off the hook, because you did an excellent job with this case. Really superlative."

"Thank you, Judge."

"This has been a very strange case, but we could use a lot more of your type of well prepared, intelligent, professional demeanor in criminal matters."

"I appreciate it, but this has been a struggle I don't think I want to repeat. I plan to slip quietly back to my corporate practice and only litigate traffic tickets."

He chuckled, then fell silent for a second. "Too bad about Richardson. He's a good litigator, but this will be the end of the line for him."

"Indeed."

"So, what's next for your client? Will this free him to fly again?"

Judith shook her head. "We don't know. He's still on unpaid leave, and the National Transportation Safety Board hearing is coming up in three weeks. It's not to set blame, but the findings will probably determine whether Mitchell gets his job back."

"Well, I wish the man well. What a horrible dilemma."

"Thank you, Judge," she said, reclaiming her hand and turning to go, then turning back.

"I...don't suppose I should ask you what the verdict was?" she said, eyebrows raised.

"I don't suppose you should," he smiled.

CHAPTER FORTY-FOUR

November — Two Months After the Trial
Churchill Lounge, Brown Palace Hotel

"I'd almost think you're holding court here," Scott Bogosian said with a chuckle as he re-packed his notebooks and digital recorder into a backpack. "You actually look like a regular, relaxing in that huge leather chair."

Marty Mitchell smiled in response. "Well, you told me last month that you love this old lounge and all the cigar smoke, and I now see why."

"I gotta get back."

"How's it going at the Post?"

Scott chuckled again. "Always be careful what you wish for. I so wanted to be a beat reporter again, and here I am, beat most of the time!"

"I take it that's an old newspaperman joke?"

"More or less. No, I'm really enjoying it, but writing your story and getting it accepted by the right publisher is going to be quite a task. Thank you again, Marty, for agreeing to help. Any word from Regal?"

Marty's smile broadened. "I'm told I'll hear from them any day now with a new training date. I'm non-current, so I'll have to go back through retraining."

"That's wonderful!"

"Not official yet, but the NTSB findings pretty much put them in a corner."

"You mean about the garbled radio calls?"

"Yes…all around. The controller was confused, we were

confused, and what it really says is that we've got to get past this seventy-year old antiquated method of push-to-talk, simplex radio being our main means of passing altitude and heading information."

"I'll bet that's a huge relief."

Marty sat forward, his expression changing to one of great seriousness.

"I lost five people that night, and injured eight. I don't care how garbled the radio was, I should have kept pressing until I absolutely knew where we were supposed to be. That will haunt me forever."

Scott nodded. "You are now, though, the least likely airline captain on the planet to ever go to the wrong altitude again."

"Very true."

"You hanging around?"

"Nope. I have a lunch date in the lobby restaurant."

"Oh. A new lady in your life?"

"My lawyer. And...yes. Maybe. I hope so."

Several blocks away in the home offices of Walters, Wilson, and Crandall, Judith Winston glanced at her watch and calculated whether she could still make it to the restaurant on time. She hated being late for anything.

The lunch invitation from Marty Mitchell had not necessarily been a surprise, but the postscript to his email definitely had been – an invitation to spend a weekend with him hiking around Rocky Mountain National Park. There was no professional purpose to be served by such an enterprise, she thought with a smile, so it had to be classified as a date. She had hesitated no more than a few seconds before accepting.

Judith was pulling on her ankle length coat when a familiar face appeared in the firm's main lobby, and she rushed to greet him.

"Joel! How are you?"

"Doing well, Kiddo," he said with a smile. "I miss spending all those high-stress, anxious days and nights with you and the team and the cold pizza!"

"We miss you, too. To what do I owe the pleasure of this visit?"

"I was just passing by and wanted to drop something off to you, for your eyes only."

"What's that?"

"A little slip of paper from the Mitchell jury that never got formally read into the record."

"A slip of paper?"

"From the foreman. Look at it later. I gotta run."

She gave the old veteran defense lawyer a hug and watched him wave as he stepped onto the elevator. When the doors had closed, Judith stood and looked at the folded note in her hand without opening it.

The praise from the senior partners, including Roger Crandall, had been greatly appreciated, yet there was still an undercurrent of self-doubt leaching away at the victory – a victory won thanks to the detective work of a good reporter and the integrity of a widower – not by the prowess of her lawyering. What if Moscone hadn't come forward? The question was haunting.

Judith forced herself to walk over to an elaborate brass trash can and open the lid. She stood there for a few seconds gazing at the still-folded note in her hand and re-checking her gut reaction that whatever it contained didn't matter.

No. I don't ever want to know! she decided, tossing the note in the trash can and turning to push through the double-glass doors, hitting the elevator call button while tapping her foot lightly, anxious to get away from temptation.

One of the office cleaning staff was moving her way with his cart, starting the evening routine that would begin with emptying the trashcans.

The elevator opened at last and Judith hesitated. The two passengers inside the car were staring out, wondering what was going on. She glanced back at the office doors, her eyes landing on the trash can, the seconds ticking by.

And just as the elevator doors began to close, Judith Winston forced herself to take a deep breath and step inside.

For More News About John J. Nance
Signup For Our Newsletter:

http://wbp.bz/newsletter

Word-of-mouth is critical to an author's long-term success. If you appreciated this book please leave a review on the Amazon sales page:

http://wbp.bz/16Soulsa

Also Available From John J. Nance and WildBlue Press

The newest aviation thriller from New York Times bestselling author John J. Nance. "A wild ride in the night sky." (Capt. "Sully" Sullenberger, author of New York Times bestseller Sully). Whoever electronically disconnected the flight controls of Pangia Flight 10 as it streaks toward the volatile Middle East may be trying to provoke a nuclear war. With time and fuel running out, the pilots risk everything to wrest control from the electronic ghost holding them on a course to disaster. "As good or better than any of his previous works. Hop aboard Pangia flight 10 - if you dare." (Charles Gibson, former anchor ABC World News)

Read More: **http://wbp.bz/lockout**

Also Available From WildBlue Press

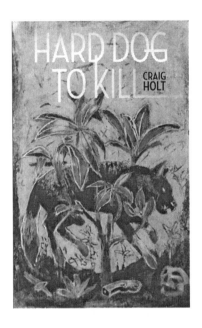

Hardened mercenaries Stan Mullens and Frank Giordano are fighting their way across the Congo jungle, having been sent to track down and kill a charismatic diamond miner, Tonde Chiora. But their victim is full of dangerous surprises, and the jungle offers more opportunities to die than to kill. Struggling to survive in the dark heart of the Congo, Stan begins to question his old loyalties – and his tenuous belief that he is still one of the good guys.

Read More: **http://wbp.bz/hdtk**

See even more at:
http://wbp.bz/cf

More Crime Fiction You'll Love From WildBlue Press

HEADLOCK by BURL BARER

A paranoid recluse lures Jeff Reynolds into a complex web of deception, where delusions are deadly, life after death can be hell, and all roads lead to the McFeely Tavern.

Edgar winner Burl Barer spins a unique and wondrous mystery from the opening paragraph to the spectacular cinematic climax featuring one of the best plot twists in PI history.

wbp.bz/headlock

SAVAGE HIGHWAY by Richard Godwin

From an internationally acclaimed author of noir thrillers comes *"the road novel from hell"* (Castle Freeman Jr., author of The Devil In The Valley). Women are disappearing on the highway, a drifter hunts the men who raped her, and a journalist discovers the law has broken down. An *"irresistible hard-boiled read that's reminiscent of old school black and white noir."* (Vincent Zandri, New York Times bestselling author).

wbp.bz/savagehighway

WHEN FALL FADES by Amy Leigh Simpson

A *"Must-Read Romance of 2015"* (USA Today). Hunky FBI Agent Archer Hayes reluctantly enlists the lovely and beguiling Sadie Carson to solve the mystery of her elderly neighbor's death and its connection to a conspiracy dating back to WWII. Results in fiery romance and chilling murder plot. *"Simpson swung for the fences."* (Anthony Flacco, New York Times bestselling author). The first book in up-and-comer Simpson's The Girl Next Door romantic mystery series. Compares to New York Times bestselling romance author Julie Garwood.

wbp.bz/whenfallfades

CPSIA information can be obtained
at www.ICGtesting.com
Printed in the USA
LVOW10s0634031117
554878LV00014B/489/P